W9-BXY-636

Praise For *Nobody Comes Back*

"Reads like a story remembered in vivid, angry detail blurted out onto the page. . . . There's no 'good war' or 'greatest generation.' Imagine *Saving Private Ryan* minus everything but the battle scenes. If Pearce had done it any more justice, you couldn't bear to read it."
—*Newsweek*

"Brutal and compelling."
—Harold Coyle,
New York Times bestselling author of *More Than Courage*

"An instant classic."
—Larry Bond,
New York Times bestselling author of *Dangerous Ground*

"The best novel ever written about the Battle of the Bulge."
—David Hagberg,
winner of three American Mystery Awards
and *USA Today* bestselling author of *Dance with the Dragon*

"Captures the confusion of battle in all its gritty detail . . . Told with considerable passion by a writer who has a unique gift for storytelling."
—*The Sacramento Bee*

"A modern classic, a bookend for *The Red Badge of Courage*."
—Walter J. Boyne,
New York Times bestselling author of *Roaring Thunder*

"Remarkable . . . I was up until four in the morning reading it."
—General Fred Franks,
coauthor with Tom Clancy of the #1 *New York Times*
bestselling *Into the Storm: A Study in Command*

"This is as good as combat writing gets. Think the hero of *The Red Badge of Courage* in the Battle of the Bulge. It's unputdownable."
—Thomas Fleming,
New York Times bestselling author of *Dreams of Glory*

Also by Donn Pearce

COOL HAND LUKE

PIER HEAD JUMP

DYING IN THE SUN

Nobody Comes Back

——☆——

A Novel of the Battle of the Bulge

Donn Pearce

TOR®

A Tom Doherty Associates Book

New York

NOTE: If you purchased this book without a cover, you should be aware that this book is stolen property. It was reported as "unsold and destroyed" to the publisher, and neither the author nor the publisher has received any payment for this "stripped book."

This is a work of fiction. All of the characters, organizations, and events portrayed in this novel are either products of the author's imagination or are used fictitiously.

NOBODY COMES BACK

Copyright © 2005 by Donn Pearce

All rights reserved.

A Tor Book
Published by Tom Doherty Associates, LLC
175 Fifth Avenue
New York, NY 10010

www.tor-forge.com

Tor® is a registered trademark of Tom Doherty Associates, LLC.

ISBN-13: 978-0-7653-6134-9
ISBN-10: 0-7653-6134-5

First Edition: January 2005
First Mass Market Edition: February 2009

Printed in the United States of America

0 9 8 7 6 5 4 3 2 1

After doing the thirteen weeks at Camp Blanding he moped away his furlough in Tampa. He made a few strolls through the hallways at school, but he only did one semester at Hillsborough High, and nobody knew him that much. And nobody was impressed by uniforms anymore; always some hero already overseas, some brother or cousin. He did see Leora once, but she was talking to a girl and didn't notice him.

He skated a little at the Coliseum, saw movies, and rode the streetcars to the end of the line, and back.

He walked down Franklin Street and saluted the drunk, happy officers from McDill Field; home on rotation, covered with glory. He snapped his elbow at an exact forty-five degrees, hand and forearm straight, fingers together, only the edge presented. He saluted their bars and oak leaves, their sexy girlfriends, their hats crushed out of shape, their wings, shoulder patches, their ribbons and overseas service stripes—just to get them to salute him back.

Some had to untangle their right arms and pull away from their girls, startled by this downtown display of military courtesy from this stiff kid in plain khakis with his infantryman's badge and the non-GI forage cap with the blue piping that he had to buy himself at the PX.

WHEN IT WAS OVER he said good-bye to Victor and Aline, Norman already in the navy. He took the streetcar downtown, got on the Greyhound, put his barracks bag in the overhead rack, and sat by the window. He listened to the baggage thumps in the bot-

tom compartment and watched the sailor on the platform getting kissed and hugged by his teary-eyed mother, and father,
and by a weeping teenage girl. The sailor came in and took the
aisle seat next to Parker, leaning over him to wave. Parker re-
clined the back cushion and closed his eyes.

HE REPORTED at Fort Meade. He was inoculated and classified,
put on a bus to an embarkation center in Baltimore where he
joined the line that struggled up the gangway of a converted
Liberty ship. He followed the guides and the marking tapes to
one of the cargo hatches, and climbed down the iron ladders to
his assigned area in the lower hold.

They were kept below for two days while non-coms yelled
and feet pounded; steam winches yammered; food stores and barracks bags were piled on cargo slings, and hoisted aboard.

On the first day out, the merchant ships in the convoy tested
their guns, the replacements grinning at the flat booms around the
horizon. They got two meals a day. The drinking water was turned
on twice for an hour and they were allowed on deck in two-hour
shifts. They took lukewarm saltwater showers every third day.

They were issued life belts and had boat drills. He was allot-
ted one of the pipe-frame, canvas-and-rope bunks stacked five
high. He could sleep in his clothes at any time during the day
from eight in the morning until eight at night, but then the alternate took over the bunk.

The ship rolled and pitched for fifteen days. The GIs
climbed the ladders through the latrine smells and the stink of
vomit to reach the main deck and get their rotation of fresh air.
They ducked away from the spray and the wind, and gaped at
the dull gray seas, the scattered ships, the navy men in their pea
jackets standing watch in the gun tubs, the destroyers that
churned around them, listening for U-boats.

But the crew was merchant marine, what Toby really wanted all along. They saw the world, those guys, and made hundreds of dollars a month—war zone bonuses, attack bonuses. You could get in at seventeen with parent permission but didn't need a birth certificate. He didn't want to ask his mother, and wasn't sure where she was then, in Georgia someplace with Bob; so he hitchhiked up to Philadelphia. But his father wouldn't sign him in either, afraid of what his mother might do. But he did let Toby stay in his apartment.

He was there a month. Daddy's brother was a third mate in the Maritime Service and worked as port relief officer. Daddy grinned and said Uncle Jack was in an air raid in London, and was too afraid to ever ship out again. But Uncle Jack knew some of the longshoremen gang bosses and got Toby into a shape-up on the south side docks. Nobody worried about his age because of the manpower shortage.

He made $1.25 an hour, humping fifty-five-gallon drums on dollies, unloading barges tied up alongside, and boxcars shunted into the pier sheds. The crates of dismantled airplanes and jeeps were marked "Teheran." He knew it was all bound for Russia and the Eastern Front.

Toby was proud of the hard, crazy work, but he ached all over at the end of the day. He pushed hand trucks. He stood in staggered lines, catching and tossing cartons, stacking and carrying boxes and bags.

One morning everybody on the dock stopped to look off in the same direction. A cargo sling had spilled over and killed a man in the hold. The gang bosses started yelling: "Get back to work, you guys. One dead monkey don't stop the show."

But Toby's arms and chest got hard. He was already five-nine and weighed one-fifty. He bought steel-toed shoes and a cargo hook, got up at five, ate at a diner, and took the subway.

He paid Daddy a share of the rent. He made his day, took a shower, and went out to eat. He would go to a movie, or just sit in the apartment to listen to the radio, or play with Daddy's shotgun from the closet, or look out the window.

His father probably had a girlfriend. He would come in late and was gone most of the weekends. They did go fishing once, renting a boat at Cape May, but Toby got seasick. Twice he sent off for birth certificates and tried to change the date with ink eradicator, but the paper always blotted. He decided to go to California. He had never been west of the Mississippi.

IT TOOK SIX DAYS, thumbing his way to Pittsburgh on Route 30, taking Route 40 from there to Wheeling, across Ohio and Indiana to St. Louis. Route 50 took him to Oklahoma, where he joined Route 66, and followed it all the way. Travel was hard because of the gas rationing, but hitchhiking was common, and people tried to help. Some drivers would point one finger across the road, an apology for not going very far. Toby would raise his hand: thanks anyway. Women never stopped.

He slept whenever he got a ride but had to pay for a room twice. He hopped a freight in Arizona once to give it a try, sat in the doorway of an empty, and swung his feet over the speeding desert. But boxcars were dirty, and lonely.

In Los Angeles, he stayed at the YMCA, worked a week at a slaughterhouse, and then at a drive-in kitchen for a month. When he saw the line outside a naval recruiting office, he got in place. But he was the only one without underwear and had to stand naked and stare at the wall clock for an hour as the line drooped around four sides of a huge room full of desks. He couldn't look at the nurse when he gave her back the cup.

But he still needed a parent's signature. He wrote Daddy and waited a week for the answer; embarrassed by the handwriting and the sixth-grade spelling; the only letter he ever had from his father; nothing else, ever, for Christmas, or birthdays. He remembered the jokes Mama used to tell, Daddy painting signs all over the South. Once he spelled it: RESTARANT, but the owner didn't notice until after Daddy got paid.

When Toby was in Seattle, it hit him. Let them do it. Go in, register for the draft, add two years to your date of birth, and volunteer for immediate induction.

By the time he had to check in, he was back in Tampa. He got a letter from the Maritime Service offering a deferment, but by then he was hung up on the idea of the navy. They had pensions and government benefits, and there would probably be a war bonus. Merchant seamen were just civilians and didn't even wear uniforms.

Victor drove him to Selective Service Board Number Four on Florida Avenue. They bussed him from there to Camp Blanding and—shazam! He had outsmarted himself; welcome to the poor, bloody infantry. But the army was better than nothing. And his father was in the army once, when he was only fifteen.

They were sent by train to Atlanta for processing, escorted back by a curious lieutenant who went over the files and called Parker over, impressed by his score on the Army General Classification Test, way above the 110 needed to qualify for officer candidate at OCS. Not finishing high school might be a problem, but combat experience could take care of that.

Toby was just worried about getting caught. He would write his mother later. He didn't want to mess this one up.

AT LE HAVRE they disembarked in a steady rain over catwalks of two-by-fours built over the side of a capsized hulk, looking out over block after block of bombed ruins. Lines of waiting trucks angled around the squared piles of exploded concrete, stone, wood, plaster, and brick.

They were jammed in standing up, and driven off, jolted, and swaying. Somebody started a moo that was picked up from truck to truck with oinks, and baas, the herd bawling all the way to the Reception Depot at Camp Lucky Strike. The drivers and MPs didn't even grin.

They rested overnight in tents in a fenced holding area and then were shifted to an intermediate depot where they went through an administrative procedure and had their personal records reupdated, again. They entered in his Military Occupational Specialty. He was a rifleman, an MOS 745.

They were issued weapons and field equipment, and were shown that same prophylactic training film, the VD special.

They marched to a railroad station, climbed into little French boxcars, and got clicked and clacked across the countryside, dangling their legs as they waved, and whistled at farmers, and schoolkids, at women on bicycles. They ate K rations, rolled into blankets, and flaked out on the straw.

Parker climbed the ladder to the roof and smiled into that winter wind of France, his first foreign country except for the quick trip across the border at El Paso and then almost up to Canada. He looked back at the men on top of the other cars and thought about all those bummed rides since he dropped out and took off.

He could have got up here quicker if he had thought up that angle a little sooner; that, and the lost training time; not the AWOL thing, when he nodded off in a lecture and that cadre broke a pointer over his helmet, made him stand at attention for an hour, and canceled his weekend pass—that week in the hospital with pneumonia. He missed three days of machine-gun training and they transferred him back a month to another company—which had already finished machine guns.

At least he did get Cary Grant's autograph. They made an announcement over the PA and he joined the line. He got a laugh when he handed Cary that TS card with numbers on the edge to be punched by the chaplain.

And now he was up front where things were real. No more squad hut inspections, latrine duty, picking up butts in the dark to police the company area. No more scrubbing garbage cans, hands and knees on the mess-hall floor with a GI brush; memorizing the serial number on his rifle, and reciting it out loud whenever some non-com felt in the mood.

No more of that *Soldier's Handbook* that told you to keep a whisk broom handy so your uniform would always be neat, and warned you that a loud noise and clouds of dust might indicate the presence of tanks.

No more standing in the dark wearing nothing but a helmet liner, an open raincoat, and shoes, to skin it back and milk it down as some sergeant strolled by. Things happened up here: history, a chance for adventure, the real stuff; promotions, and medals, men commissioned right in the battlefield. Later, people would look at him and say: "He was in the war."

And with overseas pay and combat pay, he now made ninety bucks a month, minus what they held back for the life insurance. And sooner or later, they'd give him a pass to Paris, where the French had lots of whores. His thighs shivered as he thought of what it must be like.

THEY SPENT FOUR DAYS at the Third Replacement Depot in Waremme, Belgium. They called it the Repple Depple—like living in a train station in Lower Slobovia. They did calisthenics and close-order drill. They slept in double bunks made of two-by-fours and chicken wire on burlap mattresses stuffed with straw.

There was this thing called the Replacement Stockage Report. Names appeared and disappeared. When yours was called you loaded into a truck. The rest marched off to another demonstration of the proper procedure for the field disassembly and cleaning of the M1 Garand rifle; or to another lecture on military sanitation, military courtesy, another reading of the Articles of War; or to another screening of *Know Your Enemy*, or that other one, *Why We Fight*.

Their barracks bags never caught up with them.

They sat in bleachers and got blackboard lectures, and looked up with bent necks and open mouths to watch the V-2s sputtering high with flaming tails, headed for England.

The lieutenant pointed at Toby with his stick.

"What's your name, soldier? No, you on the left."

"Parker, sir. Private Tobias D."

"Private Parker, could you recite for us the Fourth General Order?"

Toby knew better, but it was really funny and they couldn't put him in the stockade again; not now, not up here.

"I walk my post a mile a minute with an M1 rifle with nothing in it. Sir."

They all knew the rest of it; there was more. The bleachers shuddered with snorts and swallowed giggles, then got still. They sat up straight as the lieutenant glared, the fresh scar on the side of his neck a bright red.

"Anybody else?" he said.

T he bare bulbs flicked on at 0400 hours. They had shit-on-a-shingle and coffee, and fell out in full gear. Heads were counted and names called. Parker loaded up into one of the two-and-a-half-ton trucks, ten men jammed on each side, rifles between their knees, field packs and equipment belts at their feet. They divvied up the stacks of blankets but had to twist and squirm for shoulder room. Ten more stood in the middle, one hand braced on the roof frames: bare, with no canvas.

A Special Service band did a kind of slow step along the side of the road. They wore Class-A uniforms: ties and forage caps, dress shoes, and creases, some with campaign ribbons—the European Theater of Operations and the Good Conduct Medal, the one you got for going a year without catching the clap. They played a clarinet, a trombone, a harmonica, and a violin.

". . . mairzy doats and dozy doats and liddle lamzy divey."

A major looked up and down the line. He raised one arm and dropped it. The band switched to "We'll Meet Again."

The drivers and assistant drivers got in and started the motors, calculated the lag so they could get up speed, and maintain the proper interval. It took three minutes for the eighteen trucks to move out, still in the dark. The headlights were painted over in blue or showed only narrow slits, like the eyes of cats.

The men shivered. Some bragged about the souvenirs they promised to bring home, the Nazi helmets, the flags, the Lugers. Some laughed about the German pussy they were going to get. As they went around a hairpin curve, Parker could see the rest of the convoy strung out ahead, and behind them. When they went up a long grade the motors dragged down with straining moans, and made those little buzzes as the drivers double-clutched the gears, some grinding when their timing wasn't right.

Three jeeps escorted the convoy through the drizzle and the snow. They pulled over for long stops to let lines of empty cargo trucks, and gasoline tankers, roar, and swoosh the other way. The men pulled the blankets over their heads with their backs to the wind. Those in the middle squatted against knees and packs, their eyes closed.

Parker looked them over. This was his own outfit that rubbed hard at his shoulders. He was thirty men now, not just one weird kid who didn't fit anywhere, and this load was only a down payment. He could feel the muscle of that other guaranteed million closing up behind. But only one face on the other side seemed alert.

Parker yelled over, "What do you think?"

The guy shrugged, grinned, and yelled back.

"Ah. It'll do."

Parker stretched up and looked around. He sat taller than most because his height was in his torso and waist. He was not that big, but he got by. After starving himself on the road, he put on weight in the army, embarrassed by those old jokes about finding a home, and never having it so good. He shaved his fuzz every morning just to keep the cadre happy.

Men began to cramp up, to squirm and bitch. One pounded on the roof of the truck cab and leaned out.

"Hey! How about a piss call?"

The corporal rolled down the window and yelled back.

"Use your helmet."

The guy looked around and waited for the hoots, and howls, then pried the steel shell away from the fiberboard liner, hunched over, and relieved himself. He started to empty it over the side but got screeches of cowering protest. He passed it back. Two others short-stopped it to add some more.

"Hey! That's mine. Use your own, god damn it."

The helmet got passed back to Parker, who emptied it over the tailgate. The wind sent it up in a high, yellow spume. The following truck fell back.

THEY MADE ONE STOP. Five hundred–some soldiers, officers, and MPs lined up along the ditch. Some squatted to take an emergency dump. Some gagged and threw up. They did a few knee bends and side straddle hops until the non-coms blew their whistles, and yelled to mount up.

Two MPs checked for stragglers. Their jeep zipped to the rear, the bumper aerial whipping, and lashing with the quick stops, and swerves.

The convoy loosened up, the trucks spaced at five hundred feet. Their olive drab paint matched the dull green of the fir forests. It was the only color, the rest of everything a misted black and a misted white—the mountains, farm buildings, and fences. The patched, narrow road dipped through fields and pastures past war-damaged houses, curved through Hansel-and-Gretel villages, and kinked around ravines.

They passed a rusted, demolished tank and a number of wrecked trucks with most of the wheels gone, and could hear the *whoom-whooms* in the remote distance, a kind of thunder. Eyes flipped and faces scowled in the constant, light rain. Parker jerked up his chin with a smirk at the guy next to him but couldn't stop the trembles in the corners of his mouth.

MILITARY POLICE sat in jeeps at a crossroads with pistols and tommy guns and white-banded helmets. They waved the convoy off to the left and the trucks bounced, and jolted to a stop. An MP went over to the driver of the first truck and it started down a phantom trail in low gear. The rest moved on. When their turn came, the corporal yelled something out the window of the cab. Another MP pointed to a pair of worn ruts.

After another mile the truck stopped by a second lieutenant and a staff sergeant, standing together and smoking, their M1s slung muzzle down. The corporal called out:

"Is this Baker Company? Hundred-and-tenth?"

When they nodded, the corporal climbed out, saluted, and handed the lieutenant a clipboard.

"This is all? We lose fifty-six and we get back thirty?"

The corporal waited. The lieutenant looked at the sheet, checked out the men in the truck, then nodded at two of them.

"Matcovich? Levin? Hey. Good to see you guys back. You all healed up now? You're okay? So how was your vacation? Did you get good and laid?"

Parker smirked at the hospital returnees, both happy to be home. The lieutenant studied the sheet again. The corporal opened the rattling tailgate with a yell.

"Okay. Dis-*mount*. This is your drop-off point. You de-truck here. Leave them blankets behind and fall in on me."

They got out with groans and murmurs, and dragged feet. Rifle butts banged on the truck bed. Equipment scraped. Their legs stiff, they jumped or climbed, almost fell off the steps, stood in a ragged line, and waited.

"Okay. Let's go."

The lieutenant strolled off down the trail, the replacements confused by his quiet, casual order. The sergeant picked it up.

"Spread it out some. Easy. Hold it. Keep an interval."

They hiked through a forest, went around outcroppings of rock, then came to a house and barn. Two tanks were parked in

the yard under camouflage nets. The replacements crowded together in an uncertain halt. The lieutenant ducked through the
blanket nailed over the farmhouse door. A typewriter clacked
inside, a loud somebody in there royally pissed off.

"What's this shit? You mean for the whole damn company?
Thirty? And only two retreads?"

"Captain, at least they're shiny, right out of the box. No Air
Corps dropouts or stockade artists. Only one maybe."

The lieutenant came out with a first sergeant, three platoon
sergeants, and a captain, his hand and wrist in a dirty cast.
Heads bent over the clipboard and things were scribbled on
pads. The two sides looked at each other.

"Men, ah—I am Captain Stacy. Ah—some men are natural
heroes, ah. Like the movie kind. Rest of us, we shit our pants.
But then, ah—we're back up and we do our job. Of course,
there's always the paperwork."

He looked at their faces and maybe waited for a laugh.

"You're up front now and we have our own rules. First of all,
keep your voices down. Always. Voices carry. And don't *ever*
salute any officer. You don't know who's watching from over
there."

He dropped his head and turned but then came back.

"You'll get the hang of it. You'll be okay."

The headquarters staff ducked inside. The platoon sergeants
passed the clipboard around, called off names, and moved out,
leading single files in three spaced, wavered directions.

★

The replacements stumbled over rocks in the snow and skidded in muddy spots, quiet as they trudged behind the tech sergeant who scattered them around. Parker's canteen thudded against his hip. He could feel the dig of the pack straps, the weight of his rifle, full ammo pouches, and the two drooping, cloth bandoliers, six clips each, crossed over his chest.

The trail wound down the hill through the woods. Parker felt a tightness when he saw the first shell hole, black and jagged in the snow, the slit trenches, dugouts, and foxholes, sandbags stacked around a water-cooled machine gun. The veterans gazed at them with steady eyes, their uniforms faded, torn, and baggy, some of their helmets dented.

The sergeant checked his list.

"Anderson? You buddy up here with Corporal Goldhurst."

The file moved on. Nobody else, so Parker had to say it.

"How come everybody just looks at us?"

"You're new, that's all."

The sergeant dropped off two more. Parker was last. The slope was steeper, the trees thicker. Fog drifted in.

"What, nobody wants to fall in love again?"

"Just relax, okay? You bitching and moaning already, you didn't even get here yet? You're still as green as duck shit? Most guys take at least a couple hours first."

The sergeant stooped a little as they went and favored the biggest trees. Parker imitated his moves. Two guys called out through their hands.

"Look out, kid. That Headley's crazy as a shithouse rat."

Way up ahead Parker could see the back of a helmet sticking out of a hole. An arm went up, one stripe on the sleeve, a raised middle finger. Parker grouched:

"Somebody at least around here's got a sense of humor."

No answer. Parker listened to their boots drag through the six inches of snow. The sergeant stopped, gave him a long stare, lit a cigarette in the unzipped folds of his jacket, and held it backward in the cup of his hand.

"The Bloody Bucket was in the Hurtin' Forest. We got the shit kicked out of us in the Kall River Valley and at Kommerscheidt and at Schmidt."

"What's that, the Bloody Bucket?"

"That's us, our shoulder patch. Twenty-eighth Division. In September we came right up to the Siegfried line. But last month, the Hurtin'. We took forty percent casualties the first three days and around two out of every three before they pulled us out. We lasted twelve days."

"That many guys got dead?"

"No, no. That's wounded, prisoners, foot cases, nutcases. Guys missing, hiding out in Paris, or blown to pieces. The Hundred-and-twelve got the worst of it. *Nine*ty percent."

He looked down and flicked the butt with his thumb.

"Headley's one of the old originals. Been with us since Omaha Beach in July. He was a college quiz kid with the ASTP program but dropped out to volunteer. He turned down OCS. He even turned down corporal. They got him in for a Silver Star, too. Getting it now is another story. They got quotas now. You gotta be medal of the month."

"When do I get mine? My shoulder patch, I mean?"

Parker got a frown and flipped fingers—don't bother me.

"I shouldn't be scaring you with all this shit."

"Well, I guess I got to learn. Is it always that bad?"

"It varies. Mostly it's monotonous. Hurry up and wait."

THEY GOT TO THE EDGE of the foxhole. The PFC looked up.

"Headley? You got yourself a babysitting job."

"Oh, Christ. Why me?"

"You're the best mama we got, that's why. And this one's a little, I don't know. And listen, I'm getting tired of your shit. This is a fucking rest area. Come in once in a while like some kind of a human being, like everybody else? Take your turn in a regular billet? Maybe even, how do I say it? A bed?"

"My job's up here."

"We got houses. Service unit's got portable showers, hot chow, movies. Some outfits, it's just nine-to-five. Come in after dark, don't go back till just before daylight."

The PFC leaned on the edge of the hole and looked through his officer's binoculars. Parker wondered how he got them. Too busy to shoot the breeze? Hadn't shaved since never?

"O-kay. Just don't keep this poor prick up here forever."

"Dean? You put guys on the point now their first day?"

"Why not? It's quiet enough. This is the honeymoon sector. Let him get the feel."

Technical Sergeant Dean went back. The PFC thought it over. Parker wondered if he was going to let him get in.

"Better off your gear and get down here."

Parker unslung his rifle and shucked himself out of the pack, grabbed a bush, and slid down. The hole was shaped like an *L*; one leg covered over with logs, dirt, rocks, and snow, with a raincoat rigged up as a curtain: an animal's den, the bed more like a nest, just big enough to squeeze into. The short side was open and chest deep. Shelves were carved into the upper part of the dirt wall for ration cans, ammo, and grenades.

"Man. You got a lot of work in this thing."

Headley gave him a sideways look, probably thinking: Should he even bother talking to this shit? Then he surrendered with a light, sighing, triple moan.

"Yeah. Be it ever so humble, always improve your hole."

"This might sound dumb, okay? But is this still Belgium?"

"Nah. You passed that. You're in the Grand Duchy of Luxembourg. That's Germany over there across the river."

"You shitting me? Right there? Wait; who's between us?"

"Nobody."

Headley went back to the glasses, but he had to grin.

"Nobody but the OP. See it there? They have a wire that goes back to the command post. We're the flank guard. Krauts sneak across the river at night and hide out in those farmhouses. They patrol and poke around. So do we. Sometimes they even wave. And we wave back. Weird, huh? Daylight comes they're back in their boats. It's a fun thing."

"Some fucking arrangement."

"They call this the 'Ghost Front.' Wanna see something?"

Headley handed him the field glasses. A pause, and then he helped him adjust for his eye width, and the focus.

"Fog's letting up a little. See that pillbox? The three broads sneaking in? Every night, in through the back."

"Those aren't broads. They can't be."

"They sure try to be. Got big asses, long hair, and wear dresses? Keep looking behind them, don't want to get caught?"

Parker giggled and crooned, and waved one hand.

"*Guten Abend, Schatzi. Wie geht's du schöne Mädel?*"

"You speak German?"

"Not really. I had a year of it in Brooklyn Tech. Engineering stuff. Instead of 'the butterfly is in the garden,' we got, '*Ich giesse die Lösung in dem Becherglas.'* 'I pour the solution into the beaker.'"

"That's not gonna help much up here. What's this about Brooklyn? You don't talk Brooklyn."

"My sister and me used to get dumped on my grandmother off and on. Tech was a tough school, but when I was in the stockade at Camp Blanding and the PWs were right next to us? I tried to talk to some in German, but I couldn't get anywhere."

Headley took back the glasses and made a somber look.

"Trouble is, those Krauts are getting ready to put shit in the game. I keep telling them, 'Hey. Something's up.' But no-o-o. What? Railroad cars, stuff banging around all night? Those lights? That shit-eating I-know-something grin on that prisoner we picked up? German planes fly over: no bombs, no strafing, just back and forth with a lot of noise? What's that mean? But they don't want to hear about it. The Nazis are licked and this is just a rest area. My ass, rest area."

Headley took two meals out of a K-ration carton, gave one to Parker, and worked the little can opener. They ate the pork, apple, and carrot mix, and drank from their canteens.

"Okay. Trench foot duty. Time to rub our feet."

"Nothing wrong with my feet."

"Sure. You got new ones. But I been sprouting mushrooms between my toes for a month and a half."

"So go ahead. Don't mind me."

"No. Unh-unh. The way it works, we rub each other's."

"Fuck that. I gotta sit here and rub your rotten *feet*?"

"Hey. You gonna be one more of those smart-ass replacements knows all the answers but one: he'll be dead in a week?"

Headley lit up an old ration can full of dirt and gasoline. He took off his canvas leggings, shoes, and socks, and held his feet over the fire. He gazed at Parker until he unbuckled the leather anklets, untied the laces of his new combat boots, and hunched up close. They faced each other, leaned against the sides of the hole, took the other guy's foot in his lap, and rubbed, and twisted the cold, numb arches. They did finger massages between the toes and twirled, and scuffed with the flats of their hands.

Parker was disgusted. Headley grinned at him, stood up to check around, then settled back for a drag on his cigarette.

"We all got swollen feet. Turn blue, you get evacuated."

"This is really weird. I mean, sick. I think you're some kind of foot queer. I bet there's a name for guys like you."

"There is. Careful, they call me."

"You're so careful, how come you're only a PFC? Sergeant Dean told me you're pretty good at this infantry stuff."

"I am. But I only follow; I do not lead. I do not create this shit; I only swim in it."

"What's that supposed to mean?"

"I don't even know that."

They changed socks and tucked the old ones under their shirts to dry next to their bellies. Headley rambled on about the Hürtgen Forest, about artillery tree bursts. The shrapnel expands into an overhead ball, and falling flat just makes you a bigger target. Best thing is to hug a tree . . . and ditch that stupid gas mask . . . gasoline good for crabs, but keep your pants down until it dries, or you get skin burns.

Headley took another cigarette out of the waterproof plastic case that fit into his shirt pocket.

"You don't smoke? Yeah? Better get yourself a Zippo just the same for making fires. Can I have your ration, then?"

"Okay. I don't even like to touch them."

"How old are you, anyway?"

"I'm eighteen. You got to be eighteen to be in the army."

"Bullshit. Kids get in all the time. How old?"

"What am I? Small for my age? Dumb or something?"

"Listen to me. Be smart. Just turn yourself in and get out of this crap. Nobody will even notice you're gone."

"I'm telling you, I am eighteen years old."

"Okay, okay. You were in the *stockade*? What you said?"

Parker thought of bragging his way out of this embarrassment but knew he couldn't do it with this guy.

"I got pissed off and went over the hill. It was only three days and I gave myself up."

"So first you sneak into the army. Then you sneak out. You really are a fuckup, huh? Exactly what we need."

They worked hard to swallow down their grins. Parker saluted with his left hand: out flat, British style.

"Parker. Tobias D. Reporting for duty, *suh!*"

Headley returned with the slight squint and the loose hand of a high-ranking Brass Hat: casual about it, almost sweet.

"Carry on, Private."

THEY LET THE GRIN come out and shrugged it off. Headley stood up to check around with the binoculars, then settled down with his smoke. Parker looked down, then up.

"Hey, did you guys ever get to go to Paris?"

"Sure we did."

"Yeah? What was it like?"

"The Twenty-eighth took review, went right down the Champs Elysées past all the big boys at eyes right. In ranks of ten, I think it was. Took salute from old Charlie de Gaulle himself. Everybody crazy, flags and cheers, flowers, and wine. A couple girls threw their panties at us. One hooked on a guy's rifle, but he didn't faze and the crowd went nuts. Oh, yeah. We marched right through Paris. And then we marched right out the other side where the trucks were waiting to take us back to the front."

PARKER TOOK the first watch, awed by the silent closeness and the dark of the woods, the menace of it. He tried the field glasses but couldn't see anything in the fog. He shifted his feet—left, right. Left and right.

He did the two hours, crawled into the dugout, shook Headley, and took his turn curled up on the pile of fir needles, the blankets pulled over his head, hands between his knees. You need to make a bed out of whatever you have, Headley said; some insulation. Even if it's freezing, your body heat will melt through and you'll wake up in mud.

———————

HE GOT UP at midnight and looked at the rumbled, pink-and-orange flashes that murmured to the north, and tinted the vapors and the snow with delicate shimmers.

"What's that going on over there?"

"Harassing fire, is all. We did it to them, yesterday."

Alone again, he listened to those bumps and combustions over the river. He knew about palmettos and cypress swamps, but these were dragon woods. The enemy lived here.

HIS EYES DROOPED and he drifted . . . that thin, solid mattress in the attic in Richmond Hill where he looked through the tiny window of leaded colored glass at the street outside, at the cold lights, and empty slush. Then the bus and the subway to Brooklyn. And Leora, thinking about Leora again, his bicycle, Beegee, the clang of the divorce.

HE MARCHED IN PLACE and nibbled a ration cracker, his knees high, hearing that World War One song in his head, breathing it out:

"There's something about a soldier, something about a soldier . . . something about a soldier that is fine, fine, fine."

He was back in the pine needles at 0200 and up again at 0400. At 0423, he heard a loud whisper behind him:

"Monkey."

He stage-whispered the countersign: "Wrench." And then:

"It's okay. It's Lieutenant Amberly. Baker Company."

The lieutenant looked like an ordinary GI, hunkered down by the edge of the hole, hugging an M1 instead of an officer's carbine. He did wear a forty-five but had no rank insignia on his collar or shoulders, just a vertical white stripe on the back of his helmet. He offered Parker a swallow from a canteen of almost warm coffee, put it back on his gun belt, and snapped the flaps. Parker's heart was working hard at how easy he had crept up on him.

"How's it going in your sector? Everything quiet?"

"No, sir, not really."

"Keep it down. And don't call me sir. There could be a Kraut patrol out here. What's the problem?"

"There's noises and lights and stuff moving around over the river. Headley says something's up."

"Listen. Headley's . . . We got G-2 reports about all that. They're playing loudspeakers just to drive us nuts. We're only facing a *Volksgrenadier* Division. That's young boys and old men. Air force ground crews, they ran out of planes, then handed them rifles. Navy men. No more ships, the same thing. And wounded back from the hospital. They even got Polish volunteers."

THE LIEUTENANT WENT over to the left somewhere, then went back. Parker could hear him now as he made his rounds. But those cautious boots crunched into Parker's memory and he shivered as he wrapped himself with Leora in the Spanish palace. Out in the yard when he saw her alone through the open hallway of W. J. Bryan Elementary. She floated past the fountain, hugging her books.

Applause from the hibiscus and oleanders. The lady palms danced with the red and purple bougainvilleas over the rough, stuccoed arches, and clay tiles. He had that outrageous tightness in his chest. But she was in 3-B. He was only 3-A.

HIS EYES DIMMED and he jerked his head. He saw 0530 on his watch and then small, sparking flashes over the river. As he reached for the binoculars . . . a strange noise, the ripple and rumple of giant sheets of cardboard, flipped and shaken in the night. It got louder, with whistles and shrieks. The ground shook under him; snow flew up; flames flashed high among the trees. Branches and needles drifted down. It rained broken knives, sharp and hard.

Headley yelled something. He reached out of the dugout, grabbed Parker by the belt, dragged him inside, and shoved him against the far wall. The bangs came close enough to be one rolling boom. Dirt and stones sifted through the log roof. Parker's ears were clogged, his fingers electrified. The ground gave him body-punches. He smelled a sour burning and heard zings, and snarls as vicious metal chunks rustled, and whined through the trees.

Headley put on his shoes and leggings as Parker shivered and listened to that agony somewhere, the same far-off scream.

"What is this? They trying to put a scare in us?"

"Scare, hell. We got twenty-five miles of front with just out-posts scattered around? And they know all about it?"

Something big banged close. A tree landed on the dugout and the stump of a branch poked through the roof, breaking one of the logs. It sagged down between them as snow and gravel sifted in. And then nothing, only the ear-buzzing and that same repeated scream.

"It's over. Let's get the fuck out of here."

"Hang on. They just want you to run out in the open."

Parker stared at the broken log, a root in the dirt wall, tool marks, a stone. Five minutes, then ten, and then more of the whizzes, the booms, the rustles, and sparking reflections. Then nothing again. Headley crawled out into the slit trench.

"Get out here and let's get ready."

Parker squeezed up beside the tree trunk.

"First thing, admit it. You're scared shitless. Okay? We all are. Right? Now take a deep breath and ease it out."

Parker's mouth was dry and his hands were sweaty. He had to

grab his wrist to look at the watch: 0615. He was still breathing hard when a sudden moonlight broke out, a reflected glow mirrored through the cold haze. Searchlights on the other side of the river played on the low clouds, on the trees, and on their faces.

Things moved out there, a staggered line of white-on-white. Shadows of nothing took their time past the trees, dressed in loose, white cloaks, and smocks, white hoods pulled over their helmets, their weapons showing black.

"What's this? Halloween? They're wearing spook suits?"

"Winter camouflage. These guys know what they're doing."

Something exploded up front, low, by the river. There were several screams, different voices, a different anguish.

"They ran into that minefield we set up," Headley said. "They'll get through it, but it'll slow them down."

"Holy shit! What'll we do? Go tell the lieutenant?"

"He'll know all he needs to know when we open up."

"We gonna shoot?"

"Hell yes, we're gonna shoot. You want it in writing?"

Parker heard the click of the safety on Headley's M1. Headley arranged the sling over his left arm, leaned into it, and rested his elbows just outside the hole. He looked back at Parker and shuffled over to make room. Parker got set.

Fast automatic fire came from the left with yells and small flashes. Thuds hit among the trees. Whines diminished away. Parker opened up. Eight blams and the empty clip ejected out of his rifle. His heart pulsed and quivered as he fumbled to get another clip out of the drooping bandolier. Headley hollered at him:

"You're not doing what I told you. Aim first. Aim low. You see bullets kick up in front of them you got it just about right. The idea is to kill, not just make a lot of noise, like some guys don't even fire their rifles at all. Afraid they'll make somebody mad."

White figures dodged through the forest. Parker heard the roar and the wailing.

"They're coming right at us; they're gonna run over us."

"Easy. Just let 'em come. We got a few seconds. Here."

Parker was shaking. Headley reached over to grab his arm and shoulder.

"Hold it steady. Now take a breath. And—squee-eeze."

The M1 fired. Parker raised up over the sights.

"I think I got one!"

"Maybe you did. Maybe you got Maggie's drawers. Maybe he just took cover. You'll never know. You're not supposed to."

Parker got down and fired again. He stayed with Headley shot for shot until the empty pinged out of the breech. He shoved a full clip in, hit the slide forward, shot at something that moved on the right, and thought he saw it drop.

He felt a great calm, a dull but weightless confidence, the arm sling tight, the butt against his shoulder. He held it and aimed, squeezed, got kicked back, and did it again. He heard scattered screeches from the foxholes behind them:

"Medic! Over here!"

"Hold the line! Pass the word! Hold at all costs!"

"*Medic!* Medic for Chrissakes!"

A sudden brightness appeared, a new sun above the weirdness of that substitute moonlight.

"Duck down and freeze," Headley said. "Don't look at it."

The flare faded. Those ragged white clots were even closer when Parker eased up. He fired again, and again. But then he saw nothing. The noise simmered and popped. A voice boomed out:

"Take ten, you Yankee bastards. We'll be right back."

And another, from somewhere, an echo:

"Fuck you, Heinie."

Parker could hear Headley as he breathed, and snuffled up his nose. They waited and watched. Parker's fingers trembled in outraged mutiny. It wasn't supposed to be like this, so soon, so furious; and then after those few quiet minutes, cheers, and howls broke out. Weapons went off and bullets thudded around them. He heard a machine gun somewhere. Those white things were coming again. Parker had trouble keeping his voice down.

"Shit, they're around behind us!"

"No, not yet. The fucking hell's our goddamn artillery? The wires are probably blown. How's your ammo holding?"

"I got three clips left. They're close. I mean, close."

"Listen to me. Spread out one more clip, rapid fire. Then we'll throw two grenades apiece. Okay? Just toss 'em out anywhere to make a noise and then we'll haul ass. Keep those last two grenades and save your bullets. Shoot only in real, actual, close-up self-defense. You ready? Now *go!*"

Parker watched Headley, shot as fast as he did, jerked out the grenade pins, and threw when he did. He heard the pops and fizzes and ducked down. When the last grenade banged off, he grabbed at his pack, but Headley yelled at him:

"Forget that shit. Just go. Go!"

He scrambled out and slouched behind Headley up a narrow draw to a small, flat area above and behind them. Flares went off. Parker ran past a bloody GI curled up in his hole. Another was facedown, arms spread, clawed fingers still trying. Another snoozed on his back in the snow, his legs crossed, comfortable.

Parker was running and then he was down, his chest in spasms as he gagged, and whooped for air, tasting a smell of powder, and that burnt something else. Mud, rocks, and bits of branches fell around him. He got up, almost deaf, numb, most of his right pant leg blown off, and part of his field jacket.

He grabbed at a tree, the back side of it barked and raw. Headley lay behind it next to a black hole, his right leg off by itself, the shoe and legging ripped open. His face was peeled back, his mouth open, and crooked, his skull white in the red. One eye hung from something pink.

Parker pulled off his gloves, snatched at the sodden rips in the front of Headley's overcoat, and dug through the greasy sludge of cloth and flesh. He wiped at it. He thought he felt something twitch inside and then stop. He got up and took a step back to catch himself. A soldier sat nearby on the ground, crying. Two men ran around him, bent over at the waist, heads hunched down. They panted hard, struggling to take off pieces of equipment, and drop them as they went.

The barrage flashed up short glimpses of bright daylight out of the dawn, and went dark again. He couldn't find his rifle, his helmet, or his gloves. Men stopped just long enough to fire clumsy shots from the hip, and only one knelt down to take actual aim. Lieutenant Amberly came out of the fog and waved his pistol with a howling wail:

"Go back up! Hold fast! Orders have come down straight from Division. We give no ground! None! Nobody comes back!"

The lieutenant reached out to grab at one who dragged, punched, and clawed to get away. Parker dodged through the fog, limped around broken stumps, and piles of branches. Shells whumped and sprayed behind him.

He stumbled into a field kitchen with a burning truck and shot-up, overturned kettles. Dead men lay among the fires, one with a cook's apron. Another was German, his head cocked over on a red pillow of bloody snow. A half-chewed hot dog hung out of his mouth. Parker came closer and looked down at his uniform, the helmet insignia, the hobnails on his boots. He picked up the German's rifle, tried the bolt, then dropped it, and huffed his way up through the trees.

He had to stop for breath three times before he came up on a paved road that looked like the one taken by the Repple convoy yesterday. He limped along the edge of the macadam, hearing voices. A column of troops on bicycles whirred out of the electric moonlight, their helmets different, their uniforms blue. Paratroopers. *Fallschirmjäger*. He remembered those posters on the latrine wall at Blanding over the sinks, and mirrors, trying to learn the words and the insignias as he did his teeth, and took a bogus shave.

One of them sang with a martial gusto. The one in front of him went along; the one behind just mumbled.

". . . *rot scheint die Sonne . . .*"

Red shines the sun. What was this?

A tandem motorcycle swerved around the bicycles. Parker moved over, pretending he was just nobody, hands in his pockets, ambling along, as he had always done.

Brakes screeched. Commands were yelled out. Parker got some of it: ". . . dumb heads and pig dogs . . . ," already running. He dove into a ditch where he shook and wheezed, scooped snow over his legs and shoulders, burrowing into it, facedown, and still.

Boots thumped the road and the shoulder. A loud voice:

"*Hände hoch, Ami.* Hands high, Yankee boy. I shoot."

Don't move. Do like a rabbit. But then a boot hit him, hard, twice. He got up and looked at the circle of sneers.

One rammed a gun in his back. Another dug around in Parker's pockets, took his watch and his wallet, shook one hand,

and whistled in fun at the two grenades, and the clips of ammo in the bandolier. The trooper stretched out the ripped, bloody ribbons of his pants with one finger and whistled again. He unwrapped the piece of K-ration dessert bar Parker had saved, nibbled at it, smiled, took a bigger bite, and poked the rest of it into Parker's mouth.

Daylight had come and the fog was thinner. Another trooper came up, shoving three GIs ahead of him. Prodded into a single file, the four slipped, and skidded down a steep path past a body draped over a branch in a fallen tree. Most of the legs were gone and the stumps still dripped in slow beads, somehow familiar, maybe one of the replacements in the truck.

The other GIs mumbled to each other, their hands up.

"What the fuck do we do? Run for it, or what?"

"You nuts? They got us. They *got* us. We're PWs now."

"Oh, shit. They're gonna put us in a concentration camp."

Parker was first. The one behind him stumbled and fell forward, made panic noises, snatched at bushes, and windmilled down, hitting the back of Parker's knee, and knocking him over. Parker scrambled through some low, snow-heavy branches and ran, the guard swearing, and yelling. The burp gun rattled the woods. Parker dodged from tree to tree, went down the slope leaning back, spun, fell again, and got up. He stopped to look around. Which way? How?

He ran until he had to lean against the trunk of a fir, whooping for breath, gagging up a dry nothing. He could look down through a break in the woods and see bunched-up clusters of German infantry, and rubber boats hauled back and forth with ropes between the cliffs that banked the river.

He heard it, mumbled it—run, Toby; take off. That's what you're good at, getting away.

Furious, loud voices were behind him and on both sides. He

climbed back up the slope and hid in fir seedlings just below the road. He caught his breath, then ran again with the answer—hide out until dark, then sneak his way back. He got close to the ridge, and had stretched up for a look when something clubbed him across the face. He went down. His legs curled up and kicked, and his eyes watered as his fingers groped over the gush of blood.

Hands jerked, snatched, and dragged him. They would kill him now. He had no chance, none: a gun at his forehead and a German's face pushed up to his, ferocious, and wild-eyed.

"*Warst du in Normandie? Normandie? Warst du da?*"

Parker understood but didn't know how to answer. All of it came too fast. His face was gone—just gone. He was in terrifying pain and didn't know what they were going to do to him. He sounded snotty and bubbled when he talked.

"Come on, man. I wasn't nowhere. Hell, I just got here."

Another trooper growled at the crazy one and pushed the gun away. But then more came up, friendlier guns with grins.

"*Ist die Nase voll jetzt, Ami?*"

★

Firing came from somewhere on the right near the beginnings of a village, the *powf* of rifles and the chunk of mortars with the interrupted rips of machine guns.

He panted through his mouth, snuffled, and stumbled. He held one hand high as the other fingered at his face, at the gash below his eye, the loose pieces of his nose, at the agony. Tears made steady streams that mixed with the gore, and he leaned his head to one side so it wouldn't drip over his lips. He hawked and spit out the red stuff in his throat. His own bright blood was splattered over his hands and jacket sleeves, mixed with the dried, dark blood from Headley.

An officer paced in the road in a gray uniform with silver piping and embroidered rank insignia on his collar. He pointed and the wobbling line of prisoners obeyed the machine pistols, drifting into a crowd of GIs gathered in a farmyard.

More were brought up in small batches. Some wore knit caps; others were bareheaded. Those with helmets were ordered to throw them away. Some had gloves, some just one. One had bandaged eyes, his jacket loose over the sling on his arm, supported and steered by his buddy. Another had a ripped overcoat, his chest and back covered with soggy, red blotches.

Two paratroopers scuffled out of the fog with a cursing, arguing GI. They kicked and punched at him when he held back until he let himself be dragged by the arms. They bellowed at the officer, threw the GI down, yanked at his sleeves, and held up his wrists to jab at the rows of watches. One dangled something on a ribbon. It looked like a medal.

". . . *Tasche.*" Pocket, something. Parker got that. From the guy's pocket.

The GI whimpered up and around, his face molded into assorted appeals at the American prisoners who looked through him, and beyond. He prayed up at the German officer, and shifted from shoulder to shoulder, trying to see that something he knew was coming up behind him.

"For Christ sake, they're souvenirs. That's all. Those guys were already dead. That stuff didn't belong to nobody."

A shot—a squirt came out of his forehead. The prisoners flinched back, their hands shying up. But they had to look at him. They watched his arms and legs jerk, and quiver, and make marks in the snow. A slow stretch; he lay still, then shivered. One of the *Jäger* unbuckled the watches as the other handed the decoration to the officer. They dragged the body by the feet and dropped it into the ditch.

ARTILLERY BOOMED around the horizon and blended with closer, louder battle sounds. Parker sucked air over his thick, dry tongue, his sinuses swollen shut. A few GIs passed around canteens that had survived the shakedowns. Parker took that single swallow that had been contracted by eyeball agreement. Not sure if he had it right, he moved his lips in a rehearsal before he called out to the officer in a nasal plea:

"*Bitte, mein Herr? Mögen wir uns setzen?*"

The officer flipped a backhanded wave to sit down. A group groan came from the PWs, exhausted rumbles, and sighs.

The guards rotated during the day, but the forty-eight GIs were kept in the farmyard, eyes dull, and faces tight. They still made quick, fascinated looks at the body of the souvenir hunter.

They talked in whispers, and tried to relax their way into invisibility. Parker didn't see the three men who were with him in the woods, and wondered if they got away, or were shot, or were finally taken down to the river, and the boats.

They got no food or water. They had permission to piss but only on their knees. Three men took a crap but had to do it in place. They scratched at the snow with their hands and dropped their pants. Their eyes avoided the appalled, embarrassed stares.

A motorcyclist rolled up to the non-com who had taken over from the officer. He nodded, blew on a whistle, and signaled the guards, who ordered the GIs on their feet. They staggered out of the field in a herded double column, clambered into and out of the ditch past the souvenir hunter. They got back to the pavement, their arms high or with fingers clasped behind their heads, some held at shoulder height or lower. Whenever they dropped too low a guard would bark, and wave them up.

They shuffled in an uncertain rhythm past a heap of blown-up and burned jeeps, trucks, and armored cars bulldozed off the road. Paratroopers strolled beside them on one side with kept intervals and a relaxed alertness, machine pistols at the ready. The battle sounded fainter as they moved toward a new and growing roar.

Parker's face was raw, caked over with crusted blood. His bad leg was cold and numb through his flapping rags. His nose was a solid lump, and there was a swelling under his left eye from the wound on his cheek. He sounded hollow and stopped-up when he talked to the sergeant marching beside him.

"You got any idea where the hell we are?"

"The locals call this N-16. The GIs call it Skyline Drive. It goes north and south along the ridge. Marnach's back over there. Sounds like Company B's still holding out."

"Baker Company? That's my outfit. They didn't go back?"

The sergeant made a tired shrug.

Parker tried to remember those fading faces in the truck, and at the farmhouse as the droning got louder, and they went around a curve, and saw the current of traffic at a crossroads. A *Feldgendarm* kept it going with two white wands, an ovaled crescent of bright steel on a heavy chain around his neck. The PWs were brought to a halt and waited for a gap. Some tried to sit down but were ordered back up. They waited with a hopeless droop.

The German MP blew a whistle, beckoned them over, and turned them east, the prisoners and their guards squeezed over to the far edge of the road. Their shabby column rippled against the surge and flow of the advancing army.

The German column would build up to a quick pace, then stall out, stop, and wait. Some of the tanks had new paint, their crews in neat, black uniforms. Other tanks were scarred and dented; some were even towed. Waiting units of infantry leaned on their rifles and stared at the prisoners as they shuffled by. Ambulances and trucks crept ahead in low gear and stopped. Horses dragged ammunition wagons and field guns.

Out of all this came two beat-up jeeps in the westbound traffic ahead, filled with slaphappy Americans who carried weapons. But as they got closer, Parker heard them laugh and shout in German at the grinning foot soldiers around them.

The dented jeeps were marked with white stars and one had a colonel's tag on the bumper. But the uniforms were in goofy combinations: green fatigues and an overcoat; an officer's dress blouse with GI shoes; old and new summer khakis.

When they saw the prisoners coming up they saluted, and jeered with almost perfect American accents.

"Hi ya doin', old buddy?"

"Hey! Hubba, hubba, you guys. Let's get the lead out!"

"Yahoo! All the way, the Café de la Paix."

One got out of the jeep, laughed back at the others in German, ran over, and aimed a tommy gun at the PWs.

"We're gonna kill all you *Ami* bastards, you know that?"

The column began to move. He ran back to the jeep and turned to give them a farewell flip of a finger.

A klaxon screamed them off the road to let an ambulance roar back to the east, kept there by the guards until an enormous tank clanked past them in a belch of exhaust, twelve feet wide, twice the size of a Sherman, rumbling the ground.

"Royal Tiger," the sergeant said. "Biggest in the world."

"We should be bombing the shit out of all this."

"They can't. Got no visibility. This is Hitler Weather."

Parker looked at the scud, the slow drizzle, the fog.

"Aren't we supposed to be escaping or something?"

"You got your nose shot off already and you're not satisfied? You want your ass shot off too?"

"We got to try, don't we?"

"Why? Why get killed now? It'll be over in six months."

"I heard all that. Christmas, they said. Now we're talking six months in a concentration camp. We'll be pretty hungry by then, if they don't shoot us first. These shits are real Nazis, what they did to that poor bastard back there."

"He was a looter. What do you expect?"

They went by a road sign: DASBURG. The old stone bridge had been blown away, but engineers had set up a combat replacement with bolted, pre-fabricated sections of girders, and perforated mats. The Americans strolled and hobbled over the thrumming steel as dozens of rubber boats worked back and forth across the river below them.

A passing officer mocked them with his graciousness:

"Good morning, gentlemen. Welcome to Germany."

But a *Landser* broke ranks, pulled his bayonet, lunged at the PWs, and screamed insults. The column buckled, flowed away like threatened minnows, then swayed again and backed off from the guards when they raised their weapons.

The infantryman stamped his hobnailed boots and stalked after the herd with clacked, exaggerated steps. He mimed the stabbing of a stray GI who began a muted howl. The GI hobbled over against the bridge railing, went down on one knee, and rolled over on his hip, both hands still up.

One of the paratrooper guards shoved the *Landser* away.

THE APPROACH ROAD to the bridge was narrow and kinked and the prisoners and their escorts had to scramble over the steep shoulders when a tank squeezed past them. But the road got flatter and straighter as they got close to the town, and the pavement changed to cobblestone streets. Two medical men stood on the side and watched the ragged parade, red crosses on their white canvas vests and helmet covers.

The *Feldgendarm* directing traffic shunted the PW column to one side and the guards brought them to a sloppy, uncertain halt. One Red Cross man pointed at Parker and the other pulled him out of line by the sleeve. They led off the blind man, soothing his dread and resistance with pats on the back.

"McHugh? What's going on? We can't keep up, is that it?"

His buddy spoke in his ear, ruffled his hair, and rubbed his good shoulder. The German medic went up to the man with the red overcoat, pulled open the lapels, and looked inside.

The column was ordered to move off. The blind man's buddy skipped a few steps backward for a last look, then turned.

Parker tried to talk to the medics. He could only understand *verwundet* and *Krankenhaus*: wounded and sick house. He explained this to the others, climbed into the truck, and reached down to help the medics guide and load the flinching, moaning guy with the chest wound. The blind man whimpered and hesitated as Parker took his arm:

"What did they do to McHugh? Is he okay?"

"He's fine. But you need a doctor to fix you up."

"But they took McHugh."

THE CITY HAD BEEN BOMBED. Buildings had missing walls, debris still piled in some of the streets. The truck jolted over the rough, rounded cobbles. The blind guy reached out to brace himself. The chest guy grunted with each heavy bounce.

The truck went around a hotel, some of the roof gone, one wall plugged with drop cloths and boards. Sets of blankets, draped over lines of rope, made a blackout curtain that drooped around the main door. A banner hung from three windows on the fourth floor, the words *"104te Lazaret"* under the red Maltese cross.

The truck coasted through a cluster of medics hustling stretchers and stopped behind three ambulances. The PWs were led around the crowd and filed past a wall of broken, torn corpses stacked four-high in alternate, crossed layers. The bloody gray row was thirty feet long. Heads and stumps stuck out of the uneven mound with mismatched arms, and legs stuffed into random gaps.

Parker stopped and looked at the blond hair blowing in the wind, at these things that didn't feel, and didn't know. Those smiles were not smiles. Those eyes did not wink. A long shiver went over him. One of the medics murmured something and gave him a soft prod and a pull.

They were brought into the lobby, the floor covered with bandaged men who lay on litters or pallets, with only narrow spaces for the orderlies. A phonograph on the registration desk played a rousing polka. The GIs stayed close and looked down, Parker with his arm around the blind man's shoulders. But the warmth of the room brought back the pain, that swollen ache in his nose, the throb, those sharp things in his leg.

One of the Germans left a huddle in a corner, both forearms and hands in bandaged splints. The sleeves of his jacket hung empty. He crouched toward them, put his face up close, and growled something nasty. He said it again, louder. The silent GIs didn't move. The German bellowed and waggled his arms. A medic skipped over between the litters, spoke to him, and led him back.

The same medic came over with a ledger book, asked them in German for their names and ranks. Parker helped with the spellings and the serial numbers. The medic looked under the bandages of the blind man's eyes, and then at his arm, and lightly touched at Parker's face. He pulled open the bloody overcoat, turned down one sleeve to look at the guy's back, and made some notes. He spoke to Parker with simple emphasis, and went over to the registration desk.

Parker caught *etwas . . . essen, trinken . . . vor . . . nicht*. He told the others they could have nothing to eat or drink before they saw the doctor.

The windows were boarded up, the air strong with disinfectant and tobacco. Voices droned and things rattled. A soup kettle was on top of a wood-burning stove rigged up with wire-supported, floppy, round chimney sections that led outside through insulated padding. Bowls and spoons were piled on a small table. The phonograph played "Lilli Marlene" and then Bing Crosby did "White Christmas."

An excitement of smiles and happy mutterings filled the lobby as faces turned to the nurse coming down the staircase, red crosses on her apron, and the white kerchief that almost covered her braids. Heidi bragged about her pregnancy with operatic shrugs at the whistles and cheers. She posed for the applause, hands on hips, chin high, a bulged left profile.

Four medical attendants came out of a side room and balanced their way up the stairs with a stretcher case, one end shoulder-high, one end low. A fifth attendant stayed close, holding up a bottle with a tube that went under the blankets.

The side room door opened again. Parker watched a tall man float out of an intense luminescence—white gown, and round cap, a loose surgical mask, a rubber apron smeared with blood. An orderly rushed over from the desk with the ledger. The doctor flipped pages and spoke to Heidi. Parker heard her say "*drei Kriegsgefangener*"—three prisoners of war.

When the attendants came downstairs, she led them to the Americans, and helped the blind man lay on the stretcher, patting his hand as they lifted him and took him out. With a series of strained retches, another man vomited over his blanket, his boots, the floor, and over the man on the stretcher next to him who didn't move. Heidi called to another nurse who came over with a basin of water and towels.

The guy in the overcoat finally said something:

"Damn, it stinks in here. Like shit and turpentine."

"I can't smell a thing."

"You're lucky, then."

Parker tried to understand the system. Stretcher cases waited. Wounded who could still walk also waited. He wondered about a pregnant front-line nurse. Was she a war widow? Was her husband at the front, here, in Italy or Russia? He listened to Berlin cabaret singers and the "Beer Barrel Polka." The same records were played several times over before they came for the red overcoat, and finally for Parker.

PARACHUTES WERE RIGGED under the ceiling of a reception room to make a tent over a double floor of plywood sheets. Strong lamps hung from looped wires, lighting up the tanks, hoses, and instruments, the tables, bottles, basins, and stacks of clean cloths. Two men and a woman wore gray uniforms, masks, and white caps. Parker heard: *"Eins—und—drei"* and felt his stretcher swing up to a pair of high sawhorses.

They scissored away the wrecked parts of his uniform, the entire right leg of his pants, and some of his combat jacket. One sponged off his face. Another held his knee to restrict his spasms when tiny fragments were tweezed out of his leg. They dropped into a metal basin with little pings. Parker could look down and see the beads, the slivers, and congealed blood. He tightened himself hard with each probe until a wad of cotton and a mask was held over his face, and a voice said:

"Inhaling deepful. Please."

. . . GONE, STILL COASTING DOWN that long curve coming off a mountain, him and Squirt, and Mama, all singing, Daddy with a little grin.

"Oh, we ain't got a barrel of money. Maybe we're ragged and funny. But we're rolling along, singing a song . . ."

Datch and Vivian lived in North Carolina in the middle of a cornfield in a house with a rusty metal roof, big empty rooms, and wide halls, all of it bare wood, and old. One spooky room upstairs held a pile of peanuts as high as Toby's head. But he couldn't eat them; they had to be roasted first.

Datch was his daddy's daddy. He was in the war in Cuba, and Datch's daddy was in the Civil War at Antietam, where you could walk for a mile on the dead bodies without touching the ground. Datch's father tried to get a government pension after the war, but they turned him down because they said he also served in the Confederate Army. Datch said it was just some cadet militia thing.

Some kid lived on a farm up the clay road who said Toby talked just like a damn Yankee. He pointed at an old brick chimney that stuck up out of a cornfield that used to be his grandmama's house. When she was little, Yankee soldiers just like Toby rode up on horses and burned it down.

Datch never talked to Toby and children didn't speak unless spoken to. They were meant to be seen but not heard. But Vivian talked a lot. She was Toby's stepgrandmother, as big as a man, her straggly hair cut short, a wad of snuff behind her lip, always barefoot, grinning, spitting brown juice on the ground. One day she killed a chicken for dinner, took it by the legs, stepped on its head with one big, bare foot, and pulled its head right off. Blood spurted, but the chicken's wings kept flapping.

They were in the woods picking huckleberries when a storm came up. Lightning cracked down close and broke off a tree branch. Toby's ears dimmed and a strange burning smell was in the air. Vivian ran away. Toby groped through the wet bushes after her, called, and cried, not sure which way to run.

One morning Toby saw a funny car in the front yard, only a jagged edge of the windshield left, the body all soot and rust. But it was their car. Mama and Daddy were driving to an ABC store in Apex to get Datch some whiskey when a fire started under the dash. His mother's hands were raw from throwing dirt on the flames, and Daddy had burns on his arms. But the tires were all right and the motor still ran.

Later, some man drove up, wearing a thin summer suit, a hat, and a tie. He wanted the money they owed for the car. Toby stood out in the yard, behind a tree, trying to understand. Daddy and the man got mad. Then Vivian came out with a shotgun, squinting her eyes, and the man drove away.

They left that same morning, the car doors tied shut with wire, sitting on egg crates upside down, the wind blowing through, the soot flying. They drove all day, people on US 1 staring when they went by. Toby felt proud of their rusty car. They were different, and they were brave. Daddy always said: "If you can't do it, do it anyhow."

He bought two watermelons on the side of the road. The colored man wanted fifteen cents each, but he let them have two for a quarter. Toby and Squirt stuffed themselves but kept making Daddy stop so they could pee. Daddy got really mad.

AN OLDER MAN with glasses looked at Toby upside down.

"You have much luck. The ball hit the top here and continued through the nostrils, and cartilage. But with small bone fragments. I put it in good order. You have air. Maybe ugly but only cosmetic. When the war is out, ah, then. You will have pain, but I have nothing for you. Aspirin, yes."

Parker blinked at him, tried to see, and to think.

"Then I won't lose my nose? Will I be a monster?"

"Not at all. Difficult breathing, perhaps. And not . . . not until proper plastic work can be—mmm—accomplished. Not handsome. No more Gary Cooper."

"One thing, please. What does '*Ist die Nase voll?*' mean?"

He drifted, all blurry, and shuddered when the pain hit.

"The soldiers who shot me, they laughed at my nose."

"Ah, a joke. It is a joke. It means, 'Is your nose full?' But it also means, 'Have you had enough?'"

THE PRISONERS were kept together but shifted around for new arrivals, or to reach somebody to be carried upstairs, or when ambulances came to pick up wounded designated for the rear. Parker woke up cold. He felt a pressure in his thigh but deep, sharp pains in the throb in his face.

Heidi was down on one knee to reach over and give injections, read thermometers, to pass urinals, aspirin, and water, to wipe foreheads with wet cloths. She spread a German army coat over Parker, tucked it around his shoulders, and spread another doubled blanket over his legs and feet.

"*Gute Nacht, mein kleiner Ami. Schlaf gut.*"

Good night, my little American. Sleep well. Parker thrummed at her touch and her voice. Heidi's apron was smeared with blood, her stockings wrinkled, her kerchief crooked, her eyes as blue as fancy plates standing on edge in a glittering glass cabinet. But they were not Leora's eyes, those fantastic changes of green with deep flecks of turquoise, and gold.

THE SOUND OF GUNS woke him, and then the bombs: big stuff getting closer. He drew himself into a ball . . . a lightning snap and the whole room came apart. In the darkness, he heard things grind, and fall. He heard shrieks and sobs, commands that both ordered and argued, prolonged screams. Small fires were spread around the heaps of crumbled bricks, and plaster where the stove had been, the chimney buckled, and twisted, pieces of it folded.

A flashlight came on, then two. An emergency lantern loomed

through the dust, choking voices angry at what sounded like "English night bombers."

Parker had to work his arm out from something heavy and rough, still dizzy from the anesthesia, slow to understand that the ceiling sagged now, that the wall behind him had blown outward, and was gone. Men stumbled around and coughed. He felt the cold of the outdoor air, found the German coat rumpled at his feet, and put it on. But he couldn't find his boots, and felt around the broken junk, guessing at where the blind man and the guy in the overcoat had been sleeping.

"Hey, you guys—sing out. It's Parker. Where you at?"

A howl came from the stirred, black shadows. Parker heard "Heidi" and tripped his way closer to the man with the two bad arms who tried to pick up and throw away bricks. Parker helped him claw at the crumbled masonry, and splintered wood. They yelled for help, Parker gasping in the gritty smoke, and the heat, and the flashed-up horror of Heidi's twisted legs with the torn, white stockings.

They uncovered the rest of her and stood there, panting. Her hair and the kerchief were soaked in a red goo, one side of her face crushed inward, the other side bulging out.

Heavy concussions rumbled outside but farther away. A dazed *Sanitäter* with blood on his face plodded through the dust and over the broken masonry. He dragged one end of a stretcher and tried to get it over the mess of the collapsed wall. He jerked at the snagged pegs, tossing the wide-eyed patient who raised his head, and grabbed at the sides. Parker picked up the other end and they stumbled out into the yard, Parker's feet cold, and bruised by the rough chunks of debris.

They loaded the stretcher into an ambulance and went back with another. The small fires showed up a worn, scuffed jackboot standing in a puddle of soup. Parker pulled it on and felt around in the shadows for its lost mate. Favoring his bare foot, he helped the medic pull an unconscious man out of the rubble, load him up, and struggle their way outside.

As they passed the stack of frozen dead, Parker saw a right boot sticking out of the second layer that looked like it might fit. He hesitated, his fingers quivering. The medic on the other end felt the drag on the litter handles, turned, saw what Parker was thinking, and nodded. Parker made a quick grab at the boot. The leg swung out with it and he had to hold back on the knee as he pulled at the heel. The boot was a different size but was close enough.

Other things flared up when the ether and oxygen tanks in the operating room exploded. The crowd of *Sanitäter*, nurses, orderlies, and walking wounded all shouted, grabbed, and carried. Then they squatted in the yard, blistered by the heat as they watched the fire, and listened to the coming sirens.

GERMAN GREATCOATS were long enough to cover the tops of the jackboots and Parker buttoned it over his bare leg and the dressings. He took a step backward. A few men were still busy at something, but most were befuddled, and dazed.

Parker took another step, shuffled around, and walked away.

He limped through the ruins, around the holes in the street, and the heaps of destroyed buildings. Some of the houses had exposed roof rafters, the tiles shattered away. Power poles were leaning and bent, the wires sagged or broken. Snow was piled in doorways. Walls were gone.

He listened to the hobnails of his German boots as they clacked and dragged on the cobbles, and he listened to the military traffic that growled in the next neighborhood. He turned a corner and saw a stalled army creeping through the pale darkness, the artificial moonlight reflected off the cloud cover. He watched them pass. If everything really did have a place and a purpose, and if he was just standing there, bareheaded, unarmed, and bandaged, then he had to be ignored.

Until he did what he always did. When a convoy of canvas-covered trucks whined by in low gear, he stepped off the curb and put out his thumb. The men in the cabs laughed and one pointed behind them. Parker hobbled over, caught up with the barely moving truck, grabbed the corner and the tailgate, swung his good leg over, and flinched into the open space.

Two men in the next truck yelled something. He could see the grins and waves over the slits in the blacked-out headlights, convinced he was a wounded Old Hare who couldn't wait to get back, and do his bit—their kind of guy. He gave them a weak Nazi salute. He got two quick ones on the horn.

He settled into the hole and snugged the coat around his legs. The boots were warm, but the right one was tight. He rubbed the bruises and scrapes on his arm where he had to yank it out of the hospital wreckage.

When he looked out at the *Feldgendarm* pointing them into Luxembourg, he knew the bridge was close. He could feel the swerves of the sharp kinks in the approach road and shuddered with this outrageous idea of being alone in the cold woods, the Germans hunting him down with dogs. His knees shook. He grabbed his balls with both hands, squeezed with his thighs, and rocked himself. But a lot had happened since yesterday, and his nose still wasn't full.

He stared at the lights of the truck behind him. He couldn't let himself get caught again, but in the chaos maybe they didn't even know he was gone. He felt the shivering thumps of the bridge and as the convoy crawled up the long grade, he tried to think it all out. He didn't know where he was or which way to go, but not to any concentration camp.

A tank stood guard at the crossroad. The trucks turned left, away from the traffic jam. Riding backward, he couldn't read the road signs, but he knew this was south, and it had to be Skyline Drive again.

Parker leaned on the tailgate, arced both legs over, dropped, and limped along with the truck. He started a running dive but stumbled, and twisted over, slammed hard on his back, and skidded feetfirst into the ditch. The assistant driver in the next truck turned to look back, his mouth open.

Parker scrambled up and ran for the trees, crouched his way through the shredded forest, and listened for sentries, and patrols. He reached from tree to tree and fumbled over the boulders, guiding on the shells that banged and flashed on the horizon. He found a path where the walking was easier but had to drop down when he heard voices. Slow and easy, he edged around, breathing through his mouth, licking his lips.

His boot caught on something. He went down on the knee and hip of his bad leg, first winced, then made a shaken whimper when he felt the body in the snow. Brushing at it with his hands, he hesitated. But he had to do this, had to roll and pull at that thing to get off the white cape with the hood. With this he could be anybody, ignored in the mists.

The German had a flashlight on his belt. By covering most of the beam with his hands, and with help from the artillery flashes, and the cloud reflections, he could follow the battle litter, the impact patterns in the snow, the scattered junk.

A crumpled body with an arm bent backward at the elbow had one of those knit wool cowls some Germans wore under their helmets. Parker pulled it off, flipped away the snow, and rolled it down over his head, careful around his nose, and cheek, the warmth of his breath already helping with the pain.

He waded through the drifts and around the craters, and foxholes, the ammo boxes, ration cartons, and blanket rolls; the bandages, and papers, the mortar shell canisters, the spent, glittering casings.

When he reached the far side of the skirmish, the flashlight played over an American body flung over a bent machine gun next to another with his bowels kinked behind his twisted legs in a series of purses, and wads. Parker shivered over to the next one, his size or a little bigger, but with smaller feet. He tugged at it but stopped to drop down on the snow, his head on his arms folded over his knees, overwhelmed by the disgust, and the panic of all this, this being lost, and alone among the dead.

He made a few shallow, convulsive sobs, then took a deep breath, and got up. He pulled everything off the dead man, laid it all out in sequence, and planned his moves. He balked several times, but stripped off his own bloody mix of rags, to leave only his socks, and the cowl. His skin felt thick, paralyzed from the cold, numb with it. He shuddered, and jerked on the GI's long underwear, and then the two pairs of OD pants, two shirts, and a sweater.

He snatched on the German boots, stomped his feet, swung his arms, and marched in place to get control of his pulse, and his fingers. When most of the quaking stopped, he dug inside to get at the three sets of fly buttons. The field jacket had the shoulder patch of the Bloody Bucket. He found two extra pairs of socks in a pocket.

He looked down at the naked soldier lying at attention, dog tags on his chest, one eye half-open, his head ruined. Parker thought about saying thank you or good-bye—to salute; something, unable to deal with this death thing, the idea that nothing bothered them, and that he could get that way too.

HE DUCKED LOW and to one side, holding the flashlight high, and away, flicking it on and off as he moved through the trees with quick looks until he came to the remains of another skirmish. He rolled a GI over, took his M1, a half-full bandolier, and a helmet with a liner that almost fit. He left the cigarettes but took the Zippo, and canteen, the watch, and gloves.

The fog thinned, lifted, hesitated, then fell. He came to a paved, one-lane road and crawled across on his back, and on his good left side, careful about making a silhouette against the searchlight fingers that waggled over the glowing clouds.

He could hear the stalled German columns in the distance, clogged tight on the road out of Dasburg. He slogged off a slow, hard mile, felt his way up a narrow draw, and leaned, and skidded down the opposite slope around huge boulders. His boots scratched and clattered on icy stones; never sure of his direction, shaking, and breathing hard.

All around him were thickly wooded, razorback ridges and

cliffs gouged by ravines, and creeks. The only flat places were the farm fields, snuggled up to the narrow roads in broken designs. The roads here were nothing, and yet were everything. This whole thing was about roads.

TWO DARK SHAPES oozed and developed out of the fog, and the dawn, and became parked tanks. Parker crept and dodged, flinching at the idea of a sentry's challenge, his face covered by the cowl stretched over his mouth, the edge of the bandages, the cape, and the hood shrouded around him.

He would make a few crouched steps, then kneel and wait. When he got by the tank laager and the half-tracks, he came to a cultivated field, jerking back when he saw a soldier up ahead. He had been following a lone German who lagged behind a skirmish line. Parker squatted down to wait it out but went flat when the firing began. Bullets whooshed the air and riffled the snow. He felt a spasm of terror, caught in the open like this, with daylight coming.

When the shooting stopped, he heard German voices, and a scuffling. Three Americans stumbled back, their arms raised, two Krauts behind them with leveled rifles. Parker had thin, vague thoughts about making some kind of rescue, but he let them pass, then tracked the German straggler, sidling over, out of the way.

Small arms went off. Mortar shells twinkled. A machine gun flashed out tracers in curved patterns. The yells and barked commands got louder as the German patrol moved back. One of them threw a kick at the cowering straggler. Parker lay down tight against a tractor mound curved around a tuft of frozen, unreaped hay. Flashes banged and buffed all around. And then he heard clear GI voices:

"Okay. Far enough. Let's fall back."

"Hell, keep it going. We got 'em on the run."

"We're a recon patrol, asshole. Not no fucking army."

"Exploit the opportunity! Ex*ploit*!"

"Exploit your ass. They're just getting ready for a counterattack. They always counterattack. And I'm the fucking sergeant and I say, fall back."

Parker yelled out, excited but ready for the bullets.

"Hey, you guys! Get me out of here! I need help!"

He got no clear answer, maybe some cautious murmuring. The discharge from his nose dripped down his throat. He hawked but still sounded funny.

"Who are you, mac? What's the password?"

"I got half my face shot off. I got caught by the Krauts. I got away, but I need help. I gotta get behind our lines."

PARKER WAS DELIGHTED to hear familiar language and see familiar uniforms, to make it back home. But he got grim looks as they passed him from sergeant, to lieutenant, to captain. He was not a matter of rescue as much as a capture. They took away his rifle, searched him, and checked his dog tags. Then came the questions—the capital of Idaho? What league had the Cincinnati Reds? But he thought professional team sports were stupid and said so. They looked at him, hard.

What about those queer boots, the left one bigger then the right? And that cape? That thing over his head? Those paper bandages their medic said were only used by the Germans?

"German doctors use German bandages. That's not too hard. Paper? I didn't know that, but if it's paper, okay. Yeah."

They passed him to the rear with announcements on walkie-talkies. Guides took him through hidden passes, over terraces, around boulders as big as cars. The sun came out, a shy accident. He could look down into a winding gorge and see the doubled-back twists of a hardly-anything river. The road from Dasburg dropped down through suicide twists and curves.

The town of Clervaux was like a snow globe scene. Other villages jabbed up out of the scud to the north and to the east; but that had to be Sleeping Beauty's castle down there, glowering over the town with its ancient grays, its mossy stone walls, and its towers, and turrets. All it needed was a moat and a drawbridge.

They clambered down to the railroad tracks where the colonel's jeep waited to take him and two guides to Regimental Headquarters. The jeep bounced and bucked over the ballast, and the crossties. Parker hung on, looking up at the castle, and the rises of the high switchback road beyond, where four wrecked German tanks and three American tanks were burning.

The jeep washboarded through a tunnel, went over a railroad bridge that spanned the Clervé River, looped back over a humpbacked stone bridge, and passed the station. Everything was curved, sloped, and crooked. The only straight lines were vertical. Some of the houses had been hit by artillery, the walls standing alone as empty, broken shells. Twice the jeep skidded and had to slow down to maneuver around piles of fallen masonry.

"What? All the civilians already gone?"

"Or in the cellar. Most of 'em hauled ass before it even started. They're always the first to know what's happening."

The jeep rattled over the cobbles, passed a shop window filled with wooden shoes, and stopped by a small, swinging sign lettered with fancy script—*Hôtel Claravallis*.

OFFICERS SHUFFLED and dealt out messages, reports, and maps. One of them told Parker that Captain Stacy was MIA. What was left of Company B was about to be overrun. The S-2 major wanted to know more about those funny Americans in the junkyard jeeps.

"I'm really sure, sir. We're prisoners and going one way.

They got guns and they're going the other way. Happy as jay-birds, yelling at us in English like real GIs."

The major waited.

"Two of them had MP armbands, but the helmets were wrong."

More frowns, more creases, and sucked teeth.

"And they kept singing this nutty song. 'All the way, the coffee duh pay.' Whatever that means."

"That's the Café de la Paix in downtown Paris."

"You really ought to bomb the shit out of that bridge."

"We'll take care of running the war, Private."

"Yes, sir. But could I have something to eat? And some aspirin or something? I hurt pretty bad."

"Tell me again about this half-ass German uniform you're wearing. You don't look like anybody's soldier. More like something in a Sears Roebuck winter catalogue. Or something in the funny papers."

Parker waited. The major's eyebrows came together, tight.

"You *hitch*hiked from Germany?"

Parker tried a big smile under the bandages, but it hurt.

"Yes, sir. Sort of. On an army truck."

"From Germany into Luxembourg?"

"Yes, sir. If that's where we are."

"Assuming your story is true, according to the Geneva Conventions, an escaped POW can be executed if he is recaptured in combat. Especially if he's in enemy uniform. And if you're a green replacement, just came on the line, how come you already have a shoulder patch of the Twenty-eighth?"

"Everything I got I robbed from dead men around back by the river. I had to. It was really creepy, but I had to. I was freezing and all I had was this German overcoat. I didn't want to get caught in that thing. I got big feet and these boots were all I could find anywhere that halfway fit."

THEY GAVE PARKER a K-ration breakfast meal. A medic asked him when he was wounded and if he was given any morphine, then hit him with a syrette, and found him a space in the hall where he could lie down with some other light casuals. The cellar was already filled with critical cases.

The hotel was loud. Frantic men passed each other on the stairs and yelled in the hallways. Women and kids screamed and cried from the rooms above. Every few minutes another artillery round zunked into the town. A lot of message static sparked and whistled from a radio somewhere in a side room.

PARKER LAY BACK, dissolving with the drug . . . remembering, or remembered his mother telling it until he remembered: their living in a homemade house car, and traveling with a carnival. His father ran a nail joint. Bang a small nail into the beam with one swing and win a prize. Daddy showed them how easy it was.

But the other pocket in the cloth apron had nails with bent-over tips. Daddy gripped the points between his fingers as he started it in, then offered the hammer. Old-time carpenters who never missed just scratched their heads.

Toby slept through the "hey, rube" and woke up to everything in a mess. Some geezer had stuck in his hand and yanked out the kinky nails. Dish prizes were broken, Kewpie dolls crushed, silver canes and candy boxes stomped into the mud; tents slashed, and trailers overturned. His mother squatted down with a flashlight looking for scattered nickels and dimes. In the morning she had a bruise on her cheek. Daddy had raw, skinned knuckles. Toby and Squirt celebrated that day: a special treat, chocolate candy for breakfast.

He first learned the license plates by their color. Then he could read the names of the states. And then the words on the billboards, and the Burma-Shave jingles; following the white line on the gray, twisted flat concrete. He already knew it had no beginning, and no end.

". . . but we're rolling along, singing a song."

Somewhere, going somewhere—to meet Daddy, to go to New York, or to come back, something. Always laughed about Aiken, South Carolina, because that's where their feet were achin'. Mama would carry Squirt to the next corner. Toby stayed with her as Mama went back for the suitcase. She had to walk through town three times to get back to the highway where they could thumb a ride. Squirt stood in line first, by the suitcase, then Toby, then Mama so people could see all of them.

. . . into a big room with rows and rows of tables. Old men in ragged clothes and some funny old women hunched over their bowls. He and his sister ate it all, but his mother shook her head, said, "No, thank you. I'll just have some coffee." The lady looked at her and frowned.

The car had stopped and Toby raised up in the backseat. The man was trying to kiss Mama. The man saw Toby sitting up over them, let her go, and started the motor.

PARKER WOKE UP to overlapped voices: some unruffled, some keyed up—orders, questions, and numbers. From where he lolled against the wall he could see through an open door, and watch a soldier plug in switchboard connections. Others were on radios, their voices wavering from deep and steady to shrill wails. Everybody, everywhere, was surrounded, and they all needed reinforcements, and ammunition.

"I can't connect you. The wire's cut and I got nobody to send out. But maybe I can reroute you through Division."

"Able Company says without help Heinerscheid is gonna go."

"Eagle one to Eagle three. Over. No. We can't change batteries. We got no batteries. We got doodley-squat."

The colonel thundered into a microphone, lecturing with his pipe:

"Sir, I'm truly sorry if I sounded disrespectful, General. But if you really think this situation calls for some smooth-talking parade-ground artist, then send him right over."

The headquarters staff milled from room to room. Field messengers without weapons or gear huffed up the stairs. Parker tried to put it all together: the villages, the distances, the unit designations. He listened as seventeen Shermans were gradually knocked down to five. Four of those broke their tracks, or got snagged on stumps, or they were sucked down into mud. The crews climbed up on the last one and rode it to the river but then bellied down, and stalled on the bottom, trying to cross over.

". . . these the bastards shooting at the castle from the other side of the river? What do we got in there?"

"A hundred, maybe. Small arms only. Headquarters Company and stragglers, cooks, and whatnot, whatever was around. Quite a few local women and kids. Fifteen PWs in the cellar."

The colonel sucked on his pipe, listened to the incoming radio report, took out the pipe, and bellowed again:

". . . got to hold. You got to. Otherwise the whole east side of town is cut off. Look at your map. We're in a spaghetti bowl of roads and streets swirling up and down. The castle is this big meatball to the east. We're that little linguini on the west side where the river, the railroad station, and the bridge all come together. The Krauts ran over Marnach, then attacked along that top ridge. They're coming around the rim of the bowl and then down behind us."

The major stood in front of a map taped to the wall, his arms crossed, his fingers around his chin, restless, unsure.

There were booms and bangs outside. A big voice:

"They did it. They're over the bridge. They got that Sherman by the post office and the one outside is on fire. Some *Panzerfaust* team infiltrated in and they got it."

Parker hovered in and out of sleep. He was back, but that didn't solve much. Company B was lost and he wondered where they'd send him next. He could see now how it was: from here and higher, a chess game—down there, wrestling with bears.

He got up to piss, then lay back by the man who groaned, and wheezed, bandages on his head, and both hands. Two cooks grunted a kettle of stew up the stairs. Parker had no mess kit and they served it to him in one of the white hotel bowls they carried in a musette bag. The inside of the bowl had a glazed picture of the castle with the name Clervaux.

The stew was mostly potatoes, but it was filling and made him drowsy again. He put his helmet on the floor for a pillow and padded the top with the folded snow cape. Curling up on his good side . . . like pulling out those oak file drawers at the library, heavy with catalogue cards.

. . . living near a mustard factory in Long Island City where everything smelled. After that, Philadelphia; but they had to run away. Philadelphia had hollow steel telephone poles and on New Year's Eve people banged on them with hammers. Daddy had a neon sign shop, but the union said he had to hire three helpers. Daddy said he didn't need them and they wanted too much. Then his truck was turned over one night, and the store window got smashed. One of his helpers cut his hand and he and the union wanted to take Daddy to court.

They packed up late one night, the car loaded with blankets and clothes; dishes, groceries, and pots; Daddy's shop tools; compressors, transformers, and torches. Toby still remembered Mama and Daddy looking through the car windows at the empty streets, and the dark excitement of being hunted.

But it was hard to get into Florida. They wouldn't let in just anybody. As they got close to the state line, he heard the bumps of the tarred joints in the road, and watched Daddy's face, and then Mama's. Toby wondered: Were they good enough? He saw the troopers with their guns and cowboy hats. They waved down the jalopy ahead of them, others already pulled over. They were looking for Bolsheviks and Tin Can Tourists. Didn't want no Hoovervilles in Florida, naw suh.

But then happy smiles. They were in. Toby waited to see the orange trees like the pictures on the ends of those wooden crates loaded with their stuff.

. . . woke up in the car at the back of some tourist camp. Mama, Daddy, and Squirt gone off to sign the book, and let him sleep. First Miami and then Arcadia—but this was Tampa. This would be home. But on that first day, when he started out for school by himself, Mama chased after him, upset, always nervous. Give them the right address, but don't tell them he lived in a trailer. They might not let him in.

Most of the boys wore navy dungarees that had white laces at the back of the waist. Some went to school barefoot, their tough toes and heels sliding through the sand, the bell-bottoms swishing. Toby had to wear those sissy shorts and couldn't go to school barefoot. Only poor kids did that. Toby wasn't poor. He had shoes.

. . . and then Leora in the patio garden—sliding the card drawer shut with a little slam.

———

THE COLONEL FIDGETED with the radio dials, swearing at the snatches of German march music that blared back. Finally, he found an unblocked channel.

"Hell, yes, desperate. I got five tank companies gone? Three engineers? I don't know how many rifle companies. Just gone. Damn it, he won't let me withdraw to the other side of the river, and he won't send me any help. Yes, yes, *yes*. I know. Every hour does give you guys a chance to get set up."

". . . . Bastogne, that's what they want. They get through us, they got Bastogne, the hub of the whole wheel. And then, nice tank country after that . . . shit no, this is no *raid!* I don't care what G-2 says; it's a major, major offensive."

". . . five-to-one. No, not just everybody says—I mean five-to-one, maybe more. And I'm covering fifteen miles of front? And you took away one of my battalions, for a *reserve?* Reserved for what? Your birthday party?"

A tank engine dieseled in the street outside and the ground floor of the hotel exploded. The walls shivered. Smoke and dust drifted up the staircase. *Blam!* And *blam*, again. The lights flickered, went off, and on, dimmed, went off again. Lanterns were turned on. Colemans were lit. Parker heard, "What'll we do?," heard it over, and over. The S-2 major shoved crumpled papers into a fire.

The colonel let out another bellow:

"God damn it, you just don't get it. You think I'm seeing bogeymen up here. But I could piss off the roof and splash four tanks with one squirt. This is like the Little Big Horn. It's Custer's last fucking stand all over again."

Sudden calm. The colonel tapped the bowl of his pipe against the heel of his shoe, then blew through the stem. He made another radio contact.

"Captain? Best you get out of there, and fast . . . shit! Already? Well, you did a damn fine job, son. I can't ask you to give me more time, so—thanks and good luck to all of you."

"We should have blown that bridge."

"And cut ourselves off? We didn't have enough demo material anyway. To do the job would take a thousand pounds of TNT at least. Heavy granite like that?"

Two communications men ran out ahead of a small blast, a poof of electric-smelling smoke behind them.

". . . the wounded in the cellar? We got nearly fifty of them down there stretched out all over the place."

"Leave them. We have to. Let the chaplain take over."

They ducked and flinched their hands over their heads when a machine gun tore through the front door, chewed up and churned the plaster, and chips of wood. Boots pounded. Germans shouted. Four women and three kids screamed their way up to the top floor, a hobbling old man caning himself up behind them. Parker bumped through the gasped shadows in the hallways, back rooms lit up through the windows by the flares outside. Loud orders came out of the stiff but porous hysteria.

"This way! Over here! There's a fire escape!"

Soldiers and civilians jostled at the door, prancing with anxiety for their turn to scuttle down the ladder. A woman held a baby and tried to reassure a girl of about four, crying, afraid to try it. Parker squatted and offered his back.

The kid threw her arms around his neck so tight he had to turn his head aside so he could breathe. Then she knocked off his helmet and sent it gonging on the ground below. Then she slammed his nose. He shivered and sucked in his breath. She hooked her legs around his waist. He told her to hang on tight. She didn't understand him, but she knew.

The major took the woman's baby and started down with a one-handed jerk from rung to rung. They got to the bottom and ran the few yards to the face of the cliff, and the woman led them up the crude, uneven stairway, grabbing at banisters of bushes. The flares helped them find the flagstones worked into the earth, and the treads that were hacked out of the bedrock. They made it to the top, breathless, and wheezing.

They looked out over the streets below where a wind blew away the fogs. The sky glowed over a burning village on the left, two more on fire on the right. The searchlights groped through the billows of smoke.

A column of armor clanked down the high bends and hairpin turns in the east. Tank tracks sparked on the cobbles, some skidding to swipe into shop windows. Gangs of hollering Germans ran through the town and banged on doors with rifle butts. Two of the locals struggled to drape a swastika banner over a balcony railing.

The Hôtel survivors ducked down to hide from the parachute flares that popped out of the night like sizzling, electric jellyfish; then got up, and ran into the darkness. The major handed the woman her baby and sprinted for the timber with the other officers, non-coms, and riflemen. Some of the civilians veered away from the ridge toward a dark building with a carved stone front and a garden wall.

One of them rang a bell. Others pounded on a massive side door. It cracked open and in the edging of light Parker saw a glowing, flat figure in a cowl, and robe. Parker put the little girl down. Her mother reached for his hand, shook it, and said something in what must have been the Luxembourg dialect. He didn't understand any of it but felt the tremble of gratitude in her fingers, and with it a soothing quiver. She made a fluttering touch at his face bandages.

He turned to catch up with the others, his hand still buzzing.

T he others ran ahead. He heard loud talking and reckless feet that broke twigs, and kicked through piles of snow, and leaves. Parker felt his way, got his foot down to something hard before he stepped with his whole weight. The pink loom of the sky above Clervaux helped him grab at trees. He would wait for a flare or take quick looks with the flashlight.

The running noises grew fainter. Then he heard rifle shots. He faded over to his right, avoiding those sparse groves of hardwood trees with their naked branches, staying with the dense pines, and firs, until he came to a cart road that slipped away from the direction of Clervaux.

He heard tanks, flopped down, and crossed his arms over his head, swearing at himself for running off without that snow cape. Eight tanks went by like lions, long spaces between the roars that droned off into the softer, clattering squeaks of sprocket wheels in the track pads. He stayed down and waited another ten minutes, but the infantry never came.

He worked his way through the underbrush along the edge of the road, crept from tree to tree, and guessed that the direction was north. The colonel said something about Esselborn, and about a mile and a half. It took almost two hours for Parker to come to a lone village café, the door swung open: no lights, no sounds.

He skulked along the walls, bumped around the tables and chairs, and blundered through a swinging door into a kitchen. He used the German's flashlight for careful peeks and found a quarter loaf of stale bread, and a raw potato. He tried the tap in a metal sink, cupped his hand under the trickle, drank all he could, and filled his canteen. He soaked the bread and ate it with the potato. The skin had a muddy taste.

Headley said sleep whenever you can, but Parker could be trapped in here. He went out to the front windows, felt the white lace curtains, jerked them off their rods, slashed holes with the dead man's trench knife, and pulled them over his head. He draped another over his head and shoulders like a loose shawl, went outside, and slunk back into the woods.

HIS HEAD KEPT NODDING. He slapped himself but stumbled twice, and hugged each tree a little longer. Then he let himself slide down into a pile of rotting leaves. He pawed a den out of the humus, curled into it, and crawled into a sprinkle of trash thoughts that salvaged themselves; shredded memories, wishes, and sorrows; sneaking around some things with a deft shunt of evasion, unwilling to take the risk of reaching down in the dark for a lost dime, and coming up with a mushy turd.

He went back to New York, to Ridgewood. Squirt was still with Mama, but he had to stay awhile with Nana, Pop-Pop, and Uncle Boysy. He roller-skated in the street and traded bubble-gum cards with other kids, the Chinese, and the Japanese cutting each other up with machine guns, and great, two-handed swords. The German-American Bund was across the street and he saw the uniforms and flags. The *Hindenburg* floated in low to land over in New Jersey, the tail red with a black swastika.

He saw *King Kong*. Nana hated war and didn't want him to see *All Quiet on the Western Front*, but he did, finally. One day, a man in ragged old clothes and whiskers rang the buzzer and called up the stairwell. Nana told him to come on up, and she gave him a sandwich. Toby watched him gobble it down. Later he saw a chalk mark on the steps of the front stoop.

The big kids made scooters out of wood boxes nailed to a piece of two-by-four, a skate taken apart, the front two wheels and the back pair nailed to the ends. Some added coffee can lids to play like headlights. They hung ribbons on the wood handles and pushed themselves back and forth through their one-legged delirium.

A world war statue was in the neighborhood, a soldier in a helmet charging with a rifle and bayonet. Ford was one of the names in the bronze underneath. Toby named one of his toy soldiers Lieutenant Ford.

Coming home from school, Toby could see their white cat crouched on the ledge of their third-story window. At night it would sleep at his feet. But he came home one day and it was gone. Nana was upset and didn't want to talk about it. They couldn't afford to feed a cat.

An old man used to sit on the stoop, the father of the German landlady. He couldn't speak English but smiled all the time and sometimes gave new pennies to kids. The landlady's door was open one day and as Toby went up the stairs he could peek in, and saw the old man in a casket covered with flowers.

The bathtub was short so it could fit into the kitchen. You had to drop a quarter in the gas meter to make hot water.

Pop-Pop took him to a little circus, but he only had one funny half-dollar. The man dropped it on the ticket counter, tried it again, then gave it back. Toby said, "I told you it was no good, Pop-Pop. I told you." That thick hand whacked him on the back of the head and he almost fell on his face. He got hit all the way home, afraid to run, afraid to stop.

. . . up under the arms. Pop-Pop would toss him high and free, and tell him again how he would grow up to be the captain of a big black ship with tall, white sails. Toby giggled it all down, those many heavens only limited by the ceiling.

When he got older he read that small, yellowed newspaper clipping. Captain Johannes Larsen and other distinguished explorers embarked on a Caribbean expedition to find the remnants of the lost continent of Atlantis.

Out of this came the Atlantis license plates that got so much attention, the numbers embossed with a hammer and nail by Uncle Boysy; and the passport from the Empire of Atlantis and Lemuria, written in Esperanto, filled with visas from isolated consulates. Pop-Pop was convinced this was the equivalent of diplomatic recognition.

And then came the Atlantis stamps he sold in denominations of five, ten, and twenty-five skaloj, all with the Empress Marie's picture; Toby's great-grandmother back in Denmark. All this produced handfuls of newspaper clippings stuffed into that dragged, worn leather suitcase as Pop-Pop enlightened the police, and reporters in small towns all around the country.

Toby's report cards were good and he was skipped a grade. When he got sent back to Tampa he was in Leora's class. When he came in and saw her that first day he tingled all over with that crazy, squirming thing in his chest.

PARKER WOKE UP shivering. By his watch he was down thirteen minutes. He got up and swerved among the trees, hoping he was going west. He heard heavy feet and American voices.

He yelled out, "Hey, you guys!" and dropped flat.

A mumbled answer got stronger.

"Able Company. Hundred-and-tenth. From Heinerscheid."

Parker not sure. What was he?

"Company B. Marnach, I think. Only been here two days."

Six privates crashed out, loud and bold. Parker jerked when two more from the Second Battalion came out and then others:

phantoms, shy night animals afraid of each other. Twos and threes rustled through the brush, some with bandages.

"You guys got some idea what's goin' on?"

"Sure. A bunch of fucking Nazis are trying to kill us."

"Yeah, right. But which way they going?"

"Beats the shit out of me. If I knew anything for sure about this fucking situation, then I'd really be confused."

Hisses, then quiet, and a low challenge. Two corporals and a sergeant came in with a lieutenant who had a compass, and a map. He made a head count up to twenty-three, ordered them to spread out, and look for a railroad, and a river, slicing the west in half with the edge of his hand.

They bashed their way downhill but favored the thin spots, bunching up where the walking was easier. Parker held back. These happy targets were scary. But when they came to the railroad tracks they were all business, afraid of the ghost guns that could fire out of the clear perspective. They slouched over one at a time, boots scuffling on the roadbed.

The ground got marshy and soft and the scout called out:

"Over here. It's like stepping-stones."

Running feet, a little yelp, and a splash. Silhouettes congregated at the shallow place. The lieutenant waved his flashlight and hissed, and shushed for order.

They helped each other across with a stick or an extended rifle, or waded over in pairs, supporting the five wounded. Somebody started a fire and they huddled around it with stubborn arguments about the Germans seeing it, or not seeing it, and about freezing to death. They wrung out their socks and pants, swung their arms, and shivered, the lieutenant uneasy.

"No good. We're exposed here. We have to move out. You and you, take the sharp end. Come on. It's not that cold."

They groaned, sloshed helmets of water on the fire, and

made something of a formation, still wet, tired, and cold. They came to a narrow paved road with weeds growing in it and scuttled across in spaced twos and threes, hearing traffic off to their left. It had to be the Germans somewhere on the main road out of Clervaux. The lieutenant held another flashlight briefing, kneeling down with the NCOs to check the map, and compass, a raincoat over their heads.

Daylight began at 0730, a Monday, his third day. Parker's leg and face were aching as the group rambled cross-country for two or three miles, the ground rolling more gently as it rose up from the river valley. They crossed random patches of woods, but most of it was cultivated, with haystacks, and fences. The lieutenant stared long and hard with his field glasses, then led them around the isolated farmhouses.

Two GIs tottered up in plain view along a crest of high ground. Only one had a rifle. The lead scout challenged them, checked their identity, then waved at the rest to climb up the slope to a main highway. The lieutenant called it N-12. The GIs were survivors of the 106th Division, overwhelmed and surrounded when the Germans first attacked, the first combat for the Golden Lions. Two entire regiments surrendered.

"We ran, okay? We bugged out. Just too goddamn many of the bastards and too fucking fast. But we're here. We're still alive, right? Fuck that prisoner shit."

A cluster gathered close, curious and open to anybody as hopeless as they were. Then another ambled up out of the fog, a dismounted tanker from the Ninth Armored, wearing a crash helmet of padded leather and plastic, a wire, and a plug connection dangling from the earphones, his face black with burned powder, and mud, his eyes like red holes.

"I'm Jimbo. I came through a French town back there. I don't know how you say it. They said it means 'Three Virgins.'"

And then another: a tight-lipped, scowling Bloody Bucket. He glowered and hung back, his rifle cradled in his arm like Davy Crockett. Parker would guess by his look that he had been in the Hürtgen Forest, most likely with the 112th. Sergeant Dean said they got the worst of it.

The non-coms formed them up in open single files on both shoulders of the road and they began a steady march through the sleet, and the fog, weapons ready, eyes bleary, and dull.

A LOUD WARNING came from the point and they took cover with hollow thumps: a repeated chord of bangs, and tinkles. The sergeant made his way forward in zigzagged rushes and rolls, then stood up, and waved them on. The scouts had met a patrol sent out from a roadblock at Antoniushof, a junction of three farm buildings that straddled the road from Clervaux.

The patrol leader, a first sergeant, took them in past the foxholes, the knotted faces, a half-track snuggled down in a ditch with a cluster of .50-caliber machine guns. Both sides saw each other as disappointing rejects. The sergeant turned them east at the road junction, led the lieutenant to the command post, then lit up a cigarette, and waited with the others.

"We gotta hold this. Hold right here. This is the one road that goes west that can support anything heavy, and it's a straight shot to Bastogne. The Krauts gotta have it. We call this Task Force John. It's a potluck stew of leftover outfits thrown together. Odds and ends, this and that."

They gaped and stared. Parker watched him take a deep drag, cross his arms, and drop his head, exhaling at his feet as he kicked at the snow.

" 'John' is for Captain John. We're an armored infantry company, but we got a few Shermans tucked away, a platoon of armored engineers. Maybe a hundred guys from Ninth Armored. We got anti-aircraft gunners who lost their guns, drivers lost their trucks. Fucking band players lost their fucking horns."

He smiled around, appreciating the one, lonely chuckle.

"But we do have a full battery of field artillery, close enough for support. Part of the Second Battalion, the Twenty-eighth's reserve, is over by that next village someplace. We got a few machine guns. And now we got you guys."

The lieutenant came out of the house, looked up and down at a map as a captain swung his finger across the horizon, and pointed out the realities.

THE SURVIVORS were sent back to regroup and refit on the other side of a rise in the terrain. Parker limped away from the column to look into an abandoned farm wagon and came back with a rusty mattock—a perfect tool for digging in cold, hard ground. He twirled it over his shoulder and jigged with a hunched back and a gimp. A muddy curtain dragged behind him.

"Heigh-ho, heigh-ho. It's off to work we go."

He got no laughs, not even many grins.

They drifted and dragged past the outposts, the tanks parked among trees, and covered with branches. A heavy weapons platoon had dug out firing pits for their mortars, swabbing the tubes, setting up aiming stakes, and bubble levels.

The survivors filed over to a field kitchen behind a barn where they got water from a canvas Lister bag chained up on a tripod. The cooks handed out spare mess kits and they went through the chow line, the kettles steaming hot but the stew already cool as soon as it was ladled out into the air.

Medics came around to check the wounded. They sent two to the rear in a jeep and patched up the other three. Parker was declared fit for duty. They put new bandages on his face and leg and gave him some aspirin.

The SOS men had heaps of gear strewn on the ground, picked up from some battlefield by scavenger details with a Quartermaster Salvage Unit: web belts, blanket rolls, entrenchment tools and rations, muddy rolls of toilet paper. The survivors picked through it: bored, tired. They took the raincoats, folding them through the backs of their rifle belts, but most turned down the overcoats. They were warm, but they soaked up water, and got heavy.

Parker picked up an M1. Some homesick GI had carved a square hole in the butt, and sealed in a girl's picture with a fitted piece of Plexiglas. Parker put it down but picked it up again, and then a Browning Automatic that weighed twice as much with its flash hider, and bipod. He poked through the pile, looking for a lucky helmet, and found one that had bloodstains inside. It had a deep dent and a bullet hole that went through the steel pot, and the liner. He adjusted the laces so it would fit as he waited with the crowd behind a supply truck.

He stepped up for his one bandolier of M1 clips and two bandoliers of six twenty-round BAR magazines. He draped them over his shoulders and took the one black cardboard cylinder. He watched the veterans rip off the tape, drop out the grenade, spread the cotter pin wider, and button a pocket flap over the pull ring so it would dangle over his chest.

The service guy with a Blue Star patch held up a bazooka. Men ducked and waved it away.

"Unh-unh. Forget it, pal. No suicide pipe for me."

Jimbo, the tanker, stepped up, his crash helmet gone, a steel pot in its place, carrying an M1.

"I'll take it."

"Everybody's afraid of this. You know how to use it?"

"A little. Fired one in basic."

"Good enough," the Blue Star said. "You need a loader to make a team. Anybody?"

The Blue Star looked at the averted faces.

"What's this shit? No takers? So find somebody, okay? Here. You pull off the safety pin here, right? Stick the rocket in the back. Connect the wires to these posts on the firing gadget, here. The loader taps the shooter on the helmet a couple times, then ducks out of the way. It's got a helluva backfire. There's batteries in the handle and the trigger closes the circuit. All I got is eight rounds."

Jimbo picked up the clumsy bazooka tube by its long sling and shouldered it up next to his rifle, turning when the Blue Star yelled after him:

"Don't carry it around loaded, okay? Sometimes the rocket will freeze up inside."

Jimbo waved, picked up the ammo vest, and lugged it past the cluster of men. Eyes squinted at things far away or concentrated on their cigarettes with busy snuffles, hawks, and spits. Parker waited on one side. Jimbo nodded at him.

"You want to buddy up with this thing? I need a partner."

They looked at each other, asking for a silent vow of allegiance with their eyes. Could he trust this guy? Would he die for him?

"Okay. But I'm already kind of loaded down."

"I can carry the stuff."

Jimbo put his head through the vest and tied the side straps, the rockets in separate pouches, front and back. He looked down and talked to his boots in a flat tone: no associations, no prompting, just let it come out.

"I was a loader in a tank crew with the Phantoms. Up north of here. We got hit by a Tiger and did a Ronson lighter. All five of us bailed, but they . . . all but me."

Jimbo's lips quivered. A tear jiggled through the mud.

THEY MOVED OUT in a ragged single file. Non-coms pointed them off into the best defense areas; knolls, rises, cross-fire positions that concentrated on the road from Clervaux. They dug their fox-holes and emplacements up the slopes, across the fields, and along the ditches. Haystacks were scattered in some of the fields, the sides eaten around by cattle to leave overhanging caps. They looked like huge apple cores standing on their ends. Jimbo grinned.

"Don't never get behind them things. Tracers will set 'em on fire."

Parker liked that cross corner in the barbwire fences with the cattle chutes and he wanted to get away from the others. Headley said most guys got lonely, crowded up too much, and were too lazy to dig deep. Jimbo just looked. A sergeant yelled through his hands:

"What are you guys doing way over there?"

Parker yelled back:

"Flank guard. We're the right flank."

"Get over here, closer in."

Parker made a one-handed wave to go away. The sergeant glared back, his fists on his hips. They used the pick end of Parker's mattock to break through the frozen crust, the wide, curved end to pry out the clumps. They dug and dragged with their entrenchment tools, one with the blade straight, the other adjusted into a hoe.

They scattered the dirt wide to avoid that obvious hump, and then brushed snow over the exposed dirt with sideway sweeps of their arms, and hands. Parker shared his lace curtains with Jimbo, figuring out how to rig hoods over their helmets — clamping one edge between the shell and the liner, and flipping the rest of it behind their shoulders and back.

"At least now we won't look like a pair of raisins on top of the oatmeal."

AND THEN they waited and tried to hide the trembling in their fingers. Parker peeked over the edge of the hole. Jimbo smoked. They got on their knees to take nervous pisses in the bottom and dragged loose dirt over the puddles with the toes of their boots. Parker had a toothbrush and a small can of oil that he found in the dead man's jacket. They broke down their weapons and used it to clean the mechanisms.

S earching brackets of white phosphorous whirred and boomed in at exactly ten o'clock. Each hot fragment left its own trail of smoke as they stank in the wind like giant, poisonous dandelions, puffed up, and blown away. One GI screeched, climbed out of his hole, and rolled in the snow, slapping at himself, the chemicals eating into his arms.

Then the fire for effect. The ground jerked. Shrapnel whined and fluttered. Men screamed. Parker and Jimbo held their ears, bent their knees into their bellies, and kept their mouths open to relieve the pressure of the concussions.

Ten minutes of it, the impacts moving back like a dirty curtain that opened on four Panthers painted white. They whipped across the fields, threw up a spray of mud, and snow, their bow and turret machine guns firing, their decks swarmed over with grenadiers in snowsuits. More infantry ran up behind them, their war cries a shrieked insanity. Parker started those violent shivers until something, from somewhere, murmured to relax, to go easy, that none of this really mattered.

Small arms puked out into the fog along with a counterbarrage of shells that landed close among the tanks. One took a hit. A heavy shell jolted it back on its suspension and made it sway and turn. The engine raced, but it didn't move.

Parker watched the smoke cloud up. The turret hatch came open and two of the crew climbed out and fell to the ground, choking. A third got stuck at his armpits. The first two climbed back over the road wheels and tracks, pulled him out, dragged him to the ground, and away, one of his legs shredded, and flopping loose. Bullets hit around them. One fell over. The second was applying a tourniquet when he slumped on top.

Jimbo glared at all of it, screamed at it:

"That's what they did. They did that to *us*. To *us!*"

Shells exploded in the ammo racks, and the gun turret came off the hull, and slid to the ground. The other Panthers hesitated and turned back. The skirmishers kept up their advance, firing as they came. Parker nudged Jimbo and yelled over the noise.

"Not yet. Wait until they get into those fences."

The Germans helped each other spread the barbwire to duck through the gaps, to crawl underneath, or to climb the strands like steps where they were stapled to the posts.

"Stupid, dumb bastards got no fucking wire cutters!"

That trembling in Parker's fingers started again, but then the calm came back. Jimbo squeezed off steady, paced rifle shots. Parker did the Browning Automatic by the book: rocked back on the bipod after each burst of three or four, and reaimed in short scoops. He was only weakly aware of those other GIs shooting from somewhere around them.

Some Germans ran; some fell. Parker fired and got recoiled back. He changed magazines and fired again—a screaming slaughter at the fences, and cattle chutes, the Germans caught, unable to see where it was coming from. The wire glistened with a wet red, sagged by the draped bodies, the snow beneath it blotched with pink dribbles, and stains.

But all of this was at a distance, in an unfocused part of the blurred, slow-moving numbness. Parker moved the way he was supposed to move and did what he had to do. These were gallery shots; some vague scenery of black, and red, on white.

Mortars dropped around them in geysers of ice, pebbles, and dirt. An iron storm of shrapnel slushed across the field.

Jimbo's rifle pinged out the clips. Every twenty rounds, Parker pressed the release, dropped out the empty BAR magazine, and clicked in a new one. The Germans fell flat, squirmed, and paddled themselves away.

The artillery lull had a spastic reluctance. The tanks were gone. A few rifles went off. Parker and Jimbo drank from their canteens, stared at each other, and tried to grin. Parker worked on some K-ration chewing gum as Jimbo smoked. Wounded men shrieked out ahead of them, and close behind.

A German voice could be heard over and over, the accents strong, the *r* from deep in the throat.

"Medic here! Medic here! *Wir sind Sanitäter!*"

He waved a small red flag on a long stick. Behind him, an officer made a whistle signal. The shooting stopped on both sides . . . quiet, nothing. Parker could hear the sigh of the wind over the cries of agony. The German medic cringed as he raised up, wearing a white smock with a red Maltese cross from his neck to his waist and across the width of his chest.

He held both arms out, his head down, accepting whatever was decided. He waited, then called behind him. Litter teams came up in a crouch, then infantrymen without weapons. The GIs watched them drag and carry back their dead, and wounded.

A jeep with a red cross plowed across the field, a white cloud whirled up by the snow chains. It stopped at a foxhole. The two medics and a soldier's buddy got him on a stretcher, lifted it, and strapped it to a frame mounted over the hood. The jeep skidded over to Parker and Jimbo's hole. The driver ducked behind the dash and tossed them a double handful of .30-caliber clips.

"Here. All we got. This lucky bastard got hit right in the mush with a rifle grenade that didn't go off. Busted his chin all up and jammed his teeth into the roof of his mouth. Didn't even want to come with us. He was fine, he said."

The jeep scurried among the holes. They found another casualty, loaded him on the other stretcher, and went back. Parker reloaded two BAR magazines with cartridges thumbed out of the M1 clips, wiping each one off on his pants.

For thirty-seven minutes, nothing moved.

"Jimbo? What is all this? We gonna die right here?"

Jimbo looked serious, his dirty face pouted.

"I don't know. Maybe."

THE GERMANS made another charge, bunched behind a scattered line of six Panthers and Mark IVs: steady, and determined through the shelling that met them. Parker and Jimbo laid down a carpet of fire until the BAR quit, Parker stuttering, excited, feeling naked:

"I'm out. Out. That's it. I'm done."

Parker looked back. He saw two runners go from hole to hole with draped necklaces of bandoliers. But the light faded as the fogs came back, and he and Jimbo were too far out.

"We gotta move. One of our MGs has been shooting that way from over there somewhere. Let's try for it."

They left the BAR. Parker took over the vest of bazooka rockets from Jimbo and they climbed out, running an evasive pattern of flops, and rolls, quick scrambles at different angles. They made it to the remains of a stone wall, dug out, and enlarged with a riprap of burlap bags leaking sand.

Three dead men were inside the nest, another almost gone, flung beside a water-cooled .30-caliber Browning mounted on a heavy tripod. The pit was littered with ammo cans and personal gear, frozen mud, heaps of cartridge cases, a ripped jerry can. One of the corpses was in torn, dismembered, blackened, red pieces.

But the overheated gun went off by itself in one blind, continuous burst, the cooling tank steaming, the water hose blown away. The swivel latch was loose and the gun traversed, and jumped in crazy jerks. It roasted and simmered, part of the flopping belt in flames until the ammo was gone, and the barrel, and the water jacket sagged to one side.

A filtered moon glowed just once to silver up the random patches of fog and mist. Sparking, bright flashes came out of the gray. Parker ran after Jimbo. He wheezed for breath, but felt a sudden, loony pleasure, dizzy with it, invincible; laughing. He could do this thing—he could do it.

They scurried past smashed vehicles, tires burning, bodies dumped on the road, and in the ditches. They cringed over their shoulders along with other GIs, some of them bleeding, not quite dark when they got back to Antoniushof, their way lighted by the fires. They ran toward a farm building with pockmarked walls, the chimney broken off. The carcasses of charred, twisted half-tracks, and trucks, had been toppled, and dragged together to block the road.

A soldier in an outpost beckoned them on. Farther back another waved them all to a stop. "Mines," he yelled, one arm out straight, a finger pointed at a safety lane. The other arm pumped at the elbow.

They saw apple trees and compost piles in the farmyard and heard the quick scuff and scrape of frantic digging. A captain had a forty-five in his hand and pointed with it to place men in positions around the barns.

"You bazooka men! Over here! Take up a position on the second floor of that house over there!"

They had to kick away rubble from the treads as they climbed the stairs. They found four dogfaces with rifles in the bedroom partially open to the sky.

"The captain sent us up here. Where do you want this?"

"Here by the window. Best view in the house."

Parker peeked around the sash. Overhead flares dazzled the fields and he had to put a hand over his eyes. The roadblock was out front and to the right. He tried to remember the maximum range of a rocket. Four hundred yards, if lobbed up at an angle? But how far was that? He listened to the reverberations of the tank engines, the clangor of track links.

They built barricades in the two windows that were left, piled up broken furniture, dragged over a dresser, hoping a chair leg might somehow make the difference. They pulled a heavy, thick mattress off a bed and draped it on top. Parker's jaws were cramped and he spit out the wad of gum. Jimbo lit a cigarette and took quick puffs, grinning at the dull thuds that hit the stone walls of the house, and the two small wads of mattress stuffing that spurted around the room.

The first tank hit a mine in the road, reared, and skewed sideways. The next went around it, the pound of its diesel building as it made a run for the barricade, got close, and set off another mine in a big blaze. Two Panthers clanked up behind it. Grenadiers bobbed and weaved in the shadows, the twinkle of their weapons answered from every window, and hole.

Jimbo fiddled with the adjustable sight on the bazooka.

"You okay, Toby?"

"Hell, yes. I'm just getting the hang of this shit."

Parker loaded the rocket, wired it to the housing, crawled up close, and slapped Jimbo's helmet twice. Stone and mortar dust puffed all around. Rifles crackled. Two GIs in the bedroom yelled and cursed out furious challenges:

"Come and get us, shit head. Come on. Over here."

The other two mumbled to themselves, watching another medium swerve closer, a Mark IV. The ball-mounted machine gun in the bow cluttered up snow, dirt, and pieces of trees. The turret traversed and the gun fired at the roadblock.

"Shoot, Jimbo! For Christ sake, fire!"

Jimbo's fingers fumbled at the trigger housing.

"The safety, Jimbo! Thumb off the safety!"

The room filled with a hot, flashing cloud of dust, and flame from the backlash—a bright *whoomp* on the tank, the track knocked loose, a return roller wobbling on a bent shaft, one road wheel broken.

Parker scuttled around, reloaded, and pounded on Jimbo's helmet. The turret gun started to turn, and reach, but was slow at it. No push-button controls, Jimbo said. They had to crank theirs by hand. Another swoosh and a clang. The rocket glanced off the turret and gouged out a long silver scar.

"In the ass, Jimbo. Hit it in the ass!"

The next one did it. The tank torched up. Blind and tired, it made a crippled curve, and scraped against the roadblock. Its paint blistered, bubbled, and dripped tears into the hissing mud as it stalled, coughed, and canted over.

A Panther started around the end, slid down at an angle, flattened a fence, and followed a ditch to swerve back, and ram the pile of wrecks with a bang, and a high-pitched tear of metal. It backed up, hit the pile again, and shoved the center aside. Two Mark IVs followed through, the second guiding on the other's track ruts to avoid the mines. The next Panther pulled off to the side, the commander standing in the turret with field glasses.

"There, Jimbo. That one. He's looking at us."

The round fell short. They saw the commander point at the house and saw his mouth yell out to the grenadiers. Parker loaded and wired another rocket.

"Make it higher, Jimbo. Get it up."

It landed too far over, but the commander took cover. Jimbo tried it again, hit a bogey wheel, and tore off a track link. The turret gun went up and around, working over the house from left to right. Parts of the roof, chimney, and walls crumbled with every shot. Jimbo was laughing:

"Ha! We lucked out. He's using armor-piercing, not HE."

One of the other GIs fired from what cover was left, shook his fist, screamed, winced back, and cowered away. Another lay in a bloody puddle, half-covered with shattered bits of chimney brick. Another was dragged away by the arms. Jimbo dropped the bazooka, crawling, and fumbling over the wreckage of the staircase. Parker still had two rounds in the pockets when he ducked out of the ammo vest, and followed Jimbo down.

The captain lay just inside the shambles of the front door. Parker took the pistol from his hand and stumbled through the house after the other survivors, who argued, swore, tripped into each other, tried to climb through a rear window, but drew back when they heard German voices.

Four men had a quick, fierce, muttered debate, then threw their weapons outside, raised their hands, and cringed their way through the window with a white towel draped over the end of a broom. Others held back, undecided, listening.

"We give up. Comrades, okay? We're buddies now, right?"

They heard a gruff outcry of German, repeated bursts from machine pistols, and furious, terrified American screams. Bullets splatted against the walls. A grenade smoked through the window and exploded. Men went down in a fog of dust, falling over heaps of mangled household junk.

Those who were left rushed from room to room, shot at whenever they tried a window. They backed their way toward a cellar and lurched down the steps, Parker last, Headley telling him: No, don't do it. But what else was there?

They groped for a storm door, a window, a coal chute, a secret tunnel. In the midst of convulsed breathing, horrified men whimpered their misery in the darkness. They shuffled and crawled into corners, fumbled behind vegetable bins and piled boxes, and cowered under the stairs. And then they feigned an innocent silence above their heartbeats.

They heard murmurs at the cellar door, then pops and hisses. A grenade hit against a wall. Another clattered down the steps. The third came over the handrail. Parker dropped the M1 with the girl's picture in the butt and lay flat, his arms around his head. Then came the quick beat of detonations, squeals, and sniveling, a thick acrid stink.

Men whined and groaned. Jimbo was blown over on top of Parker. He gurgled into his ear, blood splashing out of his throat to run hot over Parker's face, and neck. He could taste it as he hugged Jimbo, tried to moan something to him, could feel the desperate pump, and the slacken, and the slowing of the quiver in Jimbo's fingers.

Parker went limp into a brief exhaustion, a relaxing that could be his, a sleep; but he smelled the juices of preserved apples and pears that had puddled with the smashed jars. From that syrup came a surge of wakefulness, an insistence. This would work. He could make this work.

Boots were on the stairs. A battle lantern came on and strobed up dim glimpses of terrified, demented faces. Three bursts of automatic fire flogged up old dust and masonry, wood splinters, and gobs of flesh. Hobnails scraped on the floor, crushing pieces of broken glass. A voice murmured under its breath in a casual, awkward baritone, one of those Nazi party songs:

"... *wir werden weiter marschieren wenn alles in Scherben fällt ... da heute gehört uns Deutschland ...*"

A flash moved over Jimbo's steady, wild eyes and around the cellar. Parker forced himself not to blink and let his mouth fall open in a warped sag as he gripped the captain's pistol, wedged behind his back. He cocked the hammer and wondered if any bullets were still in it.

The SS man kicked at the bodies. One moaned and raised a hand, twitched, and choked on bloody vomit. A burst from the gun, the concussions pounding in the enclosed hollow of the cellar. Ricochets spit off the hard stones in the walls.

The boots scraped and paused. Parker heard a soggy, hollow thump. The German put the light in Jimbo's gory face, then Parker's, straddled his body, and raised the *Sturmgewehr* to the head of the next man. The GI tried to avoid the light, his hands shaking as he pushed away at it.

Parker rammed the pistol up into the SS man's crotch. There was a blam, a jerk, and a gasp, an amazed grunt, and a prolonged whinny, a strangled, keening sound half-muffled, and sobbed. He shrank down into a tight, agonized squat. The lantern dropped and threw bizarre, distorted patterns over the bodies, and the stones, and the shelves of shiny jars.

Parker raised up from out of the butchered pile, grabbed him behind the neck, and pulled him down, their flat, shadowed faces close, each eyeing the interior ghoul of the other. Parker let him see the pistol. He could feel the German's strength lose its quick and leak back to fill Parker's arm. That quivering was a massage, an initiation. Parker twisted the barrel into his mouth, and fired, buffeted by a flash of wet heat as the bullet passed through.

The force of it knocked the German out of his hand, his helmet clunking off the floor, and there was a smell of shit as he seized, and wrenched. Parker watched the somber spasms of his first real kill—up close and personal. He felt a pride and an abysmal terror all at once, a passage into something beyond, a killer now, a blooded warrior.

He leaned over and whispered to the shaking GI:

"Lay still. Don't move and be quiet. You got that?"

Parker could feel the man's slight nod. He picked up the lantern and turned it off as he stepped over the bodies behind the staircase. He waited for the boots and the pause three steps down. A question Parker didn't understand, then:

"Oberscharführer? Sind Sie das? Was gibt?"

Some kind of SS sergeant. Was that him? A voice said something farther away. The man on the stairs answered and went back up. Parker waited, then flashed the light around the room, and over the scrambled bodies. His whisper was loud and hoarse:

"Any of you guys okay? This is our chance. Let's go."

The trembling guy and one other grunted and thrashed themselves out of the heap in a struggle to stand up. He turned off the lantern and started up the stairs. They followed him through the wreckage of the room and sneaked out the back door, the yard lit up by burning haystacks.

Three Germans came around the corner of the house and saw them. They hollered, all excitement and fuming energy. The GIs turned to run, but two more Germans came around the other corner with leveled guns. The GIs raised their hands. Parker let the pistol sag out of his fingers, and tried to think this through. Would they know what happened down there? Was there some way to get out of this?

"Kameraden! Nicht schiessen!" We give up! Don't shoot! The German words they all knew.

Their helmets were knocked off. They were searched and robbed, stripped of everything, then pushed, and punched around to the front of the house. A shout came from the field and they were ordered to stop. They waited for two more bare-headed groups being brought across the open, their arms high. In the dim, flickered light of the fires, Parker could see their pockets hanging inside out. One of them was the mean-faced Bloody Bucket guy who came down N-12 that morning.

They were lined up in front of three lanterns, their shadows long and weird against the house. An officer came over from a command car and paced in front of them with a nasty smirk, fists on his hips with fancy-stitched leather gloves, a silver death's head on his hat. Casual about it, smooth, he pulled at the tip of each finger and tugged off one glove. He drew his pistol and ran the barrel gently over Parker's throat and his bandages, drenched and soggy with Jimbo's blood.

Parker waited for it. He didn't much care. It had to happen. He stood at attention, his eyes straight, only a flutter inside his breathing. The officer looked at the wet pistol barrel, smiled, and wiped it off on Parker's sleeve.

With the same smile, he moved to the next man and shot him in the ear, stepping aside as he sagged to his knees and down.

The officer turned to the trembling man, nodded, and passed him by. The next one squatted down, raised one hand, and tried to crawl. The officer stalked him with minced dance steps on his toes, up close, to one side, then back. The bullet clipped the GI's fingers as it went into his head.

The others shrank back and crowded into each other, stopped by loud commands and the hard jabs of rifles. A thin tear of panic ripped through them, their eyes stretched in the firelight, mouths curled, and bent.

Another mood blazed over the officer, an incinerating fury. He pointed toward the road where seven other Americans huddled in front of a manure pile, guarded by two Germans who stood by the command car with aimed burp guns. The two groups were brought together. The officer's heels came down hard as he stormed over to the car, got in, sputtered one last order, signaled to the driver, and roared off down the road.

All Parker got: ". . . *die Zeit haben.*" Have the time.

Grenadiers loaded up into a personnel carrier and went after the command car with grins, and heckling at the three guards left behind. Parker only got an isolated word out of the snarls and growls as they argued in some dialect slang. They were young and awkward, kept changing their grips on their weapons, and gave the Americans funny looks.

One checked to see who was watching. He chewed his bottom lip, shifted his feet, and hunched his shoulders, raised the burp gun, lowered it, raised it again. The GIs groaned and sobbed together, some of them cursing.

". . . man, don't do this . . . for shit's sake . . . love of God . . . Geneva Convention—please, fella, think. Think."

The German kid jerked at his crotch as he wet himself. He turned to hide it, but the spot steamed in the cold. The other two saw it and laughed. His lips tightened up in meek bravado just as an outraged screech came up from behind. His mouth sagged at the SS officer in riding breeches, a fur collar on his open leather greatcoat, his polished boots swishing through the snow. The Germans came to attention. One said something, calling him *Herr Sturmbannführer.*

The major paced in front of the prisoners, went over to the two bodies in front of the house, and gently moved one of the heads with the toe of his boot. He came back and asked incensed, impatient questions. Each of the explanations enraged the major that much more.

"*Klar?*" Clear—yes, Parker got that one.

The major gave orders to the soldier behind him, who repeated them into a portable radio. He glared at the seventeen condemned Americans standing dumb, and limp, with filthy faces and bloodshot eyes, their hands raised. He watched the German kids push the prisoners into a column of twos, clumsy at it, anxious, not sure how tough they were supposed to be. They started them on the road to the east. The major waved at a motorcycle with a sidecar. The driver gave it a kick start and glided over.

THE PRISONER DETAIL worked its way through the junkyard of roadblock hulks and crippled tanks. They went up the sloping road, skirting craters and bodies, and approached an American truck, a white star still on the door, and on the hood. Two German military police waited for them. Parker tramped along, the shaky guy across from him, the other cellar survivor in front. Parker wondered when they would find the scene back there and if they could figure it all out.

The back of the covered truck yawned open, the tailgate down, a squared tongue ready to swallow them. The trembling guy closed his eyes, dropped his head, shook it, and moved his lips. Parker understood. Would they be taken to a PW camp or just to the next convenient field?

They were being waved over when a shell landed a hundred yards off the road. With the flubber of incoming air pressure, three more landed in the field, walking toward them in a hectic pattern. The German kids and the two *Feldgendarmen* dove into the ditch along the embankment just as another fluttered in and burst on the column of prisoners.

Three were knocked down. Four more staggered, flopped, and squirmed. Six yelled at each other and made a frantic sprint to the other side of the road to slide, and claw, and duck their way under and through the barbwire fence.

Parker tugged the shaky guy's sleeve and went with them. He laddered up a fence post, tried to vault the squeaking top strand, but fell over and landed on the back of one shoulder. He rolled, recovered, and ran on. He looked back and saw the other guy from the cellar, his jacket and pants snagged on the barbs. He jerked and pulled, then hung there limp, flinching twice, each time the guards shot him.

The rest zigzagged across the open snow toward the dim shape of a half-wrecked farmhouse. They dove into the ruins as slugs drummed against what was left of the walls. They stopped to breathe, to grab at each other, to gasp, and grunt.

"You wanna run? You wanna give up? Which? What?"

"Fuck that noise, man. We already tried that. Let's go."

They went out the back way, through the remains of a barn that connected with the farmhouse. They fanned out over a wagon trail, dropped down, waited for breath, and ran again. Bullets whispered around them but were spaced and sporadic. Just before they got to the tree line, one of the GIs started to limp, leaving a black, spotted trail.

S ix shapes scrambled up a hill and groped through the dark from tree to tree under branches bent down from the weight of the snow. They climbed through the low clouds that reflected a faint German moonlight, and got up to a ridge where the fogs made a ruffled floor below them. They came together, gasping.

"Jesus Christ, Jesus Christ. Oh, shit, *shit!*"

"We made it, man. We fucking well made it."

"Made fucking what? We'll freeze to death out here."

"If we build a fire the Krauts will see it."

"Maybe not. They're too damn busy killing our guys."

"Anyway, we can't. We got nothing to make a fire with."

Quietly, calm about it, he just slipped it in:

"I got a Zippo that they missed."

That was the Bucket guy, so ugly-looking the German kids must have been afraid to dig down too deep into his pockets. And then the Golden Lion guy with the wounded leg:

"We could use a letter I got for whaddaya call it, get it started. I was gonna wipe my ass with it, but she's worth more this way. She didn't wait long. I just about got here."

They pawed away the snow, going deep for something dry, piled rocks around dead branches, and pine needles, and lit them with the Zippo, and the Dear John letter. They blew on it, careful, anxious. The smoke didn't matter in the fog, but damp wood didn't burn well. They hunched over and toasted each piece dry before putting it in with a tender hesitation.

The guy from the cellar was still shaking, his fingers playing a nutty piano. The bleeding man had been nicked in the calf. He grabbed and squeezed at it, then moved his hands back to the fire. The big guy offered a pair of socks from under his shirt. One made a bandage pad; the other was ripped into strips, the guy with the glasses and the air cadet yanking it tight as the big guy sawed at it with the end of a sharp stick.

Nobody said much and nobody listened, but the cadet didn't need any response as he pissed, and moaned.

"I'm already in the Air Corps, New York University, precadet flight school. I had it made. My regular fifty a month? My tuition, room and board? Then they canceled out the whole program and half of us end up in the infantry. If I had turned it down, no way I'd of ended up in the infantry."

The big guy, Jensen, suggested it, a survival trick in the north woods. They slept in alternate directions, knees bent, spooned together, each one hugging the other guy's feet tucked under his jacket with his arms crossed over his chest.

They couldn't even guess at the time—maybe two hours—before they woke up stiff, and nervous. The snores and mutterings stopped. The fire was down and they were cold. They stomped out the ashes, felt around for dried, charred bits of wood to put in their pockets for later, and wrestled their way through the darkness.

They made short, careful steps, hours to make what—one mile? The point man felt ahead with a dead branch, swung it from side to side, and tapped his way through the trees. They made a chain. Each man held one end of a stick held by the man in front. The opposite hand tugged at another stick grabbed by the man behind. They chugged together with an interrupted, staggered rhythm. Sometimes a stick would jerk out of somebody's hand and they had to stop, grope around for it, and start again, trusting the lead, yet still crippled by that dark awfulness ahead of them.

After a long, clumsy time of swallowed curses, lurching away from and against each other, they got the hang of it, becoming a twelve-legged night creature with a single heart that peaked, and fluttered with desperation. But when somebody slipped and fell, a giggle would still start at the craziness of it all, the chuckles running up and down until gradually swallowed by the grunts and huffs as the line reconnected itself.

Big guns murmured all around. Faraway flashes danced on their faces, fainter from the north horizon, stronger to the west, something big but isolated somewhere in the south.

ANOTHER HUNGRY DAWN, the fourth one, Tuesday, everything mist and fog. Jensen, the guy from Minnesota, was on the point. They heard a V-1 puttering its way west above the cloud cover. Somewhere ahead of them, they heard that screech of dive-bomber sirens that every kid in America could imitate, ending it with puffed cheeks, and fluttered lips. But these ended in explosions, heavy, and real.

They looked around, still trying to understand how they outlived all those others, trying to find some bottom or top to any of this.

A brilliant, astonishing break in the weather, and Jensen was palming them down. Parker could hear the yelling of identities swapped back and forth, almost arguing about it; then Jensen stood up in plain sight, and waved. They filed out of the woods, passing scared and exhausted men with rifles.

They came to an artillery battery in a clearing. One of the howitzers probably still worked, but the other two were done. The field was pocked with craters; two trucks smashed, and

turned over with bent wheels, and ripped tires; piles of empty
shell cases, wrecked jeeps; three dead bodies laid out in a row,
maybe twenty busy soldiers. Some wounded warmed themselves around a burning truck. The survivors headed for the
heat, but a first lieutenant ran up, his eyes blinking and lost:

"You men, where are you from?"

"Here and there," Jensen said. "Twenty-eighth Infantry and
the One-o-six."

"We lucked out and escaped is what we did," the cadet said.
"We were being executed. We came that close."

"Get over here. You can help us prepare to surrender."

The ugly Bucket guy, the leg guy, Jensen, Cadet, all looked
down, around, and at each other, mumbling louder:

"Fuck that shit . . . in a pig's ass . . . never happen . . . hell,
no."

Without knowing why, without thinking about it, Parker
stepped out, and tried to sound reasonable.

"Sir? We just did that. We were in a holding action at a roadblock. They broke through and ran us over. We had to surrender. But these SS guys started to execute us; I mean they're
shooting guys in the head. Like we were wild pigs."

The lieutenant squeezed his eyes shut, wet his lips, looked
down, and up, saying:

"We had to displace from Bockholz back across the Clervé.
But we turned a gun over in the river doing it. Another two just
got bombed a while ago. By Stukas, of all things. Why is it our
planes can't fly in this weather, but the Germans can? One gun,
yes. I have one left. And seven rounds of propaganda leaflets
and four rounds of smoke."

Cadet got into it with clear, patient pragmatism.

"Sir, I don't think you appreciate the circumstances."

"All I need to appreciate is I got severe casualties. I'm all out. I'm cut off. And I got direct battalion orders to cease resistance. Spike the guns, disable all vehicles."

Parker was in front, the other five drooped and disappointed. They had managed to make it back. And now what?

"Lieutenant, sir?" Parker said. "Could we talk about this closer to that fire? We've been up all night and we're cold."

"We don't have time. And I want you away from my men. You're a disruptive element. I can recognize that."

"Give us some rations then; we've got nothing to eat."

"I can't do that. We'll need them on our way to internment in their interior. It might take several days."

"Lieutenant, they'll take it away from you. They'll strip you of everything you got. Say something smart, they'll shoot you. They might shoot you anyway, just for the hell of it."

"How do you know so much?"

"Sir, I've been a PW twice since this thing started."

"Is that right? Really? You surrendered *twice* in just four days? Oh, my."

The ugly Bloody Bucket growled into it:

"Give us some of your weapons, then. We got nothing. He just told you, we escaped. It was a fucking slaughterhouse."

"I can't go against orders, 'Cease resistance at once.'"

Cadet made small steps in place, his hands turned up.

"We got away, just by luck. But we're all that's left."

"I have direct orders. And you're attached to my unit. Where are your weapons? You just threw them away and ran?"

Parker again:

"Sir. Listen. You don't get it. They didn't *take* prisoners. But go ahead, surrender. That don't mean we got to."

"Yes, you do. Because I'm attaching you to my unit."

It took Parker a second. He didn't have to take this kind of shit from some noodle ass, not after all that back in that cellar, not with that cryptic thing seared inside his eyes.

"Attached? I don't see no umbilical cord here, Mama."

The survivors snickered. Artillerymen who had drawn closer broke into grins. Lieutenant Chickenshit stood there with a red face, pretending to watch a man smash a radio with an axe while others set up explosives, burned papers, broke their carbines. They shot up the radiators of the two working vehicles and raced the motors. They shot holes in gas tanks and set them on fire. They buried gun breeches. One beat on a gun sight with a hammer. The lieutenant turned back.

"You're out of line, soldier. This is insubordination."

Parker walked away, three others turning with him. Leg and Shaky hung back, didn't want to miss any of this.

"Now where you going?"

"I'm hitting the woods. The least we could do is be ants in their underwear."

"What's your strategy, counterattack with clubs? Get back here. That's a direct order. You got that, soldier?"

"You can go right straight to hell, *sir*."

The lieutenant undid the flap of his pistol holster and kept his hand on the butt.

"I could have you shot. Right now."

"For refusing to surrender? What side are you on?"

Two of the cannoneers stood around, enjoying the show.

"Aw rat. Le's sta't our own gawd dam wah. Nobody roun' heah knows whut the fuck hell he's a-doin' no how."

"I can't surrender to them Heinies, neither. I'm a Jew."

The lieutenant kept trying.

"So switch dog tags with one of the deceased. Your family might get notified, but you can straighten it out later."

"No. Fuck, no. If I live as a Jew, I die as a Jew."

The Jew Boy and the Plowboy went over to pick up their rigs. They waded through the snow with the survivors, but stopped to turn, and watch Parker slog back, and come to attention. The lieutenant jerked out his pistol.

"Sir? Respectfully request we requisition your surplus military ordnance. Stuff you don't want the Germans to get at. Those binoculars and those maps would help out a lot. We don't even have helmets. We got nothing."

"This is government property."

"Sir. So are we."

"Everything is to be destroyed. As far as I'm concerned you guys are deserters. I'm writing you up."

"Those glasses then. At least them."

"I want your name, rank, and serial number."

Nothing. Standing there.

"I suppose you're gonna say: 'Private Joe Shit? Number zero-zero-zero'? Let me see your dog tags."

West Point and trailer trash. Bright bars on his shoulders winked at the next sniper. Parker, a wrinkled cartoon, Jimbo's dried blood in clotted stains on his face, on the bandages, on the cowl, and the bedraggled curtain. The lieutenant turned back to his howitzers. His fingers started, stopped, then twisted the clips of the binocular case out of his web belt, and dropped it, then dropped his musette bag.

Parker grabbed it up. The others waited for the three other cannoneers angling toward them who hiked up their gear, and shifted their rifles, condoms stretched over the muzzles, more of a show than a protection from the wet, but these rifles had never been fired.

The Plowboy snorted.

"Bah the way, Gen'r'l. Wheah we goin' to?"

"Fucked if I know. Keep off the roads, is all. I'd kind of like to go south awhile. Slither through the woods at night. Coil up and sleep in the day. Pick up what we can."

"South? Everything is headed west."

"You're in a movie and there's a fire? Everybody jams up the exit. What you do, get flat against a wall, wait out the stampede, and look for some other way out. You remember that big night-club fire in Boston?"

One of the last three volunteers wore GI-issue, steel-rimmed glasses. He mumbled to Parker:

"I don't know anything about infantry. I was a clerk."

"You were in basic, weren't you? You got a rifle."

"They threw it at me. One of you guys should take it."

Somebody sniggered, awake now. Feet jiggled, ready to go. Cadet looked around, studying.

"So who's gonna be in charge here? We're all privates and there's nineteen ways to go anywhere. Who makes the call?"

The Jew Boy said:

"What about you? You with the nose? You want the job?"

"You kidding? You guys are all older'n me. Shit, I'm only a juvenile delinquent. I only been in the army four months. Somebody must have some seniority here."

The truck driver hesitated.

"I guess that would be me. I been in since the peacetime draft in 1940. Quartermaster Corps, motor mechanic until they transferred me out. Hell, I did basic with one of those old Springfield '03s. I've seen those M1s around, but I never did get to shoot one. But what's the difference? You pull the trigger, it goes bang. Right?"

"You never made any grade?"

"Lots of times. Got up to T-2 once. But I drink some."

Parker dug into the lieutenant's musette bag, found the

compass, and went through the maps. He was good at road maps, grew up with them. He diddled with the compass, turned the azimuth circle on the dial, and set it for due south. He lined up the sight line with a certain tree and gave the maps and the compass to the trucker.

"Here. If it was me I'd start out for that tree with the crooked trunk. See? These here are lines of equal altitude. When they're close you got a steep hill or a cliff. Far apart means a rolling field. These symbols here are forests. These are trails. We should be right around here above this river."

"How can you look at a flat piece of paper and see a hill and say it's that one over there?"

"I dunno. Maybe I'm naturally two-dimensional."

"I can't handle this. You better take over."

"All you have to do is think it out and make a decision. Tell us what to do and we'll do it."

"No. Better if you took it. I just want to watch out for me. It's too much to be on the hook for somebody else's ass."

The Jew said it:

"Take over, Nose. You got the balls. Right?"

"What will that make me, then? Acting corporal?"

"You can be the fucking general if you want."

"I gotta tell you guys this. It's only fair that you know. I— uh—I'm only sixteen. I lied to get in the army."

But he said it with a resonance, a dare. Jew Boy looked.

"I don't give a fuck if you're nine. You still got more balls than I got, you're bigger'n I am, and you're just as smart."

"You serious? Everybody? Jensen? You know the woods."

Jensen looked down and waved his hand.

"You guys aren't gonna do me like last time, okay? I'll think it over, and talk about it, but when I'm done, that's gotta be it. Okay? All right, then . . . let's move out."

Thermite grenades popped and burned behind them. The last gun barrel exploded into a smoking split banana. When Parker looked back from the ridge with the binoculars, he could see them raise their hands, and wave a white flag; and he could still smell the stink of the burning tires.

THE VISIBILITY closed down again. It snowed. The snow turned to rain, and back to snow again. The fog would creep into low places and leave islands of peaks, and ridges. The sun would flash, then leave them in a deep cloud while the mists oozed down. The landscapes of puzzled fields and fences blotted away into vaguely newer forms.

ELEVEN OF THEM, not quite a squad, five rifles and four grenades, Shaky still ducking that light in the cellar. Their breath smoked and plumed out as they plodded through their accordion moves that stretched into a single file at twenty-foot intervals. The point man had to step high to trample down the snow. The second had it easier, widening the footprints. When number one got tired, he stepped aside and rested, falling in at the rear, where the packed trail was easier.

They bunched up to help each other over the fences. Plowboy hacked at the top of a post with his bayonet, prying off a wedged piece.

"Lookie heah. This heah's good kindlin' wood. Old and drah, oughtta burn real nass."

He broke off a dead tree branch and used it as a club, whacking the top edge of the bayonet. Pieces of the branch broke off with every few blows. Plowboy split chips off the post, smelled them, put them in his pockets. Parker waved.

"Hey. You're making an echo all through the woods."

BUT HE GRINNED at the fantastic lunacy of all this. Not only did he have his own wild, hairy-ass guerilla outfit; he was the fucking commander. Because he had a big mouth? Or was it the blood all over him, the dirt, the oddball uniform? He kept thinking about the cellar and Jimbo but couldn't really believe much about that other yesterday.

He did remember the library at the EM club on a weekend when he had no pass, reading that line in the Officer Candidate School manual: "More officers fail because of lack of force and aggressiveness than for any other reason." But it should have been Headley or Jimbo, or that big guy, Jensen, who knew about hunting in the winter.

Parker stayed at the point more often than the others. He would take a bearing on a prominent terrain feature, point it out to the lead man, then fall back a few places. He kept telling them to just think about Bastogne.

"We get back they'll send us to a rest area. We'll thaw out and get fattened up. Maybe even get to go to Paris. Hell, maybe we'll get a medal or something out of this thing."

Couldn't admit it, but he wasn't even sure where they were. No landmarks in this misted monotony of gray greens, and dull whites, a few fences, a bare cliff, an unusual tree. Like feeling his way through a mountain of wrinkled and old, torn dollar bills. But a leader had to be the strong one, fierce and sly, had to be for real.

THEY CROSSED some open farmland but stayed away from the houses. They came to a small brook hidden by dead briars and piled rocks in the middle so they could hop across with dry feet. The five gunners shared their canteens and filled them again. They started up a wooded rise, the fog lifted, and Parker adjusted the field glasses. He could barely make out a far-off, curved column of vehicles. He frowned. A commander always frowned. Anybody with field glasses had to do some serious thinking.

They stretched out under a growth of young firs. Plowboy dressed the wounded guy's leg with things from his first-aid kit. Parker was unhappy with the cover, a few Christmas trees in a parking lot? A Spandau could gobble it right up. But they did need a ten break.

The cannoneer with the glasses wore an overcoat. So did Fred. They spread one on the ground, put Shaky in the middle, and covered themselves with the other. Jew Boy and Plowboy had blanket rolls, a waterproof shelter half rolled around two blankets. Trucker had a sleeping bag. They shared the covers and huddled close, hands between their thighs, quickly asleep.

. . . STRUGGLING AND CLIMBING but marking time in the same places. Toby still counted his money but never got past twelve dollars. The bike cost thirty-two.

In Florida again. His father built four tourist cabins, just him and an old carpenter, two miles out of Tampa on East Hillsboro, by a chicken farm where an old sawmill used to be, the sawdust pile twenty feet high. They lived in the office building, Mama and Daddy in the big bed in the kitchen, Squirt on the sofa in the front room, Toby on the sofa cushions on the floor.

Mrs. Kykendall gave them a Boston terrier pup. Toby would buy Beegee's quarter pound of hamburger at the general store on the corner, an old-time wood shack run by the owner of the chicken farm. He got cigarettes for Daddy, Wings and Twenty Grand, that cost ten cents. Sometimes Daddy wanted the expensive ones; Lucky Strike, and Chesterfield, that cost fifteen.

The neon shop was in the dirt floor garage in the back. Daddy would roll the glass tube over a burner, a cork on one end. He blew on a rubber hose over the other end. When it melted, he made the curve over the words drawn on a sheet of asbestos, the letters doubled back on themselves to make the connections. Later, these would be blacked out with paint.

He made a nick with a triangular file, then tapped it to break off a tube. Toby could still remember that one-two-three rub and that clink. Mama told him later that Daddy taught himself how to do it. He would melt two pieces, try to join them, and they would break. He tried it again and it would break again, over and over.

Toby helped with the building, picked up cutoffs, raked and swept, and ran to get things. Daddy gave him the rest of the money for the bike. He made a lot of spills but then could pedal down Hillsborough, charging along, his Daisy BB gun up high in one hand. A war had started, so big it might last until the divorce was over. He might even get in on it.

. . . THAT TINGLE whenever Leora came near him, in the same class with her now. Leora was . . . something—she lived in a regular house on Apache Avenue. He passed it every day, going up the dirt road on the way to school, standing up high on the pedals to look through the windows, and see the pictures on the wall, an upright piano, curtains, everything.

He dropped a folded note at her feet one day and pedaled away in a happy terror. It said he liked her and asked if she liked him too. In class later, she looked at him and nodded her head, but she didn't smile. Toby felt hot all over. He thought it would be nice to take her to the movies, but he wasn't old enough, didn't have the money, and didn't know how.

But he did get to tow her home once on the crossbar, his bike wheel wobbling through the thick sand. She was bigger than he was and he barely made it, his arms braced around her, smelling her hair, quivering where he touched her back.

One day he put his foot on the opposite desk seat to block the aisle, looking up at her with a big grin. She glared, and just like that; she kicked him, hard, on the ankle. He put his foot back under his desk and blinked at the tears.

HE ALWAYS HAD the best grades. When he got a hundred, Miz Ayala had him check the rest of the test papers. Leora made a lot of mistakes, but he fixed her up to a ninety with an eraser. When the papers were given back he saw Leora go up to Miz Ayala's desk. He turned cold. Miz Ayala called him outside, but she didn't say much—just watched him twist, and droop, and look out through the arches at the garden, his face hot, his eyes wet. It was his first crime.

SOMETIMES DADDY GOT DRUNK, yelled at Mama, slapped her around, and bruised her face. Toby and Squirt would be scared, hugged each other and cried. Left alone one day, Toby got a kitchen knife and dove on the back of the monster bed, swinging out of the trees to drop down to the rescue. He growled and stabbed the angry lion, but his hand slipped.

Mama asked him about the cut in the sheet and the mattress, but he didn't know how it got there. She looked at him, quiet. He kept his cut hand behind him.

. . . the divorce, choose: Daddy and Florida, his dog, his bicycle, Leora, everything—or his mother and sister, Nana, and New York. Eleven—he was eleven.

Daddy slept on the couch in the other room, always up late, renting the cabins. Toby woke him on his way to school and said he wanted to stay in Florida. Boys should stay with their fathers and girls should stay with their mothers. Daddy said okay and rolled back to the wall.

But then Mama got him outside and talked to him, slow and soft. He looked at the ground. Didn't he want to live with his kid sister? Didn't he want to live with Nana? Didn't he love his mother? He nodded, with wet eyes. He felt like a wrung out and wrinkled rag, flopped over a clothesline.

Toby had to do it on the way to school the next morning. He reached out and stopped, reached again, touched him, and said, "Daddy?" He was snoring. Toby shook him once, then harder. He changed his mind, he said, and wanted to stay with Mama. Daddy said okay and rolled over.

HE AND SQUIRT waved good-bye through the back window of the car. Beegee was scratching. No room for him, or for his bike; nothing. Daddy didn't look, just went into the office.

When it was gone, Toby turned around, and faced New York.

THE SQUAD GOT UP, shivering. They shuddered out curses and stamped their feet. Fred had three cans of K-ration beans and rice. Trucker had one ham-and-spaghetti. They shared the artillerymen's spoons and passed the cans around. Parker dug out a map, studied it again, took off one glove, and used the nails of thumb and first finger as dividers to pace off the distance. He pointed at a spot and held it high.

"Listen up. We're about here. Bastogne is over here. We're in the middle between these main roads that come together. If we went straight over we'd be in a meat grinder."

Eyes were half-shut. Heads nodded. He was just guessing, but nobody cared. Up to the leader to take care of things.

"South, then west. Farther and not easy, but better. We still got Wiltz down here. That's Division Headquarters."

"From the sound of it, lots of shit going on there too."

"We need a mile or so more," Parker said. "Then find a good spot and dig in. We have to stay invisible, and sleeping at night is dangerous. We could freeze."

Their heads wobbled. Eyes went up, then dropped.

"Okay—off and on. Off your ass and on your feet. I'll take the point."

★

They came to a fire lane, ruler-straight, an even swath cut through the forest. They crawled across one at a time and worked their way through a wooded draw to the top of another hill. The visibility was clear for that moment and they could look over a valley with rolling fields; a cluster of farm buildings with power poles, and wire, a private road covered with clean snow; but no livestock, and no vehicles.

"Maybe best we just go around all this," Parker said. Most of the others said nothing. Some disagreed.

"Man, there's gotta be some kind of heat down there and at least some potatoes to eat, anyway. At the least."

"We'll starve out here if we don't get something."

Parker studied the place through the glasses. He saw no communication wires, but two tracked vehicles had passed by, sometime before the last snow. Lines of old footprints converged at the door, swirled around, and went on. Like at all the farmhouses here, two big manure piles stood in front.

"It's gotta be a local family place, which is okay, unless they're pro-German. They speak some kind of German here. Maybe they left when the shit started, and it's just empty. Might be some food left. But what if it's full of Krauts?"

"Ah don' heah no dawgs."

"What would the Heinies be doing way out here?"

"What are they doing anywhere? What are we doing here?"

And then that sourpuss from the Twenty-eighth:

"I'm tired of always on the defense. Let's play offense. Those Heinies ain't such hotshots they used to be."

"Some're still around. Hey, what is your name, anyway?"

"Jew Boy calls me Bucket. That's good enough."

"I just wish we had the big picture of this thing."

"Shit. It's big enough already."

They stared at Parker with haggard, tight faces. The gunners sipped from their canteens, the screw caps clinking from their chains, then passed them to the Antoniushof men.

"You guys gotta listen hard to what I'm saying. We don't know what the fuck is in there, so everybody has to play his own hunches. I mean, really think. Let's try to keep it so we're all going the same way."

Parker paired up the unarmed originals with the men who had rifles. He wanted two teams to go around to the back: Jew Boy and Bucket, Plowboy and Shaky, each team with one rifle, and one grenade. He wanted two teams at the near side. Fred and Cadet would be Parker's backup with the fifth rifle.

"Listen to me. There's no cover down there, just open snow. If they see us coming, all they gotta do is wait. These dark uniforms make delicious targets. You rifle guys, you go in aimed at those windows. You see a face, shoot it."

"What if it's a civilian?"

"What can I tell you? Be careful. If you see it's a woman or a kid, no. Otherwise, shoot. Now listen. No use trying to run. They'll nail you for sure. Instead, you riflemen keep suppressive fire on those windows and you guys with grenades charge in. Break the glass first; punch it out. One grenade is all you got. You don't want it to glance off."

THE RAVINE DROPPED into a half-frozen creek they had to wade. They came out wet below the knees, numb with cold, almost crippled by it. The artillerymen piled their packs and extra gear at the fence, slipped under the wire, and closed in on the house. Parker waved them around to their places.

His stomach tightened and he felt some nausea, but the leader had to make the first move. Fred and Cadet took cover behind a manure pile. He waited for them to get set, and crouched over to a window. He looked in, then ducked, and peeked from the other side. He could only see furniture.

He took a deep breath, plodded up to the front door, and gave the knob a slow, delicate twist. The door opened. He gave it another inch, slipped through, closed it gently, and moved into the room. First he felt the crawling of bugs on his neck, and then a cold distance, a detachment. He saw himself watching his own effortless, silent moves.

A *Fallschirmjäger*, wrapped in a blanket, snored away alcohol fumes in an armchair by a window, a Schmeisser across his lap. Parker's fingers started up, but he couldn't back out, and chance the Kraut feeling that draft again from the door.

He sneaked closer, breathed as the German breathed, leaned for the gun, and tugged at it, his fist cocked, ready to punch and grab. More rattles and wheezes until the gun came free. Parker aimed it and found the safety lock. The click did it. The snoring stopped. The German jerked up and whispered:

"*Scheiss im Himmel.*"

Parker put a trembling finger to his lips and pushed the gun muzzle under the German's nose. He took away his trench knife and two stick grenades, and stuffed one into each boot, the way the Germans did it. He motioned him up, got him to raise his hands, and moved him to the door.

Fred looked astounded, then jerked his rifle up, moved closer, and aimed at the German. Cadet gawked around the manure pile. The German whirled, slammed the gun away from Parker, and ran in a dodging stagger, with a piercing shriek:

"*Hans! Joachim! Achtung!*"

Fred fired, hesitated, and fired again. The German did a quickstep and fell. Parker ran through the open door to dive down next to a sofa. A short burst of automatic fire came from the other room; then a befuddled trooper stumbled out, dangling a Schmeisser. Fred fired first. Parker shot from the floor, jolted by the speed of the burp gun, then heard Fred and Cadet yelling together in pain.

Rifles went off all around, the echoes fuzzing up the direction. Parker scuttled around the bleeding body and flattened against the wall. His fingers twitched when he heard the guttural murmurings. He waited for it. When he heard the pop and saw the smoking grenade flip through the doorway, he scooped it up, threw it back, and dove for the corner.

When it went off, he fired around the doorjamb without aiming, ran inside, and shot at two shapes on the floor, thumped flat again, and bellied his way through a haze of stink and smoke into a kitchen. Bullets came through the window and the back door and clanged off a rack of hanging pots and kettles. Parker crawled behind an iron stove, unnerved by the yells in German and English, the blurp of machine pistols, the pow of rifles; and then only quiet scrapes and shuffles. Trucker called out:

"General? Hey, General! You all right?"

"I'm in here."

"We got two runnin' out the back. Any more around?"

They went from room to room; upstairs, the cellar, and the barn. They squeezed themselves around doorways. They probed the hay with bayonets and checked the farm equipment.

An arm and hand waggled a long strip of toilet paper out of

the outhouse door, waved it around in flipped loops and cele-
brating arcs. A voice bellowed and pleaded as Jew Boy fired his
M1 four times. Wood splinters spun and flew. The door swung
open and a German sagged out, his chest gushing blood, his underwear and pants sliding down around his ankles.

PARKER SAT hard on the snow, his arms over his knees, his face
down as he shook, and tried to breathe, tried to think, to see, to
reemerge with some definition of himself.

THEY GATHERED in the main room. Fred had a crease across the
back of his shoulder. The cadet lost the first joint of his little finger. He waved his hand, grabbed his wrist, and sucked at the
nub. As they doctored each other, Parker did a head count.

"We had eleven. Who's missing?"

They found him by the barn, on his back, his round, steel-
frame glasses still in place, smiling. His chest gurgled and whistled. They pushed down on a folded raincoat and tightened the
wad with a belt. When Trucker came out with a blanket, they
grabbed him up by the four corners, and staggered with him inside to a bedroom.

They covered him, dripped water onto his lips, then
watched as his breathing became shorter, and harder, his eyes
dimmed. His world shrank to an ever-smaller sphere and came
down to a final dot.

Parker didn't look up, just murmured to anybody:

"What kind of a guy was he?"

"I don't even know. He's new," Trucker said.

"He must have been somebody's foxhole buddy, at least."

Embarrassed looks. Shifted eyes and heads. Leg said:

"You wanna take his helmet, General? You really oughtta
have a helmet."

"Yeah, I guess. I keep losing mine. Better take his rifle and stuff too."

A RAUCOUS whoop came from the kitchen. Parker ran in and saw Plowboy and Trucker throwing back two bottles of cognac, an empty on the table with four glasses, one turned over and smelling strong. Parker let out a loud curse, grabbed away Plowboy's bottle, spilling it. He whacked Trucker's knuckles with it when he wouldn't let go of his. Parker smashed them together in the sink, his jacket soaked and studded with glitters of glass. They howled back at him:

"What'd you do that for? What's wrong with a drink?"

"No booze. You guys crazy? You want to celebrate—*now*?"

"Hey, man. That was ours. Fuck knows we earned it."

"You guys wanna be a bunch of eight balls like these Krauts? Drunk and happy, juiced out of their minds? And now they're all happy and dead?"

Jensen came in and stood with him.

"He's right. This is a bad time for booze. It's dangerous in freezing weather."

"What are you, a doctor or what?"

"I'm from Koochiching, Minnesota. On the Canada border."

"Kooch, what?"

"We know about cold. And I'm telling you, alcohol will screw up your temperature. Seriously."

THEY ROBBED THE BODIES, caught up in the exuberance of survival, and the energized greed for any kind of booty. All seven of the Germans were armed with machine pistols and each had four or five extra clips. The dogfaces tugged off the head cowls and equipment belts, collected eleven stick grenades, an apronful of rockets, and a *Panzerschreck*, the shorter, paratrooper version of a German bazooka.

"Hey, guys. Only six more shopping days 'til Christmas."

Loud, happy bullshit went all around. Now they all had a weapon. Parker and Bucket had two. They gloated over the rations, the shelter halves in white instead of that giveaway olive drab. Parker played with the non-com's Zeiss binoculars and felt the better quality: half the weight but stronger than the GI issue. The snowsuits had holes and rips, all of them bloody in places, one sopping and smelly at the crotch.

Fred—half-crazy, wincing and laughing as Jensen worked on his shoulder with sulfa, bandages, and tape.

"You shoulda seen it. I'm tellin' you. General Goldilocks here? He just walks right up. He knocks on the front door like he's one of the local neighbors and he says, 'Scuse me. Is there any l'il ole bears at home today?'"

Parker smiled. Headley told him he did a good job. But Parker thought of that look in the snoozing trooper's eyes and that feeble wave of toilet paper. Shit in heaven was right.

SUSPENDERS FOR BELTS AND GEAR, knives, flashlights, trench shovels, a coil of rope; they filled their canteens and a jerry can from the hand pump in the kitchen. The Antoniushof survivor with the gimpy leg found a looted souvenir, an American officer's Colt .45 with a leather belt and a holster with a brass thumb button, the flap engraved "U.S." The handle had a swiveled loop with a short, braided silk lanyard. Three extra seven-round clips were in snap-button pouches on the belt.

Leg got down on his good knee and offered it up with the cackle and grin of a thieving crow:

"Here, General. This one's for you."

"What's this General shit, anyway?"

"After that stunt you pulled? You got a big gold star."

"Generals have silver stars."

"Maybe. But the one we see is solid twenty-four-carat."

Parker admired the old leather, fondled it, wondering if it had belonged to a high-ranking field officer, or some hell-for-leather cavalryman. He drew it out of the holster, twisted and smiled it up with his wrist, put it back and buckled on the belt, swiveled his hips a little, slapped, and patted the flap to get it riding just right. It was hard to straighten his grin.

"Okay. Fine. Now let's cut the shit and get going."

First Leg and then the others, smirks with their salutes.

"Yes, *sir!*"

PARKER WOULDN'T LET THEM take anything personal: no letters, photographs, rings, or medals. He wanted that left with the bodies. Somebody else might steal it; but not them. Burial would take too much digging in that hard ground, so he had them carried inside. Plowboy, Leg, and Finger didn't like it.

"You fucking crazy? Leave 'em be. They're dead, right? Better them than us. They'd rather it the other way."

Shaky just looked. Bucket sneered. Parker was quiet.

"I don't want some farmer somebody pass by and see them out there and blow a whistle. And we owe them some respect. They were soldiers. You guys with me at Antoniushof? You didn't already forget that SS officer who saved our ass?"

"No. And we didn't forget the one killing us neither."

"Man, shit. This is supposed to be war."

"Okay—what if they find this shit and catch up with us?"

They looked at each other but not at Parker.

"Listen. We made a deal and this is what I want done."

They lugged them into the living room, leaking blood, four

men each, awkward with the loose arms, and legs, and bobbing heads. Nobody wanted to fix up his pants for the guy at the out-house, so Parker had to do it. Jew Boy refused to touch any of them. They lined them up on their backs, hands folded over their chests. They left the dead GI in the bedroom. His dog tags read "C" for Catholic. Finger took off his helmet and made the sign of the cross with his bandaged hand.

THEY CUT HOLES in bedsheets to make up snow capes for the three they were short. They ripped others into rags. Parker wanted them draped and tied around their weapons. They looked in the barn and the sheds, found an old can of stiff white paint, and sloshed some on their helmets with a rag.

They found wire cutters, a pick, an ax. They found a tobog-gan and loaded their gear on it to pull through the snow: a long-handled spade, a maul, a brick chisel, a can of gas for their stoves. Just ready to leave when they heard a telephone ringing. They looked around at each other and geared up.

They moved due magnetic south through the snow clouds and flurries, and climbed to the next ridge of forest. Parker broke trail, worried about the battle ahead that growled louder, and wider. The vicious joy of their victory was already gone, and they were back to being fugitive murderers. Above the ceiling, another V-1 robot bomb sputtered to the west.

Freddy the Shoulder, the gunner with the name change:

"Hey, General. You said we're gonna sleep all day."

"Not *all* day. And not now. We're still in the way here."

"The cadet" had been clipped back to just "Finger." Jensen was promoted to "Koochie." Bucket still never said much, his lips puckered tight. Nothing got in. Nothing got out, his arms crossed, eyes like a rattler under a ledge of rock.

They got up through the forest cover, weaving the toboggan around the trees, and the brush, their rifles and Schmeissers slung across their backs to free their hands. They took a ten break, everybody squatting down in place while Parker looked back with the glasses.

"Let's dig in here. Make a fire, do our feet, and sleep."

"Man, fuck that feet shit; I'm tired."

"He's right. And rotate your socks and shirts."

"Who asked you, Koochie Thing? I don't remember that."

"Where I come from, this here ain't even chilly yet. But it's gonna get cold, seriously."

"When we gettin' back behind our own lines?"

"Depends on where that is. Bastogne's the bull's-eye around here. If it's still there."

They dug a shallow, meandering hole between the trees with thuds and clinks from the pick, and the ax, the maul, and chisel, until they got down to the soft stuff. They built a rim with the dirt, slapped it tight with the back of the spade, and covered it with snow.

Plowboy and Finger were still having it out:

"You sure 'nough from Noo Yo'k? With all that shit noise and stuff, ever'body shovin' each othah, horns blowin'?"

"Born and raised. You just don't appreciate us Knickerbockers. We have another perspective from all you guys out there. Things look different from the nineteenth floor."

"Shore they do. You kin lean on your elbows an' look out at all them other winders."

They made a hole in the center for the fire and warmed the cans of German chicken, gravy, and rice. They did their feet, their tour of guard duty, and slept, huddled tight with German blankets, and shelter halves, Shaky kept in the middle. Koochie made them stack their weapons outside so they wouldn't sweat in the heat, and then later freeze up.

"What happens if the slide does freeze?"

"That's easy. You piss on it. What else?"

Parker placed the guards, then climbed to an open ledge that gave him a view with the field glasses. He got a glimpse through the weather and could see the distant, heavy traffic coming out of Drauffelt, the bridge either captured whole or the river spanned by German engineers.

He got out the maps and tried to calculate their position, and best hope. He traced the villages and junctions. They had to cross three roads, then the Wiltz River, and turn west. Wiltz was getting hit hard. They would have to work around it, which meant extra miles.

He went back to the hole and curled up in his blankets, his

head covered over, warmed by his breath and his own dream. The pile of men around him quivered and moaned like a litter of pups.

. . . SMOLDERING AGAIN, that garden in his head. When Leora kicked him she knocked his compass swinging from wild left to confused right, but it always steadied on her face, and her eyes, her Idea. He couldn't even imagine her naked. She was the girl he loved. Whenever he jerked off, he thought of older, sassy, hot women with big tits, and big asses.

He looked at that picture again: his father at fifteen in uniform, with the blue-and-gray, yin-and-yang shoulder patch of Virginia's Twenty-ninth.

Victor did most of the driving. Mama helped. They all slept in the car, stopped for gas, hamburgers, and coffee, and to take a pee. They got to New York late, Aunt Toots in her room upstairs, hysterical when they came in as a surprise. She laughed and cried, and couldn't stop for half an hour.

Then Mama and Victor went back to Florida.

Toby wrote Leora once. She even wrote back. He still had the letter put away somewhere with his medal. The kids in P.S. 54 said he talked like a cotton picker, but he was the valedictorian when he graduated. The American Legion gave him a medal for scholastic achievement.

Nana would sit at the dining room table with her smocking, Pop-Pop playing his silent keyboard on his lap, blue eyes squinted over his blond and gray beard, the ivories clacking quietly as his huge fingers ran up and down the three octaves, working whatever melody he heard. This was another of Pop's ideas. Concert artists could stay in practice while they were traveling. He sawed out his prototype from a junk piano.

Pop slept on the floor in the dining room because he always

wet the bed. He would put a towel around a urinal and go to sleep with his thing inside, but it would spill over in the night. His pallet smelled of pee. Mama said he was afraid of doctors and hospitals. He had stomach trouble too, and drank a lot of baking soda and water.

They rented the second and third floors from a shy widow who lived alone on 121st Street in Richmond Hill, the high chain-link fence of the Long Island Railroad yards right behind the garage. Except for a few that had asbestos shingles, every house for miles around was covered with asphalt sheeting of brown or dark red that was supposed to look like brick. The trees and hedges only varied in their size.

The living room was a slight bump away from the dining room. The piano was there, and the sofa with the crocheted doilies held with stickpins on each armrest, and the three on the back above the cushions. Nana made them herself, and the matching, full-length curtains for every window.

The Larsen Family was a vaudeville act. Toby knew that picture of them together: Mama, always very thin, holding a violin. None of them ever talked about where they played, and he never heard his mother play the violin.

Nana's harp was in the attic where Toby slept: dirty, the strings all loose, next to Pop-Pop's stuffed iguana, his boxes of stamps and clippings, the stacks of sheet music; Boysy's paint cans, and portfolios, unfinished posters from Cooper Union; Toots' anatomy books; Squirt's shoe skates with the wrong wheel bearings for competition figure skating; rusty nails sticking through the shingle boards; all of it shaking with the passing weight and the smoking grit of the trains.

The clock on the old kitchen chair with the loose leg woke him up, the attic stairs creaking when he went down, and past Squirt's bedroom to the kitchen. He ate his cereal and went in to shake Boysy's shoulder, embarrassed every morning when he had to ask again for thirty-six cents: a quarter for lunch at school, a penny for milk, ten cents for carfare.

The stories:

Mama and Daddy used to ride motorcycles. They had wrecks and she was in the hospital once. She didn't quit riding until three days before Toby was born. Daddy and Pop-Pop never got along. Once Daddy took off his hat and rang the doorbell. Pop-Pop opened the door and punched Daddy in the mouth. Daddy put his hat back on and left.

Victor told him once about Daddy's reputation as a bar fighter. A guy would get hit three times: once with Daddy's fist, once when the guy hit the wall, and again when he hit the floor. Daddy and Vic would go to those fighting joints where they had chicken wire strung up over the bar to protect the glasses and the mirrors. You paid your money and got your beer through a slot. Daddy would stand right out in the middle, drunk, and dare the whole house to fight. No one did.

Mama's family had money once. Pop-Pop owned a ukulele factory back when they were all the rage, around the time of the First World War. He couldn't make them fast enough, wanted to expand, and went back to Denmark to ask his parents for his share of their sons' inheritance in advance.

But he stopped off in Paris and blew it all. When he got home, he told Nana he had just spent enough money to keep them for the rest of their lives. While he was gone, his partners stole the factory out from under him, and Nana never talked to him much after that.

Nana did smocking on little girls' dresses at home, puckering up the unfinished front pieces with colored threads. She had a padded ironing board with a heavy string pinned across one edge, the unfinished stock bunched on the left. After her fingers blurred their way across the pattern, she slid them to the right. When she finished a batch she walked to the bus, took them somewhere, and brought home new pieces in two heavy shopping bags. The money she got was a secret.

Boysy worked for the railroad, painting their name in gold leaf on passenger cars. Boysy wanted to marry the girl next door, but they were Catholics. She was eighteen; he was thirty. Her parents raised hell and so did Nana.

Toby collected scrap iron in the freight yard: round chunks burned out of steel girders, odd pieces, old railroad spikes. He would carry it home in a potato sack and pile it in a back corner of the yard until one day his collection was gone. Pop-Pop sold it to one of the junkies who roamed the streets in a horse and wagon, yanking on a string of cowbells. Pop-Pop got a dollar and forty cents but needed to borrow the money, he said. Toby knew it was worth more.

Boysy took Squirt to the roller rink on weekends and she got lessons from a coach. Then came the competitions. Nana made her fancy costumes and they were always taking pictures. Toby thought the whole thing was crazy: going around the same circle, the same way, with the roar of wooden wheels on a wood floor, with a bad recording of some corny organ music.

Toby never liked Squirt much, ever since when they were little in Philadelphia. She would sit in the bathroom, and yell: "Toby, come wipe me," and Mama called to him to go in, and wipe her butt. She would just look dumb and lean over, and he had to reach behind her, and smell the stink.

Nana and Pop-Pop, and Boysy, all of them, the same chant:

Your father never had any regard for anybody else, and you're just like him. All you ever do is sulk. All you want is to get back to Florida and those hicks down there so you can run around barefoot, and talk with that dumb accent.

They ate pumpernickel rye bread, boiled potatoes, lamb, and applesauce, and they drank tea. Everybody had his own linen napkin in a holder. Toby's color was blue.

Then Uncle Boysy would play some Paganini on his violin, or "In a Country Garden" on the piano. Pop-Pop would practice. Aunt Toots worked as a telephone operator and was studying to be a chiropractor. She closed the door and smoked cigarettes in her little room upstairs so Nana wouldn't know.

THEY SLEPT until dark. The fire was out. They put on their boots, stretched, loosened up, and ate some cold rations. Where the trees were thick, the point man felt ahead with his stick, the rope over his shoulder. They stayed close and followed each other, using the rope as a guide. The battle at Wiltz got heavier as they dragged their load through the swirling snow, pulling through the foggy, frozen part of their dreams.

THEY HEARD TALKING, low and close. They spread out and dropped behind trees. An old man and a boy passed by on a trail, looking down at their feet, carrying a lantern, an ax, and a Christmas tree. They must have seen the soldiers but didn't recognize them, or didn't care, knowing all about those sinful spirits that lived in the forest.

A CLUMP OF HOUSES that was not even a village, barely a farm, the dogs starting when they got close. They sank down and waited. Parker waved them up and they groped their way back through the same thick bushes, and patches of thorns.

Another hamlet, the shapes barely visible, no lights or sounds. He halted the squad with a hiss, edged behind a house, and stole up to a blank darkness, a barn or a shed, some kind of shelter. When he got closer he heard rasping sounds. He went to the wall, reached out, and felt something—a bicycle, and then another, a line of them. He went to the doorway, heard snoring, smelled hay, and a strange stink of men, a different odor of sweat, and leather, a different tobacco.

He didn't see the tank parked behind a haystack until he smelled the engine and almost walked into it. His heart thudded as he held back those urges, and kept himself to a gliding stealth. The men rose up around him, but he waved them away, went up to Bucket, and exhaled in his ear:

"Let's get out of here. This place is full of Germans."

IT SNOWED AGAIN. The toboggan dragged with a wet whisper. They spread their capes around them and became white flickers among the dark and deadly trees, the traffic louder in long, repeated crescendos, sometimes a solitary motor, and that intensifying ruckus again. Parker and Bucket left the squad behind a bushy mound and crawled on ahead, listening to the rumbles, and to the crumps of artillery at Wiltz.

The distant searchlights washed over the clouds. The blacked-out headlights on passing vehicles glowed just enough for them to see the road, the drainage ditches, and the fences. Convoys twisted up from Drauffelt into tight knots with jammed brakes and horns, then opened into a sudden emptiness. Messenger motorcycles zipped both ways around the snarls to swing off, and bounce along the shoulders.

Tanks jangled by, mediums and heavies, artillery, *Kübelwagen*, half-tracks filled with singing, laughing infantry. Ambulances and empty trucks growled back to Germany. The driver of a command car honked and yelled out the window to make way for a senior officer.

THEY SQUATTED TOGETHER, breathing hard. Each one murmured it again: his job, the password, the countersign. They had to cross over, and they had to do it that night.

"Keep to the plan, but use your head. If you really have to shoot—okay, but then haul ass. Take a position in the woods on the first ridge over there and wait up for twenty minutes. Twenty minutes is all. It's every man for himself after that. If you get lost, I don't know. Guide left and around the action up there. Maybe we could find each other."

Bucket growled it out with set teeth, glaring at everybody's bowed head and turned face. He still wanted to do an ambush. They had a coil of wire. Why not stretch it across the road and snag the next motorcycle messenger, and when the Krauts gathered around to look, then sock them with that bazooka thing?

They piled everything but their weapons on the toboggan. Plowboy and Jew Boy crawled out to the ditch. When there was a lull, they cut the three strands of wire, and dragged away the ends. They went flat and waited out the next burst of traffic, then ran across, got down in the other ditch, and when they could, they raised up to cut the other fence. They dragged away the ends, spread out, and covered the road.

Bucket and Shaky pulled on the ropes as Leg and Kooch did the pushing. They dipped and turned the toboggan, got it into and out of the ditch, skidded it across the pavement, through the gap in the next fence, and back into smooth snow.

Parker told them to space themselves, stretch out flat, and wait, peer out from their hoods, and be ready. He knew they would pant, and bite their lips as they grabbed at their crotches, rubbed their noses, and cursed under their breath.

An armored personnel carrier and three Panthers came around the bend, the commanders and drivers in open hatches, the decks swarmed over with infantry who stooped, ducked, and held on to each other by their belts. Then came a column of supply trucks and odd-looking vans; rolling repair shops, field kitchens, generators, communication trucks, bridge sections on a tractor and semi, lighting equipment, wreckers, and more guns; rocket launchers; and howitzers.

A breach opened in the column, then another short convoy of trucks. The GIs kept their faces down and waited. And then a bang in the near distance and a flare popped open to float down, the intense candlepower bleaching the countryside. Parker was facedown but watching when Finger suddenly scrambled out of the ditch with a hoarse, muttered groan:

"Shit, we got to do it now. They must have seen us."

Parker called out, "Stop. Get back here," and then a machine gun fired from somewhere, from a tank turret or a sentry post. A volley of tracers skipped and rebounded off the pavement, and Finger went down.

Shoulder opened up at the muzzle blasts with thoughtful, even rifle shots as Parker and Trucker ran out, dragging Finger into the other ditch with panted grunts. Finger's heels scraped and his head lolled. They rolled him over and saw that he was dead. The flare faded down, swinging on its shroud lines. The greens stretched and shrank in grotesque patterns lightened by the snow, darkened by the shadows of fence posts, trees, vehicles, the road itself.

The parachute landed. The core still glowed and hissed in the snow. The darkness was full of wheezing grumbles and foot sounds, casual bullets coming in as another flare popped off. Parker flopped down and looked out from under his helmet at the others. The machine gun worked over the area, searching, laying it down. A tank shell thudded somewhere in the fields, steel shards whickering away.

When the flare burned out, Parker got up, sprinted, and kicked through the snow until he couldn't breathe. When he got to the trees, he hit hard, and squirmed around with his rifle up. He heard fast feet in a scurry around him and to the front, and made the challenge:

"Task Force?"

"Crazy."

Kooch stumbled up, fighting for breath, he and Bucket dragging the toboggan. Parker helped them pull it off to the first rise, then settled in behind some trees, and waited. Leg limped up. Stray bullets rustled through the dry bushes like something terrified. Shaky was quiet and calm until the shivers came again, stuttering to himself out loud. Parker hugged him with a blanket, patted his back, and looked over his shoulder at the road. Shaky was weeping.

"You gotta promise me. If I ever lose an arm or a leg, you gotta shoot me. Promise me. I know I can trust you."

"Fuck that. You'll change your mind. Everybody does."

He looked back with the glasses at the weak headlights and silhouettes flitting by. He checked his watch. After ten minutes, he took a swallow from his canteen; after fifteen, he dug through the triple layer of pants, hunched his hips to get at his cold, shrunken peter, and took a piss. He scanned the field again with the glasses and saw something that moved.

He pointed it out to Bucket, who went over and came back with Jew Boy, whimpering curses. He had stumbled over Plowboy, crumpled up, a bullet in the back of his head. Parker tried to talk to him. Jew Boy snarled and slugged him away.

"Get the fuck away from me, all right?"

They agreed to give Trucker and Shoulder an extra five minutes. Parker made it six but then started off. Shaky got up to follow him, then the others, on a track that would skirt around the shimmers, and flashes in the sky above Wiltz, that pink and evil beacon, a flickered neon with a bad electrode.

They could see dark, blurred houses up ahead. A quick look with a flashlight showed them crooked road signs on a bent pole. WILWERWITZ was upside down and in any direction you liked. A splintered, shot-up MP sign warned them: BRIDGE AHEAD UNDER FIRE. They saw a wrecked Sherman with a tiny fire under it and smelled burnt paint, and cordite. As they got closer, they heard a weak, choked voice:

"You guys GIs?"

They dropped, their weapons shouldered off and ready.

"Hey. It's me. Who are you guys?"

"We're bits and pieces. Who are you?"

"I'm the engineers. They grabbed us into this defense platoon for Division. 'Special Troops,' they said. My ass."

"Come on out where we can see you."

A short T-5 tottered out, dragging a shelter half and a blanket. He wore a knit cap, the earflaps down, a ripped overcoat. One gloved hand rubbed the other bare hand.

"Where's your weapon?"

"Ain't got none. Ain't got nothin'. You guys headed for Wiltz? There ain't no Wiltz. It's Heinie City now. Kaput."

"We're trying to make it to Bastogne."

"Shit, that's another eight miles. As the Kraut flies. Twelve, for real. You got any spare water? I'm eating snow."

They gave him an extra canteen to keep. Parker asked him:

"What are you doing this way, so far out?"

"What way? Nobody knows which way is up. We're down to the paymasters. Telephone guys. Fucking chaplain's assistants. Made the medics take off their red crosses. I'm *road maintenance*. You dogfaces don't *realize*. We're operating two sawmills and a gravel quarry . . ."

". . . I got it. Okay. They broke out the Yellow Pages."

"Field artillery keeps getting towed in, but then, *whoom!* Tanks? Zapped and burned. What's left turns tail and runs. Krauts everywhere, house to house, street to street. They scream like lunatics. Everything is blowing up and on fire. It started at two this afternoon and was over by midnight."

"You wanna come with us?"

"Just leave me alone. They'll come get me pretty soon."

He plowed his feet, dragging the shelter half, and blanket; fell down, and swayed himself back up. Parker called after him:

"They might shoot you. They do that. We happen to know."

The engineer waved and crawled back under the tank.

"Be sure you keep that canteen under your coat."

"Shall we catch that crazy bastard?" Koochie said. "He doesn't know what he's doing. One blanket? Sleeps at night? He'll freeze to death out here."

"Let him fight his war his own way. Besides, we're not doing so hot our own selves."

P arker got under a raincoat with a flashlight. He tried to concentrate on the map, but his eyes kept tearing, and he kept counting the faces of the men who were gone. Maybe Trucker and Shoulder were just missing. They could catch up. Maybe they got cut off, or got wounded, and decided to surrender. But this made five. He was doing this all wrong. General? General FUBAR, maybe.

The map showed the next road as narrow and secondary. It came up from the river at Wilwerwitz with kinks and crooked curves, crossed the valley over a filled-in causeway, then switched back, and jacked itself higher. But it held no traffic. Bucket and Jew Boy climbed the sloped retaining wall of stones to check for sentries, and to stand guard. Two blinks of a flashlight and the rest picked their way up, crossed over, and picked their way down.

The valley was all snowed-over fields and fences. The going was easier, but they were exposed, and vulnerable, so they drifted back to the heavy progress of the forest. They ate cold rations without talking; that high, loony energy evaporated with the smoke of their breath. Parker thought about being really warm again, counted the four men he just lost, ticking off their names—their real, Task Force Crazy names.

They laddered up to the ridge through a cold, misted world of dismal cathedrals supported by dim, black columns. Every move was involved, stalled by the thick growth. Their breath panted out in clouds. Sweat leaked under their shirts. Jew Boy grabbed a pine bough that dumped a load of snow on his head.

When he let go, it snapped up, a cascade plopping over him. They yanked him out, but there was no banter, no jokes.

Push, pull, pass the toboggan and the gear from hand to hand; or gather around it, lift the whole thing to the lip of the next ledge; or haul it up a steep slope with the rope, making grunted heaves until somebody took up the slack around a tree. Parker tried to remember how they got where they were, and why they were doing all this.

. . . TUGGING HIS WAY through Richmond Hill, entering that contest the *Long Island Press* held for teenagers. He won a ten-dollar first prize for his essay arguing that bad luck and hard knocks in life would build good character. He bought a pair of jodhpur shoes for six dollars and spent a dollar on movies and ice-cream sodas before Pop-Pop found out about it and borrowed the last three dollars for carfare to the city.

Twisting over to shut off the alarm clock, he looked through that attic window at the cold street outside and got dressed with a flashlight.

Brooklyn Tech was a prestige school for boys only, an honor just to get nominated by the grade school principal. He took the entrance exam with hundreds of kids in a monstrous auditorium. Only one out of three was accepted.

Some of their courses were college-level and grades were a ferocious competition. Three thousand names and their scores were printed in the school paper in descending order. He was number three in his class with an 82.6 average. The number one kid had 83.1. Somewhere in the building, pickled, and hidden away in a jar, was some brain who had a 94.2.

Toby was okay in math, but then came geometry. He couldn't understand the relationships between forms and shapes, not even the triangulation of himself. Boysy was the sine of Nana who was the cotangent of his mother and Pop-Pop was the square root of the Empire of Atlantis.

When he transferred first to Lakeland High and then to Hillsborough High they translated all his grades to Cs.

. . . dogtrotted with bare feet down Fortieth Avenue. Norman, Calfrie, and Dominic had feet like leather, but his had gone tender. The blacktop was hot and he blistered and limped. The dam was out because of some hurricane, and they treaded and floated all the way downriver to Sulfur Springs. They walked and jogged home, delirious and happy. When summer ended, the guys at Tech said he talked like a hillbilly.

PARKER LOOKED BACK into that flat, shadowed face in the cellar, his mouth tasting like old pennies when he pulled it down, the pistol shot soft and fuzzy to his deafened ears.

HE TOOK THE POINT and scouted ahead but still glowed with the muted crunch of his own footsteps, remembering that heart-thumping thrill when a car would pull over, and he had to grab his stuff, and run before the guy changed his mind. That old joke actually happens: "Tired of walking? So run awhile." Ha, ha, as he pulls away.

And that abandonment when the guy said, "This is as far as I go." He would thank them, polite, gallant even, a knight of the road. And then back with the thumb and the traffic whizzing by. Their eyes looked at him with pity or distrust, but mostly didn't see him at all.

SOMETHING WAS OUT THERE. Parker hissed and held out both hands. He circled them in, fading over to Bucket. Koochie felt it and came close. He breathed it in their ears.

"Any you guys smoking?"

Shakes of the head, palms up. Parker sniffed, stepped away, and came back to mouth it.

"That's Kraut tobacco. I know that smell."

He pushed down on their shoulders and crawled ahead, using a small draw for cover, careful about loose rocks, and dead branches, until it leveled out on a wide ledge. The trail was only a tunnel through the trees, but that smell was stronger, and he heard voices, clinks, and scrapes.

Parker watched through the glasses. Two Germans talked and smoked by a campfire. They wore soft peaked caps with the earflaps buttoned up, and white parkas. Their white pants were tucked into short, laced boots with mean-looking cleats, and ski socks folded over the tops.

That poster again, on the latrine wall: *Gebirgsjäger*.

He saw four white helmets, four sniper rifles, swivel-stacked in a pyramid, two other men in sleeping bags. Soft radio static came from a tent. Something like a surveyor's transit was set up on a tripod with open sky beyond it, the overcast fluttering with reflections from the fires in Wiltz.

Feet scuffled on the trail behind him. Parker got down, drew his legs up under the cape, and burrowed his face into a snow-drift. He watched the sentry lumber up to the camp, put his rifle down, and sit by the fire, then toss back the hood of his parka, and fill a cup from a pot. When Parker saw the lightning-shaped SS runes on the side of his helmet, he crawled back, and let himself down the draw to the squad.

"It's an observation post. Sticks up into nothing like an eagle's nest. Must be for long-range guns. There's five of 'em. We can take them or we can go around."

"What's there to observe in this shitty fog?"

"You've seen it clear up. A few minutes could mean a lot.

They look like SS mountain troops. Probably tough bastards. Not like those drunk pussycats at the farmhouse."

They were quiet until Jew Boy, the cannoneer, whispered:

"Those fuckin' SS creeps. The thing on that tripod is an azimuth circle for taking bearings. They gotta have a range finder too. Some kind of officer; a radioman, and a driver. Couple of guards. They must have hid their vehicle somehow."

"Might be hitting Bastogne. If they can see that far."

"How long before somebody catches on, before, you know."

"When they're due to check in. Or if the weather clears."

"Wanna vote on if it's worth it?"

"Hell, we got the surprise. We can bushwhack 'em."

"It's risky. We shoulda stayed down in that valley."

"And run right into an army like last time? Now we're stuck. We'd have to go all the way back down again."

"That trail could shortcut us back to the next road."

"Bite off more'n you can chew and it comes back, and bites you on the ass."

Dark hands moved up to dark faces. Parker had to imagine the eyebrows and pursed lips, the thumbs dug into temples. He had already lost five, and now what? First Headley, then Jimbo. Getting back alive should be good enough. But even so, they'd just be put out on the line again. Bucket breathed out with a husky hiss that had to come from a wicked grin.

"Let's harass their ass. Let's kill the Nazi fucks."

THE TOBOGGAN WAS STASHED at the head of the draw. They had at least two hours before dawn, and were getting good at moving in the dark, but they chomped on the worry of that guard being loose somewhere out in the woods.

In their own way, Leg and Shaky were both wounded.

Parker put them in the center, hidden behind the toboggan and some fir saplings to cover any surprises. Koochie and Bucket crawled up to the camp and got ready to jump. Parker and Jew Boy left their M1s on the toboggan, looked at each other, then started a stroll down the trail: straight, casual, burp guns under their snow capes. Jew Boy pulled Parker to a stop and whispered:

"Right there. He's sitting on a tree stump."

Parker kept going. His hands were wet and his heart burned and punched at his chest. His stomach felt stuffed. His rectum started to leak, but he tightened it off. Jew Boy picked up the pace. The guard took a long drag on a cigarette, crossed his knees, murmured something, a song or he argued with himself. His head snapped and his eyes went up when the two white figures wafted out of the mist behind him.

Parker growled it out, strong and outraged. He kept the vowels long, grated his throat, and made the *r* heavy.

"*Was machst du hier?*"

"*Was meinst du? Und wer seid ihr?*"

What are you doing here?

"What do you mean? And who are you?

Flabbergasted, the sentry snatched at his cigarette. Jew Boy knocked him off the stump with one short burst, the butt still in his fingers as he slid backward down the slope into a drift of snow and dried leaves.

Automatic firing flared up at the observation post and then came repeated, single rifle shots. Parker and Jew Boy ran up the grade past Leg, who was trying to yell something about Shaky. A bullet shooed past them and thwacked in the trees. They crawled the rest of the way and passed Shaky, facedown in the trail, a piece missing from the bloody back of his skull. They worked over to Bucket, flat behind a tree.

"Me and Koochie were in position okay and when it started,

we let go. We got the two in the sleeping bags. I don't know how come it happened, but the one taking a piss, and another one is just wounded. He's shooting back, but I can't find the fuck. Over that way somewhere. He's good too. Don't take no chances. Shaky was behind us. He got it right in the face."

"Shit! Shaky was supposed to stay back there with Leg."

A bullet barked a tree close to Parker. A German inside the tent repeated frantic orders in a rising keen.

Jew Boy was yelling:

"Those crazy bastards! If they're calling down on their own position, we're fucked!"

"Can they do that?"

"Not like here, no. You do it when you're desperate, but you're dug in good, and the other guy is out in the open."

A tracer bullet hit a small tree next to Jew Boy's head, went through it with a spray of sap, bark, and wood fragments. The hole sizzled with a puff of sour steam.

"Where's that goddamn fucking sniper at?"

Kooch was in the woods on the other side of the trail. All four of them kept shooting at the tent, but they could still hear those frantic orders.

"That guy must be low. In some kind of a hole."

Parker and Bucket rolled over on their backs, unscrewed the caps on two stick grenades, nodded, rolled back, popped the strings, and swung their arms to send them spinning off. One landed in front of the tent. The other slapped against the top and slid down. When they went off, the canvas collapsed. Pieces started to burn around the German who lay in a shallow pit. They could hear him screaming out numbers.

Jew Boy rose up around a tree trunk for a clear shot but got knocked backward, his chest spurting. Parker pressed into the snow, his face in it, wheezing. He wriggled and slid his way over, and reached over to pull Jew Boy down by the ankle. Jew Boy's eyes fluttered, but he wasn't breathing.

They heard long, colossal rips in the sky. The artillery came in with the sound of square-cut nails dragged across a window-pane: one shell ahead to the left, one behind them, and to the right. Both crump, carumped in the treetops. Shrapnel snarled through the forest.

Parker felt the kick, the good side of his face flattened as he flopped over, rolled, and lay still, feeling around for his helmet through those seconds of dark numbness. Bucket and Koochie called out, their voices thick.

"General? You okay? You hurt? Hey!"

Blood ran over his face. He tried to control his breathing as he pushed back the wet cowl, and fingered the cut where a sliver of his scalp had been zipped off. As he checked himself out, an-other bullet whirred by, close.

Bucket cursed and raved as more shells came in. Parker swung the glasses back and forth until he spotted two huge rocks close together on the crest of the ridge. A rifle poked out with an attached telescope. Parker waved at Bucket and pointed it out, then fired at the space between the boulders.

"He's right there. Can you see it? You cover for me!"

Bucket used his M1 with slow, intense aim, calculating the angle shots that chipped fragments off the boulders. Parker had to worm his way back and over the trail to get to Koochie, and point out the sniper.

"You okay, General? You get hit?"

"Yeah, yeah. Listen. Slide back down the hill . . ."

A shell hit the trail, then another.

"When you're in the clear, run back to the toboggan and get that Kraut bazooka from Leg. You can shoot it, right?"

Parker sucked air in and out, his mouth dry. He was drinking from his canteen when another concentration of shells walked the trail. Dirt, snow, pebbles, and branches flew up in acrid fountains. He couldn't just lay there and wait.

The trees grew thick up to the edge of the flat shelf that made the trail. He kept himself low and hidden, defiladed from the sniper as he crouched, and crawled, finally coming out on the sloped edge of the cliff. He followed it until he could see those boulders, and the rifle barrel with his glasses. The sniper's boots stuck out on the other side.

He felt calm about it now, decided his moves, got himself set. He uncapped a grenade handle, got up, and ran. When he was close enough, he yanked the silk string, flipped the thing over the boulder, and flopped down. When it blew, he scrambled up on top, and burped down at what was probably already dead.

He slid to the ground, grabbed the boulder, and coughed against those pains in his chest. He stepped across the gore to reach for the sniper's rifle, and pulled off his ammunition belt. Parker cupped his hands, his voice high and hoarse.

"Bucket! I got him. All clear. Come help me here."

Bucket ran up and they went into the remains of the tent, rolled the dead officer away from the radio equipment, and shot into it with the machine pistols. They wrecked the range finder and the aiming circle on their tripods with close-up shots, and checked around with a few anxious, uncertain steps.

"Let's go. We got it. We're done."

They stopped by Jew Boy and then by Shaky, looked at them a moment, and ran down the slope, skipping, and sidestepping around the shell holes. Parker skidded and went down on his good knee by the toboggan to stare at Leg's random shredded slabs, his rags, and raw flesh studded by splinters of bone. Parker banged his fist against his chest.

"We could have gone around! Damn it! Why not go around? We could have. Somehow, that's all. We didn't need this."

Bucket pulled at his arm, snatched up the toboggan ropes, put one in Parker's hand, and gave him a shove. Parker shuffled, then staggered, then ran with it.

"Hey! Wait up!"

Koochie came up behind them, but he dragged one leg, blood on the side of his head.

The fog was thick again, the air warmer. The trail thawed in muddy places that made the toboggan grate on pebbles, and hard to pull. They dodged through the woods but were loaded down with more than they could drag, and had to throw things off. They kept their ammo and blankets, some of the rations, but dropped the extra weapons, and the tools, the jerry can of water, and the one of gas.

Koochie's gimp got stiffer and slower. Then he quit and just looked at them, his face like a tired, old dog. His head cut was probably worse than Parker's, but the worry was that fragment notched deep in his hip with a purple swelling.

They bandaged him with what they had, shot him up with morphine, wrapped him in blankets, and a tarp. They strapped him down on the toboggan, dreamy and limp, his head propped up, and padded over the bent curve at the front. They stacked their gear at his feet.

They couldn't just wait for darkness, or even take a long rest. This was the third mark they had left behind, and a detachment of mountain troops could already be scouting its way up that logging trail. It was full daylight when they reached the high grove of snow-heavy pines where they could take cover, and watch the convoys surge along the road below them. Motorcycle riders passed both ways, and they could see three sentries posted every five hundred yards around a double bend.

They took ten and ate some of the German ration goo. Koochie hummed out his misery with even-spaced groans, his face crumpled up. They tempted him with a piece of D-bar, coaxed him, held up his canteen.

Parker sat with crossed legs to look through the field glasses, but had to turn away from Bucket to hide his shivering. What a piss-poor general—fucked up beyond all recognition. Nothing worked right; one disaster after the other, and now eight of his men were gone—*eight*. His head still hammered with those shells on the trail. What? Artillery registered on their own position?

They hauled their way across the folded grade, around the curved hip of a hill, and kept looping back to check the road.

THE CONGESTION EDGED FORWARD with a sprinkling of scraped, dented American trucks, and jeeps, even a Sherman, the white stars slapped over with crude black crosses. But the march got into a sluggish detour around some furrowed paving and two burned-out American tank destroyers. It flowed several hundred yards through both ditches, then angled back to the hard surface, and picked up speed.

Parker played with the adjustments on the telescopic sight on the sniper rifle, this thing that had killed Jew Boy, and Shaky. He could see the *Feldgendarm* standing on the outside of the curve. The Zeiss binoculars were stronger and he switched over to study the marking tape held up by kinky iron stakes made for combat barbwire; the black-and-yellow pennants with a death's head; and the signs: *Achtung! Minen!*

Bucket saw it too; tried to hold the GI binoculars with one hand so he could steady his quivering leg, then leaned back against a tree.

"Hey, General. All we gotta do here, switch around them signs and that tape, and shit. And then—ta-ta and ka-boom!"

"No more of that General shit, okay? Let's just scram the

fuck out of here. They're on our ass, and we got Kooch to take care of."

"Think a little. They ride along, happy as hell. *Whoom!*"

"Some other day, when we're patched up and rested."

"Wait for the right gap in that Heinie parade, is all."

"What is this, Bucket? You average out at about six words a day. All of a sudden, you're some kind of blue jay?"

"The action, man, nothing like that good, hot adrenaline."

"We just lost three of our guys. *Another* three."

"So? Tough shit. You want war? Try the Hurtin' Forest."

"What's the Hürtgen got to do with anything?"

"The death factory, man. Heads this way, legs that way. Really, really thick woods and the Krauts dug in deep, and mean, all zeroed in, and booby-trapped. Dig in, you hit a mine. Stand up, an MG gets you. Lay there and they drop mortars on you. Artillery? We had guys crying like babies."

"Hey, breathe a little. When you gonna come to a period?"

"We lost all our company commanders, *all!* Three just went nuts. The MPs arrested this one lieutenant for refusing to order his platoon to attack. *Arrested* him! Hauled him off!"

Bucket hesitated. His voice dropped.

"We all believed in God. We had no choice. Not there."

"And you want some more of that? You need more?"

"Hell, yes. It's our turn now. Let's do it."

"You're crazy. We get over the road, that's good enough."

"What? We're just gonna bug out? We're wet sissies now?"

"Two. We're down to two sissies that can still walk."

THE NOISE DROPPED into one last clink-clink of a rattling bulldozer. Parker squatted with his elbows braced inside his knees, the sling snugged around his arm, three fingers and his thumb tight around the small part of the rifle stock.

The *Gendarm* was lighting a cigarette, cupped the match in his hands and leaned into it. Parker wondered if that breast badge he wore could deflect a bullet, and brought the crosshairs just above it. He could see the bob of his own pulse.

Breathing easy with a loving finger, he willed the trigger to move. Surprised by the recoil, he saw the German go down. He hopped up, slung his weapons, and took the toboggan ropes.

"Let's go. Now, Bucket. *Now!* Koochie? You okay?"

Koochie was asleep, out of it as they lowered him down the incline, hit a rock, rolled him over, and tumbled the gear. They set him right, threw everything back on, and maneuvered to the ditch, and the fence. Bucket cut the wire. They panted and heaved to scrape the toboggan over the slush, and the bare spots on the pavement where the snow was squished away by the determined wheels, and tracks.

The other ditch—one last fence, Parker sprinting through the gap Bucket made with the wire cutters. He saw the snow puff up on both sides before he heard the rifle shots but kept it going, reached the tree cover, turned, and wheezed, dizzy for air.

"Oh, Christ! Man—we did it. We made it."

Bucket was gone. Parker saw him running back through their own tracks. He screamed at him:

"You wacko! Come back! Get over here!"

A column of horses dragged guns and supply wagons to the start of the curve just as Bucket raced down the road to cut the marking tape, and pull out the warning pennants, and the signs. Parker gaped for a moment, then jerked when a bullet spurted up the snow. One of those sentries wanted his ass.

He dragged Koochie deeper into the trees, looking back to watch Bucket peel the minefield open, working an iron stake to get it loose, carry it with the drooped marking tape to the ditch, and hammer it in with a rock. He retied the tape and switched the warning signs.

Parker unslung the Mauser, braced his right shoulder against a tree, and shot at one of the horse teams, bolted out the cartridge, and rammed in another. If he could keep the Krauts busy—keep them blind, put down something in between.

Bucket jiggled out the other stake and carried it to the opposite ditch, dragging the tape. He almost had it, hammering with the rock when his body made a slow twirl into the air with the shattering rip, and echo of an exploding mine.

PARKER GROWLED AND WHIMPERED the toboggan up the hill in a back-and-forth slalom through the tree growth until he reached the steep, sudden drop of a cliff, and ravine. The running stream gurgled over huge, glistening boulders, the Wiltz River swirling around snowy banks, and over shoals of gravel. He stitched his load back down the hill, looking for a ford, and found a level place, an icy backwater marsh.

"Koochie! I can't get this thing over that. You'll have to let me walk you across. Hey, Kooch! On your feet. Hey!"

He pulled back the blanket. Koochie's face was a deep red purple. Parker wiped at his eyes with the back of his wrist. For a long time he tried to look at Koochie, and tried to not look, his head up, and down, his eyes open, and shut. He sighed out a deep breath, and let himself slump.

HE PUT A REASONABLE, light load together, rolled three blankets inside a white tarp, and shoved two stick grenades under his belt. He put two ration cans in his pockets. He took ammunition for the Mauser and the Schmeisser, a canteen of water, and one of gasoline. He left the rest.

He waded into it gradually, the river coming up to his crotch. He held his boots up, one in each hand, his pistol and belt stuffed into one, canteens in the other. He felt with his foot, wiggling into the gravel, and around the stones before he tried the next step. One end of the blanket roll dipped in and got wet.

He heard explosions back on the road—one, then two. The river didn't seem that cold until he got out, stopped to put on his socks, and boots, staggered into the open air, and climbed into the woods on the next hill.

He looked back with the binoculars through a break in the mist. He could see the stalled column and a burning vehicle. It looked like a line of men hunched over on their knees, feeling ahead of themselves with bayonets.

His legs stiff and numb, he made it to the cover of the back slope. He pawed through the snow around a tree to find loose twigs, and forest mulch, dug into his jacket pockets for some charred bits of tinder, doused it all with gasoline, and flamed it with the Zippo.

Smoke and steam mixed with the fog. He dragged over a dead branch and stomped it into short pieces. When the fire got going he squatted over it, turned, and twisted his butt to toast one leg, then the other, sat down to pull off the boots, and rub his feet, stood up, and turned again. When he got mostly dried out, he lay back, wrapped himself with blankets, got drowsy, and went off, snapping awake every few minutes to raise his head, sleeping, but not sleeping, the dark memories flickering in, and out.

Why did he keep slurping on this stale vomit? He didn't need to see Pop-Pop again in that old suit, sweater, and greasy tie, standing on the sidewalk outside a delicatessen in Kew Gardens, going up to people in the crowd, selling their ration stamps for butter, and meat to get carfare, and lunch money for another of his meetings.

They had moved again, next to the Long Island station, a dark, steep, narrow stairway to the tiny two rooms, and tiny kitchen. It would be compact, like living on a yacht, Boysy said. He made a drawing board out of thick plywood for his designs, and built bunks out of twelve-inch planks, and four-by-four posts that went up to the ceiling around the walls. He rigged up fluorescent lights under his own bunk for his work. The window in the fourth wall looked out on soot-covered vents, rain gutters, skylights, and roofs.

Pop-Pop and Nana had the other room. Toby and Squirt had to get up on a high stool, and then climb into bed, hearing the slide and the rub of the gum eraser on Boysy's pencil sketches; his breath when he blew away the crumbs; the clink of brushes in the jar of water. They felt the train vibrations, and heard the laughing and the whoops, the jukebox in the bar downstairs: "Chattanooga Choo Choo," over, and over.

"Track twenty-nine. Boy, you can gimme a shine."

But then they got bedbugs and Toby scratched, and got welts. They painted kerosene in the wood joints and cracks, but they still itched, and had to smell the kerosene too.

He was at the movies when the picture stopped and the lights went on. The manager came out on the stage with a microphone and announced that all armed forces personnel had to report to their bases immediately. Toby was surprised at how many soldiers and sailors sidled out of the seat rows to swarm up the aisles. When he got home he heard about Pearl Harbor.

He walked through the rain one night from the library at Richmond Hill, went around the curves, and under the chestnut trees, two books under his belt to keep them dry, so happy that day he got an adult card, and could take out any book he wanted, not just the juveniles.

He was tearing up newspapers to stuff into his wet shoes.

Pop-pop came in and wanted to feel one, said it was ruined, and got upset because Boysy had to work so hard to get the money. When Toby turned his back, Pop-pop gave him a hard whack on the head with the heel of the shoe.

He got an after-school job delivering clothes for a dry cleaner. No wages, just tips. His first real job was the summer they lived in Somerville, New Jersey, where they had some cousins. His mother worked as a telephone operator in a defense plant. She met Bob there, a construction foreman.

After Victor drove them to New York, Victor went back to Tampa and divorced Aline. But then Victor married Aline again and they had a baby girl. Much later, Toby caught his mother hiding those scars inside her left wrist.

Defense work and the draft caused a manpower shortage and Toby got a job on a farm making a dollar-fifty a day. But then he heard about this weekend estate owned by some rich doctors. They needed somebody to mow and rake the two acres of lawn, but he couldn't believe they'd pay *five* dollars a day.

When the caretaker asked him if he had his driver's license yet, he had to tell him he was only thirteen. The guy thought he was a lot older, hired him anyway, but only paid him three dollars. He had to work hard and fast, and was always stiff and sore, but he grew four inches that summer, and saved a hundred dollars. Only later did he think about the caretaker putting that other two dollars in his pocket.

He spent the next summer with Victor and Aline and their son, Norman. Toby got a job as an outside machinist's helper for Tampa Shipbuilding. He had to be sixteen, but they took his word for it. He paid Victor and Aline what was fair for his room and board. His shift was four to midnight and once he worked all night on overtime, installing a propeller on a minesweeper being built for the Russian navy.

Most of it was dodging the government inspectors checking up on the cost-plus-ten-percent war contracts. The machinist ran him back and forth to the toolroom while he smoked a cigar, and waited for Toby.

A welding rod banged off Toby's hard hat one night. He looked up and saw a girl in overalls waving, and smiling down from the deck above. The machinist told him she was flirting. He should take her out, buy her a beer, and get laid. But Toby didn't have a car, had never tasted beer, and never even kissed a girl, except spin-the-bottle once, when he was a kid.

He bought a pair of cowboy boots in Ybor City, a bull's horns and roses stitched across the front. The guys at Brooklyn Tech were flabbergasted when he clattered down the hallway on his hard riding heels. When they wore down he took them to an Italian shoemaker, but he put on old lady's heels, shorter, wider, and curved at the back instead of straight and narrow. He never wore them after that.

Pop-Pop was a teetotal atheist. Nana was Protestant. Once he caught her praying in their little room, and blew up. He tore chunks out of the Bible, yelled curse words Toby didn't think he knew, switched to Danish, and back again. He spit on it, jumped on it, then ran into the kitchen, threw the teakettle on the floor, and jumped on that too, bent it out of shape, ran down the stairs, and outside.

Toby was making a peanut butter sandwich when Pop-Pop came back. Toby looked away, almost holding his breath. Nana was still in their room, but her crying had stopped. Pop-Pop picked up the ruined kettle and turned it in his hands as if he were holding a relic, his bushy gray-blond overhanging eyebrows pulled together tight. Toby wondered what he was thinking.

. . . Toby little—he was really little. He could remember that part: running wild through the darkness, his bare feet wet from the dew, gathering sticks, making long, curved, happy swoops to drop his load on the fire and run off again.

But Mama had finished cooking the grits and beans. Daddy used a board to pick up the spare wheel they had used for a stove, and rolled it away to cool. Toby descended through the glory, hair in his eyes, his shirttail, his flag. He dropped his donation and zoomed off, one foot down on the hot wheel, and then the other, screaming away in crazy circles. Daddy had to run him down, like catching a rabbit.

He didn't remember much of the rest. He was in a large white room and a pretty, nice lady in a stiff white dress was washing his feet in a basin. She put on something greasy and wrapped them in bandages. Daddy carried him to the car. He was in the rumble seat under a blanket, and they were going down a rutted dirt road: home, or somewhere. He lay on his back, looking up at all the stars, his feet tingling.

PARKER LOOKED AT HIS WATCH. Ten minutes. He wanted more sleep but had to push away the drowsiness, had to move. He kicked snow on the fire, picked up his gear, and stumbled into still another wilderness, groggy, and numb, small, and alone — alone now, again.

Caught in the open, embarrassed when the sky blazed out into a brilliant clarity and the sun torched him with the sudden, sharp, black-and-white focus of it all. But Luxembourg was still cold and empty, and only pretended to be a Christmas card. Off somewhere, a machine gun imitated cracked sleigh bells. A buzz bomb went over, its spreading trail showing the way west. To his right, smoke hung over the remains of Wiltz.

A farmer trotted among the haystacks in a fenced pasture with his arm around a cow's neck. The sky closed down and the sleet and the pale in-between came back. The woods were like leaking baskets of fog. Parker made an easy stroll across two empty roads a quarter mile apart.

He first saw the dog and then the body, then the gaping wound it was tearing at with bared, bloody, foaming teeth. The dog snarled and he swerved aside. And then he passed abandoned weapons, equipment, shell casings, muddy holes, paper— everywhere paper: reports, orders, the news; letters in different languages that expressed business, love, and cheer to the wind. Walls had broken apart and poured into a buried lane, a curtain caught on the edge of a shapeless window.

A jeep was upside down and pretzeled over a black hole. The front and back fenders almost touched and trapped the GI driver whose frozen intestines dangled over his face.

Everything was a silence. As he climbed over piles of chimney bricks and splintered wood, he could hear his hobnails crunch and click. He stepped around a coffeepot, part of a traffic signal, a baby carriage, a sofa, toys, books, roof tiles, tangles of military phone wire of different colors.

Local people walked around a dead horse harnessed between the shafts of an overturned two-wheel cart. Its belly was bloated and all four legs were stiff and pointed up. Parker saw a piano, a steamer trunk spilled open, a cardboard box full of pots, and dishes, an armchair. Villagers pushed wheelbarrows along the road, full of household goods and children. They pushed bicycles loaded up like burros.

An old man with a high, felt hat walked by with a small dog on a leash, a bedroll over one shoulder, a stick and a bundle over the other. A fat woman clumped by in loose galoshes. She wore a coat with a fur collar and leaned on a cane. They ignored Parker and ignored the two workmen who shared a bottle of wine, and then spilled over a handcart full of dead civilians, tumbling them into a pit. The cart had iron tires that rumbled on the road along with the clacking of their wooden shoe soles.

Parker threw back the hood and the folds of the snow cape, and hoped he could reassure them with his American helmet. He passed a woman crying in front of her tumbled stone house, the next house with a corner gone. A pattern of missing steps in walls papered with flower designs made flights from missing floor to missing floor, ending with a closed door at the top.

He crept into a cellar hoping for something to eat, the Schmeisser ready. He saw shapes in the dim light from the dirty foundation windows and flinched back on the steps. He turned on his flashlight. An old peasant couple sat in a corner. He held a rooster in his lap; she had a hen.

He swung the light and caught a staring grandmother, mother, and daughter together on the floor with quilts, wadded clothes, and boxes. A kid, about three, held a cat that peeked out of the covers.

He saw a basket of potatoes by the wall and held one up. "*Bitte?*"

All he got was eyes. He wiped the dirt off on his sleeve, put it back, hesitated, picked it up again, and bit into it, chewing as he left. He dodged a shell crater in the yard, the wall of the barn splattered with an exploded compost heap. A cow and two goats were restless in their stalls. He went up a ladder into a hayloft but paused at every rung. He found a deep hole among the stacked bales, fixed his blankets, used his helmet for a pillow, and went to sleep holding his pistol.

. . . BACK AGAIN but couldn't remember how. He must have been in Florida when the Larsens moved to Forest Hills: a country house of wood isolated in a sea of pavement, and row houses with the same brick steps. It had spacious hallways and stairs, a mansion in its day but paintless and dirty now, an unlikely scenery prop from *Gone with the Wind*. They lived in two rooms on the second floor. They could smell the stable of riding horses on the other side of a dirt yard.

Toby had read all the books about the old west frontier, learned about the slaughters at Sand Creek, and Wounded Knee, having trouble believing Americans ever did such things. The Indians used to travel for days in a slow, loping shuffle, barely leaving the ground with their feet. Toby tried it, got winded but gradually got up to a feeling of lightness: a joy. He would jog a mile and a half to the subway for school, his shirt-sleeves rolled up, without feeling the cold. People stared at him, wearing mackinaws, fur collars, and gloves.

One of his teachers nodded him out to the hall, scowled, and asked him why he had no coat. Toby shrugged it off—didn't need one, he said—but embarrassed. He told the teacher he wanted to be an aeronautical engineer, not quite sure what that was. But he had to go to college, which meant money. The teacher said he might get into West Point, but his congressman would have to endorse him.

. . . trying to remember being warm—Leora on her porch swing in a bathrobe, maybe getting ready to go out. He sat on something wicker. She pouted and picked at her nails. All he could do was smile, his cheek muscles in a knot. He tried not to stare—those eyes she had. He could see around the robe's lapel at the top of one of her breasts. He waited. What was love supposed to do? Be charming and amusing, like in the movies? How did you do that?

PARKER HAD TO STUDY his watch long and hard to realize he had slept fourteen hours, not just two. This was 0643, twenty-first December, the sixth day. He drank from his canteen, cut open a ration can, and ate a German form of egg and ground-up sausage. He felt rested, but with the relaxation came the hangover stiffness of accumulated scrapes, and bruises, and the agitated cramps of revived bowels. He was aware of the pain in his nose, and cheek. That caked swelling on his head throbbed under the helmet liner straps.

He took his first crap in a week in a corner of the loft, squeezing out hard, steaming lumps. He wiped himself with handfuls of hay, but grabbed up his drawers and pants when he heard voices. He crept down the ladder and over to a high window in the cow stall. He heard hobnail boots outside, felt for a grenade but let it go, and sneaked back to the ladder. He geared up and slipped out a rear door into the dawn, first an orchard, then again, back to the woods, and the fields.

The snow was heavier and dunes were piled and rippled by the wind. He checked the compass and stayed west. When the weather was clear enough, he could judge the course of the river by the thicker tree growth and took shortcuts across the bends. He tried the railroad leading to Bastogne, the hard, straight surface of the crossties making easier walking. The tracks crossed the river and recrossed it three times over trestle bridges, but the risk of the exposure was too much, and he went back to the woods.

★

Something crunched and squeaked through the frozen snow crust. He sank behind a tree, narrowed the hood, and folded himself into a white knob in the landscape. He heard boots rustle and bump through the bushes, and aimed the burp gun at the shape that slogged its way out. A branch heavy with collected snow was pushed down and a face appeared.

"*Fritz? Bist du das?*"

A German stumbled into the clear, his rifle at high port. The tail of his greatcoat almost dragged on the ground, the torn sleeves hanging down over his knuckles. He had no helmet and his ripped head cowl hung useless behind his neck. His blond hair and the dried blood looked like straw, and cow flop. Parker held back. He didn't know what else was out there and a shot could give him away. The German saw him and cringed until his face expanded into a blooming grin.

"*Amerikaner! Ich will mich ergeben!*"

He aimed his rifle with one hand at a vague sky that he knew he might miss. He dropped the gun but forgot to raise his hands, rubbing them instead.

"*Nicht schiessen. Bitte?* Okay—you Joe?"

I want to surrender! Don't shoot. Please? Like, think it over, maybe? Parker told him in German to put his hands against a tree and patted him down. The guy was living out of his pockets and Parker felt all sorts of cans and boxes, and lumped wrappings, but no knives or grenades. Parker found three clips of ammo that he could use for the sniper rifle.

Parker explained: he only knew a few words of German, and

could speak better than he understood. He asked him where he was going. The guy nodded and smiled, started with slow, distinct baby talk, then picked it up, and started to jabber.

He said, or maybe he said, he was looking around, trying to give up. Two of his buddies were wounded that morning and taken prisoner. He managed to get away with a little something on his head, but he lost his helmet, his pack, even his gloves. Then he figured maybe he had enough of this baby-shit war. It was almost over anyway. Why be the last man killed?

He peppered in a lot of *weisst du?*'s, and *verstehst du?*'s, but Parker did not know, and didn't understand. He used to spend hours in front of the mirror, trying to get "*fünf*" and "*acht*" and "*zwölf*" just right. But the mirror never talked back. And this country goof had some kind of hayseed accent.

Manfred Klaskin, almost sixteen, a *Schütze* in the Twenty-sixth Volksgrenadier Division, a buck private in a people's foot-soldier outfit. Seventeen thousand men and five thousand horses. He was with them in Russia for two months until they were shipped west in September. He looked down at Parker's German boots, frowned, then smiled, and shrugged. Corn-flower eyes and big freckles: all he needed was a guitar and a Gene Autry love song.

Parker knew the best thing would be to just shoot this bastard, that he was going to complicate everything. But this simple face was not the one in the cellar. Who could kill a Mortimer Snerd like this? A baby, even younger than Parker?

THEY WADED THROUGH THE DRIFTS, Klaskin in front, his torn coat collar turned up. He tried to drape the shreds of the cowl over his crusted head, and slumped forward, rubbing a bare ear with one hand, and putting it back in his coat pocket, then rubbing the other ear with the other hand.

Shots sounded ahead of them and to one side. Klaskin motioned Parker to get down and they lay without moving until voices came closer, then trailed off; and the sound of running feet faded the other way.

Parker closed up and they hunkered down together. He handed Klaskin his canteen, then slipped off his bedroll, and pulled out a blanket. He folded it double, and gave it to Klaskin to wear over his head like a shawl, the ends around his hands tucked under his armpits. Parker put down his weapons to hoist the load back over his shoulder.

Klaskin smiled at him when he turned; wagged one finger, then fired it—boom, boom. A big grin and a chuckle, but Parker had trouble grinning back.

The goofball leaned over to admire Parker's face, shook his hand, and whistled, then checked the graze wound on his head. Parker looked at Klaskin's oozing, crusted hair, and flipped his hand.

They got up and tramped on, the clouds low again, the snow slanted into their faces. Parker heard the lilt and rhythm of American voices somewhere around them, then saw silent banshees streak from tree to tree. The field glasses didn't help in the murky visibility. Parker cupped his hands.

"Hey, you guys! I'm stuck out here. I'm coming in."

Only soft sighs of the snow and then, funneled by hands:

"Who's that? You better sing out, buddy, loud and clear."

"It's me! Company B, First Battalion. Hundred-and-tenth. Twenty-eighth Division. I got a POW here with me."

They came out of the woods, rifles alert, bearded, muddy, and wet with bloodshot eyes, some with bandages. One had a civilian child's sweater draped over his head under his helmet. One wore a sleeping bag with holes cut out for his arms and legs. Some had clumsy, crudely sewn mittens cut out of blankets with a hole for the trigger finger.

A staff sergeant shifted to one side as he skulked closer, almost on tiptoe. He reached out for Parker's dog tags, a ready carbine in the other hand. He glared, jerked his carbine, and had them march down a trail through the firs. Helmets showed in the underbrush. Rifles poked out. Some wiseass snickered:

"You're dead meat, Nazi baby!"

They came to a cluster of huts, the command post low in a dugout with a roof of poles, and branches, a signboard propped up for a table. A smoking piece of rope burned in a can of gasoline next to an open case of grenades. The lieutenant had dirty whiskers. His eyes drooped over the top of his glasses.

"Where you been, anyway?"

"Up past Skyline Drive, down by the river. They took me into Germany, but I got away. I'm on the run six days now, fighting my way back through Clervaux, and Wiltz and everywhere else. I can't tell you how glad I am to see you guys."

"Where did you get this bum?"

"Back out there in the woods. This morning."

"You're on top of his hole? He's fresh out of ammo and *then* he decides to give up?"

"No, no. He just up and surrendered. Fair and square."

"Well, tough shit. We got orders, take no prisoners."

"So what do I do with him?"

"You take him back out and you shoot him. What else?"

"Hey, wait. I can't do that. You serious? I don't believe this. I've killed Krauts and then some, one right in my own hands. But this guy surrendered. Those SS pricks came close to killing me when I was forced to give up. Shit, we're Americans for crap's sake."

"We take a PW, we got to guard the fuck and feed him. If he's wounded we even got to nurse the bastard."

"Come on. That's Nazi shit for fanatics. Not us. And he's just a kid. What kind of way is this to save the world?"

"Listen. You're just a kid your own self. You don't know what war is all about yet. We're desperate here. Bastogne is under siege. We're surrounded for fuck's sake. You want this to be a direct order? Is that it? Or you want somebody else to do it? I'll get somebody else."

Parker looked at him, at the other eyes, the wildness.

"No. I'll do it. But not here. And I don't want no witnesses around watching me."

"Hey, Benny. Take this guy over with those other Krauts."

"No. This one's mine. If it has to be done, I'll do it."

"You let him get away, I shoot *you*. You got that? Huh?"

PARKER JABBED KLASKIN with the burp gun, snarling:

"Let's go, asshole. End of the line. *Mach spielen.*"

Klaskin frowned. What did that mean? Parker gave him a shove, got him away from the dugout, and the stares, and followed the footprints to a patch of briars where two Germans had collapsed into a frozen wilt. Klaskin knelt down, muttering something about his comrade. He lifted a head and stared into the face, the man's eyes sleepy in the gloom.

Klaskin looked over his shoulder at Parker. His hands went up and quivered. Parker spoke with quiet, slow hesitation as he tried to glue the German words together.

"Hear me. Play shooting. You beg and screams. I shoot the air. We run the both."

Scream? Was that *schrieen*? Or *schreken*? Or what?

The German kid wasn't getting it. Parker turned and yelled back with a dramatic fury:

"Right there, you son of a bitch! That's far enough!"

He urged Klaskin to come up with something, waving his hands like an orchestra conductor. Klaskin's mouth hung open. But then his lips pouted and his eyes got shrewd. He started a shrill, passionate scream:

"*Nein! Bitte! Um Gottes willen! Ich bin nur ein Kind!*"

Parker fired his pistol twice in the air and conducted up a final scream. He grabbed Klaskin by the coat and yanked him into a run. He could hear a yell in the distance behind them.

They got into a snow-covered thicket of bare briars. They lay flat and listened to the usual combat noises, but heard nothing close. Parker took a swallow and passed his canteen to Klaskin. He checked his compass, pointed to the east, and told him to go back, he was free. "Take off" didn't work in German. He jiggled his fingers, then closed his eyes tight, hung his head, and waved, and scooted his hands. Klaskin didn't move. Parker glared up at him, saw him smile, shrug his shoulders under the blanket, and cup his hands.

"But I am your prisoner," he said, explaining it all.

TANK DESTROYERS NUDGED out of piles of tree branches to cover the withdrawal of the trucks, and half-tracks that bumpered up, loosened, got jammed again. A Sherman chattered by, GIs on top, the commander in the open turret. Parker flagged him down to a crawl and he and Klaskin jogged alongside.

"Hey. We need a ride."

Two of them reached down to give him a hand.

"What's this you got with you?"

"He's a POW."

"No rides for no Krauts. Didn't you hear, take no prisoners? Shoot the fuck and climb on. Hell, I'll do it myself."

Parked stepped in front of Klaskin, his arms out. The tank stopped and the commander aimed his pistol.

"Hey! No! This is my personal prisoner."

"What? You *own* him? You won him in a crap game or

what? You gonna ship him home for Christmas? Okay, fine. So then you both can walk."

The exhausts puffed out a rancid cloud. The dogfaces stared back as they hung on to whatever they could.

PARKER GUIDED HIS WAY west on the sound of the guns as the fighting converged and got hotter. He was at the extreme left of the lieutenant's last detail map, probably off the edge at the lower corner by the printed arrow, and the word—Bastogne. This area had more farmland, the terrain a gentler roll. The railroad crossed the river again, but he decided to stay on the south bank, putting them somewhere close to the town of Neffe.

They found an abandoned two-man foxhole with a roof, a rug in the bottom, and a doormat rigged on a board as a backrest. They made a fire, got themselves dry, and comfortable, grinning like bad little boys in their secret clubhouse. They passed Parker's canteen, but he had nothing left to eat.

Klaskin pushed out his lower lip and frowned, scratched around deep inside his overcoat, and came up with two ration cans. He held them up with emphasis. *Eisen Portione*, he called them. Iron rations, forbidden to eat except—in something, an emergency, probably. Klaskin tried his best pidgin German, grabbed one wrist, and made a hauling-away kind of motion. You had to write a letter explaining why you ate it, or you would be put in a penal battalion. But this was now the right time to do it.

Klaskin heated one in the fire, opened it up, and offered to share the lard, and pork that tasted like cat food. Parker had to gag it down. Hard biscuits were in the other can.

Klaskin kept talking. Parker never understood him the first time but could get at least something after a few tries. Klaskin must have been an orphan. No father or mother. Or they were killed. *Bomberangriff?* Air raid, maybe he meant.

Klaskin showed off his dog tag, a metal oval with three slot perforations, his unit, his initial *K*, and his serial number inscribed on both halves. If he was killed, it was broken. One half stayed with his body, the other half sent back. And then his *Soldbuch*: the pay book with the eagle and swastika on the front, his picture as a recruit inside, his service record.

Klaskin's German got exasperated, fast and crazy.

"*Ostliche HKL—Hauptkampflinie. Ha-ka-el.*"

Practically yelling it, so maybe he would understand:

"*Ostfront! Russland! Schwerpunkt!*"

"Okay. You're on the main battle line, the Eastern Front. In Russia? On the point? And something happened?"

Again, Klaskin reached into that enchanted, vagabond coat, and came out with a small cardboard box with worn edges. It held a parchment, a ribbon, and an Iron Cross. Klaskin presented it with a gentle hand, smiling. He unfolded the citation and read it in deep, severe tones:

"'*Im namen des Führers verleihe ich dem Schützen*'"—he paused to spread his hand on his chest. "'Manfred Klaskin—*das Eiserne Kreuz zweite klasse.*'"

Another pause before he read the name and rank of the general who bestowed it and finished off with something about carrying his buddy on his back as crazy Russian bullets zinged all around. They grinned at each other. Parker could hear the oompah band in Klaskin's head, the cheers, could see the salutes, the flags. He offered his hand and they shook.

THEY SQUATTED DOWN at the edge of a firebreak that could be a Kewpie doll gallery for a machine gun. They listened to revved motors and shifted gears, boxes, and crates dropped on the ground, and stacked. Men were digging in. With the Zeiss glasses, the rims of fresh foxholes showed up in the foggy background. Parker thought about infiltrating, sneaking through on their bellies. But so close to Bastogne, the ring had to be thick and tight here. Better to be open about it.

On his signal, they both got up and went in, arms high, hands open. Parker's voice was loud, sharp, the snow cape thrown back to show the OD greens and his helmet. Klaskin cowered behind him.

"Hey. This is Private Parker, Tobias D. A-S-N four-four-zero-zero-seven-four-nine-nine. Coming in from the Twenty-eighth Division, infantry."

No answer. No shots, no challenges.

"Private Parker coming back from up front. Skyline Drive. I got a POW here with me. Hold your fire. HOLD YOUR FIRE!"

Nothing. Damn.

"Company B. Hundred-and-ten. Captain Stacy. We got cut off and run over at Marnach. I'm coming in with a prisoner."

A sudden, ragged volley zipped and slammed against trees, clipped twigs, and combed the snow. Parker was out flat with a numb pain that throbbed on the back of his left arm, just below the shoulder. He screamed:

"WHAT THE FUCK YOU GUYS DOING?"

Another hit near him, then another. He flopped over in the cleared lane and looked back at Klaskin, tumbled into a wet, red ball. Men came up, galoshes, boots, and leggings close by Parker's head. He saw gun muzzles and fierce glares. One of them nudged him with his foot.

"Hey there, Superman. Welcome to Bastogne."

Feet shuffled to one side.

"What have we got here, Nathaniel?"

"Lieutenant, we heard about suspicious Krauts over the walkie-talkie from a patrol. And then they just waltzed right in. Probably those counterfeit sons of bitches. Coupla that guy

Skorzeny's SS commando creeps. Hey, you. You hear me? Hey. What's Mickey Mouse's girlfriend?"

Parker was hurting, holding his arm, trying to sit up.

"You fucks. You shot us. You just murdered that guy."

"I asked a question. What's it mean, I say 'dem bums'?"

"You playing baseball cards with me at a time like this? We were coming in. I know you heard me. I yelled it out."

"You better answer me like I tole yuh or your ass is mud."

"Go fuck yourself, asshole. And the horse you rode in on, the horse's mother, and your mother, you son of a bitch! You shot us down, like—just bang! Like that. Like wild dogs."

He was crying as he held his bad arm. He fell over and rolled from side to side.

"Sarge? He's okay. He's only a kid."

"Hey, Lieutenant. They're all kids. Wha'? Look at that other one. Hey, you. You're a lousy Heinie spy. Admit it."

"What the fuck you talking about?"

"You're in half-ass Kraut uniform? What's that white helmet mean? You're carrying Kraut weapons and you got German boots? Chrissake, you got two potato mashers in your *belt*?"

"I lost my boots in Germany. And then again all my gear when these SS were out to kill me. Every damn where. I found the weapons. Besides, they're better'n ours."

"Oh? So you were in Germany?"

"Yeah, for a while. But I got away."

"Uh-huh. You got away."

"I been on the run since the start, shit head. Scrounging around, doing best I could. So I'm funny. Does my face look funny too?"

"Never mind that. Where d'ja get that spook suit? And that's an officer's pistol. Where d'ya steal it from? Whattaya got those white rags tied around your weapons for?"

"If you can't figure that one out, forget about it."

"Hey! Smart-ass! Those are *not* authorized weapons!"

"And I'm not authorized either. So what?"

The lieutenant jerked at Parker's combat jacket, dug down inside his shirts and long johns, and pulled out his dog tags.

"He's okay, Nathaniel. Only a real GI could swear like that, anyway. Send him back to an aid station and mark this other one for the buzzard detail."

The lieutenant turned to Parker.

"You picked a good time to come in, kiddo. We only got patrols out working right now. But listen. That Schmeisser? It has a voice of its own. You could get killed by our own guys shooting that thing."

"What about him?"

"We'll take care of it."

"He's got personal effects, a medal. That's no souvenir."

"Yeah. All right. You got that, Sergeant?"

The sergeant squinted at Parker, jaws tight. He dragged him up and shoved him down a dim path.

Half of Parker's right boot heel was shot off and curled under. His gear hung from one strap on his good side as he squeezed his bleeding shoulder, hobbled, and hopped. The sling of his rifle slid down his arm and he tripped and fell. He had to struggle to get up. When he looked back he saw them going through Klaskin's pockets. One held up the Iron Cross and pointed at it with a laugh.

They came to a jeep parked behind some bushes, the driver nodding off with his mouth open. He jerked when the sergeant touched him.

"Charlie. Take Superboy here downtown. The first MP you see, dump him out."

T he jeep bucked, bounced, and jangled. The driver shivered, steering with one gloved hand, the other under his crotch. Parker stretched the cowl up over his nose and down over his forehead before replacing his helmet. But he didn't feel the cold, just a low volume of numbness, a faint current of not much of anything.

"Fucking no windshield on this goddamn heap. Took 'em all off 'count of the reflections. Now we freeze our ass."

The driver dodged shell holes and piles of wasted junk in a destroyed village, angled around the square with its World War One monument to the local heroes, the church with the top half of its steeple gone, a few stores still intact but closed behind steel shutters.

Beyond it, tanks poked out of treacherous shadows. After a mile or more, Parker could see Bastogne through the breaks in the overcast: black, and ominous on a high plateau. The full moon showed up the hectic hills, the chipped, checkered squares of farmhouses, pastures, and tracts of firs. Some of the woodlots were cultivated plantations laid out in neat rows, the lower limbs trimmed up.

"So this is the big city we've all been dying to visit?"

"Yup. It's what all the hootin' and hollerin' is all about. They got five highways. At least that's what *they* call highways. And three also-rans. All come together right here in the main drag. Can't live without it. You sound disappointed. D'ja expect home sweet home, or what?"

"Never had one of those. But I didn't expect to end up still surrounded, or get treated like some stray mutt either."

Over the Wiltz again into the stone and brick outskirts of
the city, over a railroad, past a straight line of ragged tree stumps
on the edge of a boulevard. They were in the wreck of the main
square, in two-way traffic, headlights painted blue or blacked
out with just a slit remaining. Parker looked at the dark, battered
buildings, most of them four stories high with the windows
blown out, the shops boarded up.

The signs were in French now. They passed a movie theater
with one wall missing and a bare light inside. He could see the
blank white screen and the empty seats and a pair of lady's shoes
on the stage.

A street sign: *Place de Carré*. A deuce-and-a-half filled with
a massed pile of corpses growled through the moonlight, the
frozen arms and legs jostled by the bumps as the clinked song of
the snow chains rose and fell with the potholes. Another truck-
load followed behind it.

The jeep driver pulled up to an MP on the corner.

"Got yourself another straggler, old buddy."

Parker climbed out and limped over, his bad arm angled
out. He dragged his webbing. The MP came up behind him,
close enough to see the Screaming Eagle patch of the Airborne.
Shiny leather boots beat a slow, precise cadence as Parker shuffled and hauled down the path shoveled through the rubble.

A stenciled sign in front of the building: STRAGGLER COL-
LECTION POINT. Two MPs, bundled in overcoats, sat smoking in
a jeep by the door, one galoshed foot on the dashboard.

"They'll give you a bowl of stew or something here. Then
they'll send you out to an aid station."

One of the MPs in the jeep called out:

"Don't be eyeballing that door too hard, okay? Some of you
stragglers get a night's sleep and a couple squares, get thawed
out good. All the sudden you get straggly again. Next thing

you're in Paris hijackin' supply trucks. Some straggle theirselves all the way to Fort Leavenworth for twenty years."

Parker smelled nicotine and foul bodies. Eyes went up as he came in, blank hangover eyes like Orphan Annie's: eyes that had seen so much of everything but now saw nothing. Parker showed his dog tags to an MP at a clerk's table by the door. The MP wrote down his name and serial number.

The warehouse was heated but had no windows. Men sat or lay on the floor in a cigarette cloud of murmurs, and snores, some wearing the Bloody Bucket patch or the Golden Lions; others, the Ivy Division, the Checkerboards, the Indian Heads. Dismounted tankers from the Tenth Armored wore padded helmets and coveralls. The field artillery was there, the engineers, probably two hundred grimy, bearded derelicts who had filtered through the battle lines, starved, frozen, in shock.

Some had no weapons at all. Some wore a full rig, ready to move out. One pumped a cleaning rod through the barrel of his rifle with a slow, dreamy motion. He looked at the patch and ran it through again.

The clerk pointed Parker to a cluster of wounded gathered near a coal stove. One was groaning, still lying on the half-scorched door somebody had used as a stretcher. A soldier on his hands and knees babbled about the Germans who would kill them all, any time now. Nobody bothered to shut him up.

"Latrine" was chalked on the back wall with an arrow pointed at an iron door. Parker went outside, walking on the ball of his right foot away from the torn heel. An MP with a tommy gun in the courtyard. Piled snow on three sides was dotted with tints of yellow stains, piles of shit, and scraps of paper. He saw a German propaganda leaflet, wrinkled and smeared brown.

"Hey, buddy! Think of your family!"

———

Two new stragglers came in. Medics arrived. Names were called. A four-man kitchen crew lugged in three kettles in tandem. A chow line formed up with a medley of rattled mess kits, scraped spoons, bitching, and moaning about the soup.

A sergeant with the Blue Star of the supply guys said:

"You're lucky; at least I found a few onions, and we still got some salt and pepper. But we're running really low, I'm telling you. A few more days, we'll be boiling our boots."

Parker hobbled over and stooped to the ladle, holding away his bloody arm. He found a place to squat just as a T-5 medic came in with a helper. They checked with the clerk, moved the groaning man on the burnt door to a stretcher, and carried him out. They came back for another. The T-5 yelled out:

"All you other wounded, off and on. You can still walk."

Parker was on the floor, huddled over his kit and spoon. The T-5 charged over.

"Hey. Come on, mac. That means you."

"I had to wait this long, another minute can't hurt."

"Hey, eight ball. Let's go. I mean, like *now!*"

After another spoonful, Parker wiped his mouth, leaned over, pulled out his forty-five, and let it dangle over the back of his wrist.

"Not eight ball," Parker said. "FUBAR. *General* FUBAR. Stand at attention when you talk to me."

The T-5 looked around, but only two or three others saw it, and none were interested. Out of habit, he came to a sloppy, uncomfortable attention. Parker holstered the pistol and went on with his soup, feeling stuffed cramps, forcing himself to finish. He got up with awkward moves, almost losing his balance, limping, his left arm held out stiff.

He threaded his mess kit and spoon together with the handle, dipped and shook it in the hot soapy water in the first kettle and into the rinse water in the second. Using one hand and his knee, he folded it all together, and snapped it back in its pouch. He hitched up his gear, picked up his weapons, and dragged past the T-5 to the door.

Six of them were loaded into an open truck and driven around the square. They were taken out at a department store and brought into an enormous room, the display counters shoved into rows, and covered with blankets, bare, dirty mattresses, or unzipped sleeping bags. A medical T-2 went around with a stethoscope and a clipboard, taking pulses, and temperatures, making notes. He stooped over, put a penlight in a man's eyes, and flipped a blanket over his face. He held up his arm, called out, and pointed his fist, thumb down:

"Lennie!"

Parker watched the two orderlies come over with a body board. The generator outside made a hungry roar when they kicked open the exit bar on the door. It closed with a swallowed gulp and roared open again when they came back empty.

Frank Sinatra crooned through a loudspeaker about a paper doll he was going to buy that he could call his own. The walking wounded squatted and leaned along the walls under big dripping numbers painted on with hurried, thick paint. One man thrashed inside an air cargo net that hung from the ceiling, draped, and roped tight around the display counter.

Parker saw that T-5 peek at him as he mumbled to a master sergeant with a Red Cross brassard. The T-5 got excited when the sergeant shrugged him out of his way, surly about it.

"I'm telling you. He's half past eight, that guy."

Coleman lanterns hung from the walls. A tent was set up as an X-ray darkroom. Nurses and technicians mingled and moved apart, orders given, supplies brought in. Stretchers were carried through the white curtains strung up into a brilliant, glowing

arena where four angled lights over an operating table were reflected by the shiny insides of two five-gallon cans, cut in half
lengthwise, from corner to corner.

Parker watched the moving shadows inside go from dark to
dim. He watched as an elevated leg drifted away and left its owner behind. An orderly came out with an awkward object wrapped
in bloody towels. The back door roared open.

PARKER WAITED, so warm . . . thinking he should have written
his mother, maybe ask her to get him out. But how did you mail
a letter from here? And the army took forever. It would be over
by then. Besides, this was his own hole he had dug.

She was in Savannah now, married to Bob, selling hand-
tinted picture enlargements, door-to-door, almost all of them to
colored people. He had finally convinced her to take him out of
New York. First it was only to Lakeland, but when their territory
petered out, they moved on; and at last, he was back to Tampa,
staying with Norman, Victor, and Aline. Mama must have paid
them for his board or something, but he didn't know.

He transferred again, this time to Hillsborough High. Every
morning the class stood at rigid attention, facing the flag outside
while the school band played "To the Colors." But they couldn't
see the flag or the band from where they were standing. It was a
matter of faith, like facing Mecca.

Leora had another homeroom, but he did get to pass her in
the halls. She said he talked Yankee. He gradually realized that
this Tampa wasn't the same Tampa he knew, and he had a sick
sinking in his stomach. But he did hang out with some regular
kids at the Coliseum, everybody skate crazy by then.

And that day at the beach? The beach—he didn't remember
it all, didn't want to; he couldn't. A year and a half ago and not
remember? He had a new driver's license and somehow per-

suaded his mother to let him borrow her car. And Leora said yes, sitting beside him as he drove over the causeway to Clearwater with Junior and Nita in the back, overwhelmed by his own inspired maneuvers. Leora! He tried to play it casual, but he had waited all his life for this.

Leora looked thin when she came out of the dressing room in a one-piece bathing suit, but he never thought of her like . . . her body to do with sex. Junior and Nita fooled around in the surf, squealing, laughing; but Leora wouldn't go in the water, just lay on a beach towel in the sun with closed eyes.

Toby lay on his side, head propped by his elbow, looking at her face, her hair, her legs, her small breasts, his fingers jittering as he thought about touching her hand. He couldn't get her to say much, so he scribbled "I love you" in the sand, then palmed it out before she could turn and see it.

On the way back, he kept glancing in the mirror at Junior and Nita smooching in the backseat. He smiled at Leora, but she just looked at the road. He grabbed the wheel tight, thinking, wondering—then pulled over, telling Junior he should drive awhile. They both grinned. Toby got out and went around. He sat next to her, actually nudged her with his hip. He put his arm over the back of the seat. And then, hissing it, vicious:

"Whut do you wont me to do? *Kiss* yuh?"

. . . trying . . . remember the rest of it, driving back over the causeway, dropping off Junior, and Nita, then taking Leora home. She didn't say anything. She didn't invite him in. He was never inside Leora's house.

Later, as he worked at the skate room, he heard stories from other guys who went to Hillsborough. Leora's brother was an A.B. in the merchant marine and she was engaged to a sailor on a submarine in the Pacific somewhere—engaged. *Engaged!*

Toby went to the men's room to wash his face and stare at his swollen eyes in the mirror, stunned, bedazzled by that tall, blue-eyed blond in his dress blues, and ratings, the guy with his jokes, and his smiles, who drove his own red Oldsmobile convertible—who could tap dance in the rain and do a running jump into a saddle.

Toby carved it into his left forearm, the lopsided scars unreadable after the scabs fell off, the razor blade cuts shallow, and uneven, deep scratches really. He felt no pain.

Mit alle meinem Herzen, Liebchen—ich liebe dich.

A coded signal of a secret love in an enemy language; worried about the grammar—but nobody noticed, and the message was lost in the healing.

THEY HAD HIM pile his weapons and rig, and peeled him down. Dirty socks fell out, a plastic match container. Everything was stuffed into a barracks bag. They helped him on a litter and covered him with blankets.

"Jason? He needs boots. Pretty big, like twelves. See what you can find. And maybe a medium overcoat."

He looked up at the faces under the lights with their caps and masks. They sopped and blotted his head, his face, and shoulder. He felt the needles and the pressure of the instruments but had to shut his eyes against the lights. The doctor kept up his monotonous, slightly amused, cynical commentary.

"Ah . . . not bad. A little chunk out of the deltoid but no ligament or bone. Get these stitches out in a week, ten days. That's a nice, clean job on your nose, but you're going to need some plastic reconstruction back in the ZI."

The doctor smiled and said, "The Zone of the Interior to you, yardbird, the USA. Who did it? Where you been?"

"Behind the lines most of the last five days. In and out. A doctor in Germany did my nose and my face, and my leg. I was a POW there, but I got away. I just infiltrated in this morning and got shot by one of our own guys."

"In Germany? Yeah? You must have seen a lot of action."

"Kind of."

"You by yourself?"

"Not always, no. I had a whole squad once. But I'm the only one now, the only one."

"Huh. You probably earned yourself a helmetful of medals. Trouble is, you need witnesses to verify. I've seen it. Men out there in unrecorded, isolated actions; but very often they had no witnesses. All of them killed or hauled off as a PW."

"Never thought about that. But it doesn't matter."

"Kind of ironic. You get a Purple Heart when your own people shoot you? You might squeeze out one more for the rest. You can't exactly prove it didn't all happen at once. For what it's worth, I'll write you down as having two previous—no, maybe three."

"One problem I ain't got. I'm not in the medal business."

"Come on, soldier. You shitting me? Everybody wants a medal. Impress the girls? Everybody? Throw out your chest and strut your stuff. A *medal*? Hey!"

"I used to, I guess. Yeah, I did. But all those guys I left out there, all they got was the Distinguished Order of the Wooden Cross. One guy out there did get one, but he . . . It's all bullshit anyway. The officers get most of them."

"Not exactly true. At the very top? Probably. But the casualty rate for line officers is higher than for the ranks."

"We shit ourselves scared. We kill people. Our friends get torn up and die. And the lucky ones who are still left standing say, 'Hey. Look at me. I'm a hero.'"

"You're a little young for this kind of attitude."

"I used to be, yeah. But that was six days ago."

The doctor hesitated as he probed the head wound.

"Your leg isn't much. Your head is superficial. Could have used some stitches but too late now. A greenstick fracture possibly but not—ah. Scalps always bleed a lot. The scar will be bigger and you'll have a bald spot is all."

The doctor shrugged and crayoned FFD and RTU on the tag.

"You're fit for duty. I'm returning you to your unit."

"What's it take, a bullet between the eyes?"

"Ordinarily, I'd send you to the rear for a couple weeks at least. But there is no rear. We're surrounded. Keep that sling on and try not to bend your arm too much. When the Novocain wears off get the medic to give you some aspirin."

"How am I supposed to hold up a gun?"

"Hey. North of here they had an aid station in a stable. They lined up everybody who could stand up, and passed out rifles at the door. This morning it got overrun. We're draining blood from dead men for transfusions. We're recycling urine to retrieve the penicillin. Orders are, if he can walk, nobody comes back."

He made a face.

"It's a shame, but then that's the shit of war. Good luck to you, pal."

The man in the net fingered one of the meshes, squeezing the strands, looked at it close, then checked above and around him. His mouth drooped open, thinking.

T he medics helped him dress. The grimy cowl was glazed with a black crackle of blood; his and Jimbo's. They tried to take it, but he pulled back. They gave him a pair of used combat boots, fixed the arm sling outside the overcoat, and tied the diagnostic tag to the buttonhole. The coat had holes in it and the shoulder patch of a war correspondent. Parker had them cut it off. The boots were too big, but he could tighten them with wads of newspaper.

Four of them shambled off on their own, over and around the piles of wreckage, back to the straggler point. The clerk checked their tags and made entries on his clipboard.

Parker asked him; quiet and dejected:

"Does anybody know where the Twenty-eighth went to?"

"Should'a got here yesterday. Took out maybe three hundred to regroup down south, to get replacements and rest up."

"That's all, out of—how many thousand?"

"Not exactly. There's some more around."

"So what about me? Where do I go?"

"You? You're Team Snafu. They'll put you on some shit detail or send you out to man a roadblock somewhere. Draft you into some outfit that's short, which is everybody."

Parker lay with his bad arm against the wall, so nobody would kick it, restless, in pain, unable to sleep or dream. The MP had a civilian radio tuned in to the Armed Forces Network. "Tuxedo Junction" blasted out, two guys jitterbugging while four others clapped and danced with their shoulders.

Most of them had that same look: empty and battle-numb.

Parker knew he looked like that too. The guy next to him gob-bled down the K-ration breakfast meal, chopped eggs and ham. He wore the patch of Jimbo's outfit, the Phantoms.

"Don't take no shit off these paratrooper fucks. The new ones? They volunteer and make three jumps in one day. Just one day. They go up and they jump, and they go up, and they jump. Three times and they give 'em their wings and a pair of boots. They sew a Screaming Eagle on their shoulder and dou-ble their pay. That's it, a one-day wonder. Didn't even pack his own chute."

The radio roared on:

"This is the GI jive, man alive, it starts with the bugler blow-ing reveille over your bed when you arrive. . . . Roodley-toot, jump in your suit, make a salute. Boot!"

"D'ja hear what the Krauts are up to now? These comman-dos are dropped in with parachutes, dressed up like priests and like nuns? They speak English like you and me. Neat, huh? All the nuns around here gotta lift up their skirts and prove they got no dick. But the MPs caught some of those guys, tied 'em to a stake, and boom!"

A kettle of coffee was ladled out into canteen cups. Parker heard some far-off shelling. Stragglers dribbled in. Some were called out. Guys shot the breeze and smoked. Some were inco-herent, their eyes on things a thousand yards away. Exhausted GIs flaked out against the walls or curled up in knots, sad sacks, all of them. They all knew sympathy was only in the dictionary, somewhere between *shit* and *syphilis*.

But some were wild, happy, drunk with their own bullshit.

"What we did, the Krauts left the hatch open, and we sneak up. We get on top of it and tippy-toe over, give each other the nod, and drop in two grenades. But we blow ourselves up with it. Didn't get hurt none, just flew off, and we landed in a ditch. Knocked the breath out of us for a while."

And another:

"There was five of us on the gun. We got seven tanks, one right after the other. Boom, boom, boom."

"Come on, man. Who you shittin'? *Seven?*"

"I don't mean those Panthers or those Tigers. I mean the medium ones, the Mark Fours."

Another one had triangles in his eyes:

"We're pinned but didn't know where all this MG shit was coming from. He got four guys to peek up as high as they dared to, and he jumps out, and waves his arms, and yells, 'Hey, fuck face! Over here!' He jumps back in. Nothing happens. He jumps out again and wiggles his ass. 'Manny, manny boo-boo.' They couldn't resist that one. They open up and we spot their location, call in, and got them with our mortars."

"So what happened to the guy?"

"He bought it the next day. Opened a booby-trapped door."

The radio:

"We'll meet again, don't know where, don't know when, but we will meet again, some sunny day."

Parker sang it to himself over and over, his eyes wet.

A 101ST AIRBORNE lieutenant staggered in, braced one arm against the doorjamb, hung his head, and breathed deep. He rubbed his nose with one knuckle, two sergeants and a corporal behind him. He handed some papers to the MP who flipped through his clipboard, and stepped to the center of the room.

"All right! Everybody at *ease!*"

He folded over the top pages and tried to look mean.

"When I call out your name, I want a column of twos on

me. Glatz. Stewart. Axelrod. Bachelard. Stanislaus . . . Quarles. Ogden. Burke. Wilson. Clayton. McCrory. Biagini . . . Wysong. Olsen. Okay. Front and center."

Groans, mutterings—the line drifted together. A sergeant made them sound off with their names as they came by. Parker was in the next batch and joined the lame, wilted formation waiting in the street. The lieutenant looked them over. Parker saw disappointment but no surprise.

"I am Lieutenant Stoklosa. Three-twenty-seventh Glider Infantry. Our company is a provisional, ah—part of a thing called Task Force Browne put together with the Four-two-O Armored Field Artillery. That probably doesn't mean much to you. But— uh, we've been ordered in to defend the perimeter, and the gun batteries set up in our area. The Germans have swung around and, uh, we expect them to hit us from the southwest."

He stopped and looked down with two swipes at his nose.

"I won't bullshit you. This will be tough. Questions?"

"How far off are they?"

"From right here? About three miles."

"How many your men are left?"

"About two hundred. We started with six. We have two artillery battalions and nineteen tanks from the Tenth Armored."

"How much front do we cover?"

"Two miles, give or take. The front is, uh—fluid."

An undertow of curses murmured, and rippled all around.

"So, you mean. It's like what? Every man for himself?"

"Not that, no. But we do need individual initiative."

★

About a hundred Snafus fell into a route step, hiking through the drizzle and over the dirty slush. They went through the traffic past parked vehicles and mounds of broken masonry, picked their way over a fresh pile of rubble, and around a bulldozer clearing the street. Smells came from all directions: things burned, things dead, gunpowder, gasoline, and shit.

They passed a tank, frozen to the pavement. The motor labored. The crew poured gas around the tracks and set fires, watched the flames, and the steam, and yelled at the driver:

"Okay. Now try it. Hit it hard."

The tank twisted and strained. The tracks broke free.

The Snafus reached the suburbs; farms, a demolished, smoldering house with a dead girl in the yard, about six, legs reached out in a running step. She held a doll by the hand. In her other hand she held the hand of her dead mother.

Bits of forest were jigsawed into surging hills, the land flatter here than in the Clervé Valley. Shell craters with crumpled rims pocked the snow like a virulent, black acne.

They went out on a hard road for two miles, passing a frozen, flattened, fossilized German who had been chopped, and pounded by columns of tank tracks until the grotesque, distorted outline of his body, his boots, and helmet were ironed into the macadam. They went left at the village of Ile-la-Hesse, went another half mile on a secondary road to the front line at Senonchamps, and cross-country from there, north.

They marched past scattered tanks dug-in and hull down, the crews slapping them with whitewash, some parked across spaced logs so the tracks wouldn't stick to the ground. A lathered-up lieutenant squatted on a rear deck and dipped a razor into his helmet water. Burrowed into pits walled with sandbags, guns hid behind veils of camouflage nets.

An exuberant corporal, one of their guides, sang out:

"Welcome to the hole in the doughnut, you guys. But us airbornes are always surrounded. Shit, we like it that way."

"At least we got lots of artillery."

"Oh, yeah. Short barrel, long barrel, big barrel. What we ain't got is something to shoot. We're rationed down to ten shells. Not per hour. Per *day.*"

Supply trucks waited to issue them ammo, weapons, K rations for two days; small blocks of nitro starch with fuses, and detonators to blast holes out of the frozen ground. They got the day's password and were dropped off in fours and fives along the perimeter, getting bad looks from the glider men who stared hard at these stumbling, sad sacks of shit.

Unhappy, dull green birds, they rustled over their miserable nests. They scraped away the snow. They shared small picks that a few carried with their gear, the head and handle dismantled, and strapped together on their belts. Others whacked on the top edges of their shovels to make holes big enough for the quarter-pound blocks of TNT with a short piece of primer cord. Or they fired eight shots into the ground at the same spot, dug out the dirt with a bayonet, and then put in the TNT. They lit the fuses with Zippos, ducked down for the bang, then got up and dug.

Axes and bayonets thunked and chipped. They dragged over saplings and big branches, arranged them with spaces left to shoot through, and openings at the back to get in, and out. For two men it had to be three feet wide, six feet long, and four feet deep. A long **L**-shape was best so a tank couldn't grind down on top of you or gas you to death with its exhaust.

Parker couldn't dig with a bad arm. He was an unpaired odd number and had no help. He went beyond the prepared positions, got down under his cape, waited, then made a one-handed crawl. He judged the distance by the bangs of the TNT and the hard, crisp cracks of axes. He came up to a clump of small trees, an outpost dugout protected by scattered foxholes, and barbed wire. An erratic net of chicken wire was strung up high to ward off hand grenades.

"Halt! Advance and be recognized!"

Parker yelled it out: "Humpty!"

"What's the rest of it?"

"You're supposed to give *me* the rest of it, dumb shit!"

"I'll shoot your ass."

"How about, 'Dumpty'? How about, 'Had a great fall'? How do you like, 'All the king's horses'?"

A sergeant stood up and waved from his hole.

"Get over here. I'm Platoon Sergeant Blavatsky. We can't identify you in that white outfit. What makes you so touchy?"

"Nobody knows. Nobody."

"You any good with that sniper thing you got?"

"Not especially. I liberated it, mostly."

"Then get rid of that Kraut shit. Get yourself an M1."

"Up your ass get rid of it."

They yelled at each other, screaming their outrage:

"What the fuck did you just say?"

"I'll shoot whatever I want to shoot. I killed thirty-eleven Germans, so far. What else you want?"

"Are you nuts or something? You can't talk that way to a non-commissioned officer."

"Hey! *Sir!* I been cut up and cut off, shot, and shit on, starved, and froze stiff. So now what are *you* gonna do?"

The big sergeant's eyes squinted somewhere under the dirt

and the dark of his brows. Parker gave his eyes right back, pissed off, furious:

"This is supposed to be a war, not some square dance."

"You're tellin' *me* what's a war? Armies make a war. Discipline. Organization. Not some half-ass Errol Flynn mountain bandit. And *you*—are now a four-star member of my shit list."

"That's fine with me. A nice, steam-heated court-martial sounds real good. Just spell it right—Parker, Tobias D."

The sergeant glared. Parker wandered away and looked for a used hole but was already beyond the point. A derelict Panther was farther out in the fog, whipped, deformed, spun around, the turret blown off, the long 75 with the muzzle brake tilted into the ground. A fire smoldered in the engine compartment and made black, greasy smoke. He squatted and thought about it, and checked around. Hide inside a burning tank? Why not? The fire was a nothing and who would suspect?

He looked again with the Zeiss binoculars, got down, and hopped like a three-legged dog. When he got closer to the wreck, he dragged the Schmeisser and the Mauser by their slings, and side-stroked over the snow. The Panther was cocked over, the right side exploded, and burned, the track broken, some of the road wheels snapped off.

The turret was like the lid of a can, cut out and bent over with a lollipop stuck to the top. On the bottom was an open capsule that rotated inside, providing a deck for the gunner and the loader, with a pedal-and-rod firing mechanism.

Parker clambered over the bogies and the track, grabbed at the pad eyes, the racks of auxiliary hand tools, and spare links, and got himself over the jagged gap—leery of the sharp edges. He lowered in his weapons, snaked over the gear ring, and slid inside with short, clumsy moves, careful of his arm.

It stank of burnt paint and fuel, burnt anti-magnetic plastic that had been stroked over the hull with a notched trowel. Most of the interior was gone, but live shells were still in their racks behind a sliding door on the left side. He had to lean against the slant of the bottom deck. The engine compartment bulkhead behind him was still warm.

He saw a thoughtful, posed camera portrait of a young woman taped to a spot of surviving paint. Another bulkhead separated the fighting compartment from the driving compartment. He climbed back out and teetered over to an open hatch, a mangled, burnt hole on the right where the other hatch had been.

He let himself down into the driver's seat, looked around, and played with the controls, pushing and pulling at the pedals, and levers. Taped to the slanted armor plate in front of him was a picture of two naked whores feeling each other up as they leered at the camera. A shaped and glazed porcelain mug hung undamaged on a wire hook. A troll grinned around a tree trunk and through some vines.

The gearbox and an instrument panel separated the driver from the machine gunner. Smashed radio equipment, the gun—everything was covered with soot, and sifted snow that had turned into black mud. There was some kind of viewing glass in front of the driver, but Parker couldn't see through it.

He stood up on the seat, scanned the splotched horizon with his field glasses, and made out a smudge of foxholes. He propped the Mauser on the edge of the hatch and adjusted the scope, putting the crosshairs on a *Landser* drinking from a canteen. He could almost taste the guy's thirst. Then he let himself slump: like shooting a rabbit, but a long shot. Picking off one wouldn't be worth the risk of giving himself away.

He put his flashlight into dark corners to check everything out, startled with a little yelp when he realized that the charred stump on the right used to be the machine gunner. His uniform and skin had burned into a black glaze, but the open, bony hands still covered the pistol grip, the eyeballs intact, huge and white. Its teeth sneered at the gun sight.

Parker's heart thumped hard and each throb made an echo of pain in his face and shoulder. He turned away from the dead thing and laid out spare clips on what flat places were handy, found a spot for the burp gun, and the grenades, a footrest, and something to lean against. He could feel the flashing heat from those fires when the wind shifted, and heard the whisper of bland notes sigh over torn holes.

Darkness came with sputtered shadows, reflections of the flames fed by drips from a ruptured fuel line. Murky flickers glimmered over the snow, over the gunner's eyes, and his smirk. Parker closed the hatch cover, wrapped himself in his blankets, and sagged down in the driver's seat. He put on his flashlight and reached up for the lucky beer mug, rubbed his fingers over the grinning elf, hung it back on the hook, poked it, and watched it swing.

WHAT WAS IT HIS FATHER SAID, the last time he saw him?

"Whatever you do, be good at it. If you're going to be a bum, be a good bum."

. . . semitrailers going south in Louisiana, low-boys loaded with new tanks. Brakes, gasps of compressed air.

"Where you going, sir?"

"Can't tell you that. A slip of the lip can sink a ship. But I can give you a ride. Where you going?"

"Can't tell you that either, 'cause I don't know."

"That's okay, kiddo. Hop in."

He could see khaki forage caps and shirts in the windows of the troop trains that rumbled across the Arizona desert, parallel to Route 66. He dropped nickels in the Pepsi machine at the gas station across the road. He threw rocks at bottles in the ditch and muttered at every car as he threw up his thumb: "This one will stop. This one." Trucks, busses—their motors and tires had their own personalities—the buzzing buildups, and then the drop.

Parker jerked awake, then nodded off again.

. . . Aunt Toots and her baby were living in LA, Toots a chiropractor by then, married to a Hungarian who was in the Army Medical Corps. Toby stayed a few days, answered the phone, and watched the baby while she was out. Western Union called and read him a telegram. Pop-Pop was dead.

Later he found out there was a big fight and Boysy threw him out of the house. Pop-Pop actually got a job somewhere as a baker, the trade he had when he was a kid in Denmark. And he did finally go to a hospital. He died there the next day of uremic poisoning. Toby remembered when Daddy's mother died. They were in Miami then.

. . . the rumble and vibration of that stern-wheeler. He made two trips as a deckhand from Seattle to Mount Vernon, up Puget Sound through the islands and then the Skagit River to load up a cargo of canned evaporated milk. He registered for the draft in Seattle.

He was good at close-order drill at Camp Blanding and they made him acting corporal, better known as an acting gadget, a safety-pin promotion, a black band around his arm with two khaki stripes. He had the responsibility but no authority.

Loaded down with a dozen carbines over his shoulder, lugging them to the supply room when he saluted that passing captain with his left hand. The word got out. He was Piss-Poor Parker from then on.

. . . that nurse lieutenant when he had pneumonia. Made them stand at attention in their pajamas, dizzy fevers and all, yelling, and screaming she was an officer. Drag the beds around. No way could they get them straight enough.

HE WOKE UP CRAMPED, cold, and hurting. The hatch cover hinges were spring supported and it opened easy. He stretched up, worked his legs, and punched out with his good arm. At 0600, he took three aspirin and snuggled back down.

HE JERKED WHEN the splash of the steam-driven stern paddles turned into the rumbled chug of German diesels, and the jangled clank of cogs, and wheels. He looked out at a fleet of tanks painted white with spotlights that prodded through the falling snow. He counted seven. The wail of sirens cut in and Parker's fingers shook at the fiendish malice that screeched through the howl of the wind.

Two of the mediums passed around him. The next would come closer, a Royal Tiger, a straining, crippled monster, like a mobile house with a telephone pole sticking out of the upstairs window. But Jimbo said they had underpowered engines.

He could see reflected outlines of grenadiers ganged together on the deck. He eased his bad arm out of its sling, propped up the Mauser, and steadied the stock with his chin and right shoulder. He fired. He grabbed the bolt up and back. The cartridge flipped out and plinked behind him. He reloaded, aimed, and fired again. He thought he saw the first one slump on top of the Tiger. The second might have fallen off backward and dragged the first one with him.

The sprocket wheels cranked by. Bow and turret machine guns threw up snow flurries wherever a light beam pointed. He grabbed the burp gun, shoved the extra magazines into his pockets, and hauled himself out to the deck, the stitches pulling in his shoulder when he fumbled for handholds. He climbed into the knocked-over turret and leaned his hip against the commanders seat, one foot braced against the gun breech as the other pawed for traction at an instrument panel. He had a crooked view through the open hatch in the cupola.

The Tiger found the American outpost with its spotlight and fired two rounds. The clump of trees huffed up in deviled clouds. The demented sirens wailed again and again.

The grenadiers cut away the wire, and shot down into the foxholes, their war cries modified by the wind. Parker braced the Schmeisser by the clip and the skeleton-rod frame, remembered its fast firing rate, and short range, and aimed a little high. He shot off a thirty-two-round clip in even bursts, lighting himself up with the flashes.

The grenadiers would know the sound of one of their own weapons, but this came from their flank, and the *Amis* weren't supposed to be out this far. The in-and-out moon and the tracers helped him see brief silhouettes, the world a flickering picture book of afterimages. White shapes tumbled and faded away. The reflected loom of the spotlight went out. The Tiger rattled and whined off to the rear.

Artillery counterbarraged both ways. Shells spluttered overhead. Scenes of tanks and running men flashed and shimmered with whiplashed booms. He scanned behind him with the Zeiss when searchlight beams wiped the skies over Bastogne. He heard the ack-ack guns and the throb-throb drone of the Luftwaffe. Rumbled bombs drummed the city. When they were gone, he climbed back to the driver's seat and nibbled on a cracker, avoiding eye contact with the black mummy beside him.

THE SUN STARTED UP, the sky clear, the air drier. Bright glints came off the snow. Parker swept around with his glasses and made out two half-tracks full of *Landser* coming across an open field, and from behind the defilade of a farmhouse.

He sank down and took a pull on his canteen. When he

twisted to put it back, his head touched the beer mug. As it swayed, the wire made little squeaks. He watched it swing, then stared at the cremated gunner. When he stood up to check with the glasses again, he saw two officers behind a command car. One shaded his binoculars and pointed at the wrecked tank. Parker dropped down, deciding not to take the shot.

He collected his gear and squeezed his way out, crouched behind the gun turret, climbed single-handed down the burnt, blind side, and got around the hot places. He flipped the snow cape, dragged himself away, and slid into a shell hole just as two mortar shells hit the ground like enormous slapsticks, bracketing the tank. The third one was a hit.

With his glasses he could see the attack line forming up. The *Landser* made short, quick advances, covering each other with suppressive fire. Parker braced the sniper rifle on the lip of the crater, but his one hand shook and he couldn't aim. From somewhere behind him a machine gun opened up. When the Germans took cover he fished, and crabbed his way out, and to the rear. His ears still rang from the mortar blasts, but when he got closer he could hear that mean, big-city, Yankee roar.

"Somebody get out there and help that son of a bitch in."

He twisted around and saw two paratroopers crawling in the snow, and held out his good arm. A trooper locked wrists with him, dragged Parker out, got him on his knees, and steered him through that last, running stumble to a dugout. He missed the last step of the junk ladder, tilted, and collapsed into the hole, flailing for support with his good hand. Blavatsky grinned, pulled him up to a squat, and offered him a canteen of lemonade made with a K-ration powder.

"You crazy shit! That was you saved our ass last night. They had us pinned. We got two deads and six other casuals, but they would have got all of us. I'm puttin' you in. You'll get some fucking color on your chest for this one."

B lavatsky took out six at a time and let them filter their way back to a camouflaged field kitchen behind the gun batteries. They had to plow through the drifts, the windchill about zero, the sky clear, the sun low but strong. They got thin soup, coffee, one slice of stiff bread, and went back.

One of the Tenth Armored Tigers side-kicked his left boot with his right, the right boot with the left.

"Hear about yesterday? These Krauts come in under a pillowcase on a drapery rod? They demand, I mean they *demand* that we gotta surrender? And they want it in writing or else? The general? He says, 'Nuts.' That's all he said. One word. And the Nazis, they speak English and all, but they don't get it. 'Vas iss dis nutz? Iss dot negatiff or affirmatiff?'"

THE NON-COMS PASSED the order down. The Third Battalion had to withdraw from a salient to keep from getting cut off. The Germans would come right behind them, but when the perimeter was evened up into a neat circle the First Battalion would go around, and hit the German flank. But they had to be careful with their ammo and the big guns were almost dry.

THEY WERE STANDING by at ten minutes to twelve. The sky began to hum and drone, high, and wide. An armada of airplanes came over, low, heavy, more C-47s than they could count. German flak barked and boomed. Black puffs shot up among the parachutes.

Red ones were for gasoline, yellow for food, blue for ammo, white for artillery shells, orange for medical supplies. Canopies snagged in trees. Bundles bounced and dragged over the fields. Some hit hard and their loads split open.

Hundreds of GIs climbed out of their holes to shield their eyes, and look up at the Gooney Birds that came over in flights of twelve, three flights to a group. They waved their arms and yelled, or just stood with their mouths open. They applauded. They whistled. Men took a whack at the sky and screamed. Men danced a hootchy-kootchy as the trucks bounced out into the fields to retrieve the dropped supplies.

Mustangs and Lightnings prowled in long sweeps. Parker heard their engines strain as they climbed, and groan when they dove. Thunderbolts went after the ack-ack with machine cannons and bombs. Three C-47s started smoking but stayed on course. One engine burped and stalled. The others drew away from them, gaining altitude after they dropped their loads.

The cheers stopped when a C-47 was hit and a wing came off. It fluttered down and exploded in the woods.

And then a different roar went up as the Third Battalion came over the rise in columns of trucks and jeeps, field pieces, trailers, and armored cars. GIs scrambled and dodged. Tanks and SP guns crashed over to turn, and cover their rear.

Whistles blew up and down the line. Team Browne went on the counterattack to support the retreat, and to recover the supplies. They moved in a low, boxer's crouch. Parker tried to keep up but had to stop, his chest heaving as he watched it happen. He counted six parachute packs drop from each C-47 but could only guess at the weight. Men unbuckled the straps and cut away the cords, unloaded the nets, passed containers, and threw them into trucks and jeeps.

One of them gathered up a white parachute and stuffed it into the cab of a six-by-six. Parker heard him yell at the driver to pass it on. It was for one of the civilian volunteer nurses in town, he said, at the department store. He promised it for her wedding dress. Parker stood in a muffled blur . . . standing . . . all this frenzy, not sure where he was supposed to be, wondering the why of it all. Blavatsky something . . . for hours.

. . . COULD STILL GET killed up here but didn't know if he cared that much. If Leora loved him—maybe. He tried to imagine being dead and Leora sorry. He could see her crying.

WHISTLES BLEW. Blavatsky howled:

"Keep moving and spread out! Do *not* bunch up! Do *not* stand still! *Run!* Run and spread out; keep running; keep moving. I shouldn't have to tell you shit heads all this!"

Vapor trails scribbled the sky overhead with expanding swirls and crosses. C-47s blew up in flaming globs. B-26 Marauders followed tracks in the snow that lead to camouflaged German bivouac areas. They dropped napalm. The woods caught fire. Smoke billowed all around Bastogne.

Blavatsky was still screaming in his ear:

"Come on, kid. Let's get the lead out! You can still shoot that burpy thing one-handed. I know you can do it!"

Parker looked at Blavatsky and wondered at the soft voice.

"Hey, kid. Hey. I said, let's go. We got 'em going."

Blavatsky sucked his lips in tight.

"Parker? That's you, right? Tobias? Come on, kid."

With jerks of his head, Parker shook himself into it. He joined the whoops and rebel yells. Mortars slammed around, the concussions sucking the air up into the sky. The craters smoked and steamed from bits of scattered hot metal.

Parker fumbled over a dead medic and dug under his jacket, sweater, and shirt. Somebody told him they carried their morphine taped under their armpits to keep it from freezing. He found two syrettes, pulled off a cap, punched through the layers of uniform, and squeezed one into his leg.

He caught his breath and followed the attack, jogging after a machine-gun crew. He ran on electric now, with the full joy of the movement, the risk, no casino ever as good as this. The assistant slammed down the tripod. The gunner ran up with the MG, a half belt of ammo draped over his neck. He knelt to lower in the pintle. Parker swerved away from one of the ammo bearers who lugged up two cans.

He heard it coming and dropped into a hole. The shell landed close enough that he could feel the shock wave and the heat flash by. He went deaf. He looked out and saw one of the crew flip, and jerk, an arm stumped. Another thrashed out and tore up the snow. His surviving leg curled and twisted, half-rose, scuffed, and danced.

"Oh, my God. Oh, my God. Oh God, oh God, please, God!"

Parker did not hear an order to fix bayonets, could see but not hear them drag, and scrape out of their scabbards, rub over the rifle muzzles, and clatter, and click onto the studs.

A GI carried an SCR 300 radio on his back with a carbine over his shoulder, following a lieutenant who murmured into a walkie-talkie at the end of a wobbling, stretched coil of wire; his head turned, his breath clouding off to one side. A smoke screen was generated from large steel tanks and mixed with the overall, lingering stinks of cordite and white phosphorous. Men choked in it. Some vomited. Flak guns opened up, the tracers erratic, swerving away in strange arcs.

Parker shuddered, the muscles in the back of his neck drawn down, and cramped between his hunched shoulders. Two men screamed at him as they scrambled past him to the rear:

"Hey! Jonesy got it! Jonesy! He's fucking dead!"

As Parker ran ahead, they looked at each other, and followed him. A German tossed out his Mauser, climbed out of a fox-hole, but stumbled under a whip of automatic fire. Jonesy's buddies held their rifles on him. Shot in the belly, groaning, he tried to stand up, and raise his hands.

"Im Namen des Gottes, ich bitte dich!"

Jonesy's buddy made a long thrust with his bayonet, the way they did it in basic on a stuffed barracks bag. It went in the German's thigh. He screeched. Jonesy's buddy made the withdraw and followed with the short thrust. Another shriek. The upper-cut missed, but the butt smash thudded and the German went flat. Jonesy's buddy finished up with the downstroke, then flinched into the on guard position.

Jonesy's other buddy tried it, the German down, grunting, trying to breathe. He looked at the blood on his hand and then at the two GIs. They took turns doing it again.

BY LATE AFTERNOON the guns were quiet, only isolated, mean-ingless rifle pops far out and over. The waver of airplane engines faded. Lieutenant Stoklosa watched them fly away, talking to a staff sergeant, Parker in a nearby hole.

"Somebody at Battalion got the word from Division. They have to do better than this. We still don't have enough thirty-caliber. We still don't have enough blankets. They dropped twenty-five thousand K rations? If we stretch that hard, that's two days. But maybe they can get back tomorrow."

BLAVATSKY TOLD PARKER to spend the night in the platoon com-mand post dugout, guiding him down through the opening cov-ered with a loose canvas flap that saved some of the accumulated heat. Blavatsky chewed on some gum as he watched Parker jab, and squeeze the other syrette into his left thigh.

"I glided in at Sicily. Then Normandy, and then at market

Garden. I seen other guys like this. It's probably to do with how bad they've been through it. And then like how much time with no break. We'll all go off, stay at it long enough. Everybody. I sort of had it a couple times."

Parker's back was against the slope of the hole, his legs drawn up. He felt light and soft, and listened to the buzz bomb as it went over, put-putting like a cheap motorcycle. Blavatsky wouldn't let it go.

"You start to itch and shake, scared all the time. You need some ups and downs. Because otherwise you get stale, and being scared is all you can think about."

BLANKETS AND UNIFORMS WERE WET. Water seeped through the sides and the bottom of the hole. It all turned to mud, melted by their own body heat. Blavatsky got by on quick naps, up and down all night, muttering about guys in open foxholes. He had to keep everybody awake so they didn't freeze to death.

Parker watched the guard climb down the three steps of the ladder nailed together out of scraps of rough lumber. Before he could shake Parker's shoulder, he rolled out of the three blankets on top of an overcoat. Then the guard fell into it.

Parker trudged forward with his partner to relieve the other outpost guard, checking the shadows along the way, reacting to wind noises. They changed every two hours, terrified by those screams they could not ignore, never knowing if they were wounded GIs or a German trap—repeating the day's challenge and password to each other so they wouldn't forget.

The wet spots on their uniforms turned to ice. They held their weapons ready, made no lights, and never talked, just stared into the darkness, listening for that combat patrol that would sneak in for the kill, or that intelligence patrol without helmets or weapons that would slide in to catch them asleep.

Full daylight came at eight o'clock. Soldiers climbed out of their holes, stretched, cursed, and kicked their feet. They draped their blankets over bushes to dry, threw ration cans into small fires, and went to the straddle latrine. Four other men squatted over the narrow, ten-foot trench, always face to back. Better to look at a man's ass and watch his shit steam in the cold air than to look him in the face.

ALL ALONG THE FRONT, men gazed up at the sky. When they saw the planes coming, they pointed, and hollered, like announcing the arrival of Santa Claus. More C-47s flew over and made their drops. When the Germans sent up their flak barrages, the fighter-bombers went after their guns. Skirmishers from both sides squabbled over the parachute bundles.

Blavatsky had kept Parker in a rear foxhole to guard the CP when he heard a trooper yelling to clear the way ahead. He shied up to the command post, holding his rifle behind a German officer whose head was bleeding through a towel tied on by a strap. One arm was in a sling. He held his free hand high.

The lieutenant climbed out and looked him over, spoke into the walkie-talkie, and waited. He acknowledged, then told the trooper to take him in to Regimental Headquarters for questioning. No jeeps were available. He'd have to walk it.

Blavatsky ambled up from one of his rounds and Parker watched them talk. Lieutenant Stoklosa glanced his way and said something, and Blavatsky beckoned him over.

"Better you take this Kraut in. He's got some heavy rank on

his collar and even if he's not in much shape he might try to scram. One guy with a rifle, semiauto and all, could miss. But he knows what that burp job you got can do to him."

The lieutenant groped into his musette for a pad and scribbled out a pass. Blavatsky waited for him to climb back into the CP, then grabbed Parker by the back of his neck.

"Lissena me. You might bum yourself a snack at Regiment. Hey, Christmas Eve—you know. Any case, goof off a little. Relax some. You'll feel better."

THEY PASSED A FILE of infantry moving up. Heels hit a solid 120 a minute on the pavement, making a tinkled, chimed rhythm with the spoons in their mess kits, and the buckles on unfastened galoshes. All eyes watched the crippled PW and his crippled guard.

Half-tracks chattered across the fields from one colored parachute to another. A wrecked C-47 had gouged through some trees and a fence to break up across the road. Parker and his prisoner had to go around it. A naked woman and "Sweet Sue" was painted on the nose. A pair of baby shoes hung in the smashed windshield. A detail winched away the pieces as two men peeled the leather flying jacket off a dead flyer. Another admired a white, silk scarf.

They passed crumpled buildings and got into heavier traffic. A tank was parked on the side, the left track disconnected, and rolled out flat. The crew yelled back and forth as they worked with pinch bars, and wrenches to attach mud extension clips on each link.

A sign was stenciled with an arrow and the word WATER. Slimy engineers in rubber boots worked at a portable purifying unit, a two-stroke gas engine pumping from a wellhead through rubber hosing to a filtering apparatus, and then to a bulging, shoulder-high, collapsible canvas tank. There was a strong smell of chlorine. An engineer filled rows of jerry cans in a utility trailer hooked up to a jeep.

The German officer walked erect, his shoulders back, right elbow held high, his tired hand drooping, then snapping up. Parker held the Schmeisser down at his side. They swerved together away from a truck dumping gravel into a large shell hole. Four soldiers waited with push brooms and shovels. An MP guard at a crossroads checked Parker's pass, the German PW standing with a steady look. The MP pointed out a medieval seminary. They could already hear the singing.

Parker had to walk his prisoner across the transept floor covered right up to the altar with a crowd of senile and injured civilians wrapped in blankets and folded parachutes. Some mumbled along with the choir of soldiers who stood in the chapel, helmets under their arms, holding hymnbooks.

The sun glinted through the sagged rips in the tarpaulins rigged over the cracked and shattered stained glass. Powdered snow caught the colors in the light as it blew through the holes. Guns quarreled out their authority on the outskirts of the city. An occasional shell landed closer in.

A huddle of women and old men lay on salvaged mattresses. Little kids squealed. Four teenagers giggled over a card game. An old lady rapped her cane and told them all to shush. Nuns in their tall white hats with the starched wings bustled around. Over their habits were dirty, blood-spotted aprons.

"We three kings from Orient are. . . ."

Parker motioned with the muzzle of his Schmeisser and followed the PW up the stone staircase to the third floor. The sentries let them in after they checked Parker's dog tags, and his pass, and searched the prisoner. The room was full of officers: several majors, captains, a bald and skinny colonel, assorted lieutenants, all of them shaved, and lotioned, their hair slicked back.

A major came over, waving away Parker's salute, crooking a finger at a lieutenant.

"Harold? This the guy they're talking about? You want to do him? You *parlez-vous* the language and everything. See if you can get somebody to clean him up a little."

Parker waited at the door by the Christmas tree set up with ornaments, and lights, hung with icicles of tinfoil chaff that had been scattered by bombers to confuse the radar below. A small doll in a Red Cross uniform hung just under the star. It had a chipped nose and both arms were missing. Somebody had decorated it with a Purple Heart drawn with a pen.

Folding cots were lined along the walls with air mattresses, and sleeping bags. Radio signals squeaked and yowled on the other side of a closed door. A situation map was tacked up with several layers of acetate overlays marked with red and blue grease pencils.

Desks had been pushed aside, folding tables laid out with china, and silverware. Platters on typewriter tables held cheese and jelly, sliced ham, crackers, and salmon. Hard candy was heaped in paper-clip bowls. A private worked as bartender; two others served. A phonograph played Benny Goodman as two army nurses and three Red Cross volunteers did a jitterbug with senior officers, tipsy, giggling, their faces made up.

Parker stood at a loose, battlefield parade rest, weapons muzzle down, his good thumb hooked under a sling. He moved his toes and feet from side to side, and up, and down, feeling the warmth of the room soak through. He had sweat on his forehead and his heart was working. Once he thawed out, these people would smell how rotten he was, his breath, his uniform, and they would know about the skid marks in his pants.

HE COULD REMEMBER another really cold, cold night. He and his sister and his mother going wherever—always going somewhere, catching up with Daddy, who had gone ahead to find work. Toby shivered in those long, brown, sissy stockings with the garters under his short corduroy pants. They crossed the road and went into a general store. His mother asked if they could come in and warm up.

Four old farmers in bib overalls sat around an iron stove. They spit tobacco juice and snuff. Each one had his own can. After ten minutes, Mama thanked them. They went out and crossed the road again, and waited for a ride.

HEADQUARTERS SMELLED OF LIQUOR, perfume, and cigarettes. The last meal the service guys brought up to the front had been a cup of cold, watery soup. No seconds. Parker had counted seven white beans.

He stared at a mirror on the wall, his face smudged black with gunpowder, and encrusted blood, his red eyes blank, and spooky inside purple rings. The bandages were filthy. He had rips in the grimy snow cape and holes in his jacket. The paint was worn off the edge of his helmet and the steel shined like some goofy, wavered halo. He kept jerking himself awake.

Two Red Cross women swooped past a major who shuffled through a stack of record albums. They tottered over to Parker, cigarettes, and glasses flared out.

"Hi there, soldier boy."

He looked straight ahead. They fingered the snow cape.

"What a cute outfit, but who wears white after Labor Day?"

They giggled and smirked.

"Do you always carry all that stuff around with you?"

THE LIEUTENANT PULLED the prisoner through the party by the sleeve, the German officer trying to walk straight, and proper. His head was freshly bandaged.

"We're done. Can't get anything out of him. Might as well take him to the provost marshal. Turn right at the door; go two blocks, and then left. It's the city jail."

The colonel twisted his loose fists back and forth.

"Come on, Harold. Give the guy a drink at least. Gotta take care of our boys. Samuel! Some Cointreau over here."

"No, thank you, sir. I don't drink. Besides, alcohol is bad for you in cold weather. You can freeze to death."

The colonel blinked down at his glass.

"But some of that candy would be nice. Sir?"

The major came over and offered him the bowl. Parker took one. The major jiggled the bowl. Parker took two more, made one step back, and saluted.

When they got outside, he gave one piece to the prisoner and wished him a merry Christmas in German. The officer smiled, probably at his accent, maybe at his rank. He made a slow bow, clicked his heels, and thanked him.

THE SIGN READ: *Gendarmerie*. The MP at the desk copied down the German's name, rank, and serial number from his dog tag. A civilian guard opened a barred gate, led the PW down a corridor, both sides lined with wood doors fitted with peepholes, heavy hinges, and locks. From inside the cells came muffled, boisterous singing:

"*O Tannenbaum, O Tannenbaum, wie grün sind deine Blätter.*"

Parker watched the German officer being locked up.

"Do I need a receipt or anything?"

The MP didn't look up.

"Nah. S'okay."

H e headed back, still tasting the peppermint, hearing the carols a block away from the police station. He stopped, and turned to listen. As he took a leak on a pile of broken bricks, a jeep charged up behind him. The squealed brakes and the sudden challenge made him wet himself. Two MPs hopped out with ready carbines. Parker twisted around to shrug his hip and do the buttons. He dug into his pocket and showed them his pass. The MP flipped at it with the back of his fingers.

"That was yesterday. Today you go our way."

"Bullshit, yesterday. That was this morning."

"This thing could be forged. We see it all the time. We got orders, pick up any and all stragglers."

"I'm not a straggler. I'm with Team Browne. Lieutenant Stoklosa signed it right there. Special assignment."

"Team Browne? They're all Snafus, those guys. Get in."

"I brought in a PW to the station over there. Ask them."

"Yeah, yeah, yeah, yeah. Hey. Just get in."

"They're gonna put me down as a deserter."

"Naw. Just MIA."

BACK AT THE STRAGGLER POINT, Parker joined the chow line, shuffling up to the cook who was doling out one boiled potato and a D-bar until strange airplane engines pulsed with the drone of a different meanness. The AA started to pump up their ack-ack, and the warehouse shook with the whistles and booms. Somebody yanked open the door and veered inside with a flash from the magnesium flares in the sky behind him.

Parker heard a crack of timbers, the grinding of stones; the room fogged with dust as a close concussion sucked at the flames in the stove. The slams moved farther away, then rolled back. The building rattled. Something fell from the ceiling. One of the stragglers reached up with clawed fingers and blubbered, and bawled.

THREE ROUGH, exasperated sergeants jostled through the door.

"Listen up. You guys are now proud, honorary members of the Five-o-two Parachute Infantry. We got a truck out here."

The paper-and-name game again as another Team Snafu grated and dragged outside. Searchlights beamed at a thing in the sky, airbursts sparking around it. They were jammed tight into the truck. Two were draped over the fenders and hugged the hood. Two more rode on the running boards, their backs to the wind. Two were left behind with their smiles and shrugs.

The tires clinked their chains through the town square. Buildings burned. A cluster of soldiers and civilians dug into the destructed heap of the aid station at the Sarma department store. They tossed aside chunks of rubble and reached down through the cellar windows to hand up bleeding survivors.

The truck took the right fork where the signs read HEM-ROULLE and LONGCHAMPS. Savy was just a few rough fieldstone houses a mile from Bastogne. Another mile and they turned left at a crossroads, bumping down a rough dirt trail to Rolle, even smaller than Savy. They went cross-country in low gear with the headlights out, slowing down when they heard the heavy diesel but almost colliding with an ordnance evacuation unit: an enormous self-propelled crane, an M-19 tractor, and a low-boy trailer with a crippled Sherman on its back.

The truck stopped. The three sergeants dropped the tailgate, ordered everybody out, and lined them up with impatient shoves at the slow, and the clumsy. Team Snafu was led off and scattered into the darkness, broadcast like mildewed seeds across a furrow of gun pits, shattered trees, wrecks, foxholes, and craters.

PARKER HUNCHED THERE with three others. A sergeant climbed out of a hole and looked at them.

"What's with you?"

"Got it in the face and the shoulder. Few other places."

" 'Sergeant' would be nice."

"Yes, Sergeant. Sir."

"What's that supposed to mean? Sir?"

"Nothing, Sergeant."

"You carry a lot of iron. Can you still do any good?"

"Sort of. But I don't do holes. Not with no one arm."

"But you can walk, right? You can do a patrol? Thing is, we know they're gonna hit us tonight with a big Christmas special. But the question is: Exactly where?"

"These guns get any ammo dropped in?"

"Yes, some. Finally. A good day's worth anyhow."

The four Snafus followed the sergeant into a hardened gun pit lined with racked shells with colored numbers and piles of fiberboard canisters. Five men on their bellies made a sheriff's star with their legs and boots, their heads and arms under a shelter half. The sergeant kicked at their feet and yanked up the cover, his flashlight showing the blanket, the money and cards, the candle stump welded on the butt of a bayonet handle.

"Let's go. Time to earn that big, juicy jump pay."

"Owww. Hey, you're lettin' in a draft."

"And I got a full house. Where'd my ante go at least?"

The sergeant snagged three more out of foxholes. One of them reached up to shake hands.

"Sergeant Dexter? I'm pretty sure I'm not gonna make it tonight. I can feel my number coming up fast. I just want to say, you've been okay by me all along."

"What the hell you talking about? Get your ass up here. Patton is on his way in right now. Old Blood and Guts himself, personally. With the whole fucking Third Army right behind him."

"Well. Then, Merry Christmas, anyhow."

"Yeah. Merry Christmas. Now let's go."

THEY CROUCHED and crawled on the scout's signals and got out a slow, quiet, painful mile. They heard trucks. They counted the sounds of tanks that started up to keep the engines from freezing, and to rock their tracks out of the ice. Germans were singing Christmas carols to each other from their foxholes, the fields dotted with dead men mounded over with snow like overlooked air-drop bundles that had missed their marks.

The full perimeter was scorched with arbitrary blazes, house and woods fires started by the Luftwaffe that day. And yet sleet blew into their faces. Ice formed on their helmets.

"*Wer da?*"

An anxious challenge from a German sentry made everybody slump down, and gradually shrivel back, and go around.

And then those picking sounds as boots creaked through the snow crust. Pick, pick. Pick. When everybody was aimed and ready, the sergeant shot up a pistol flare.

Right in front of them, a German *Sanitäter* was on his knees, chipping a body off the ground with a bayonet. A second medic swept the snow off another body with a broom. A *Kübelwagen* and trailer behind them was piled with corpses twisted into wicked, frozen shapes. Four others held a grotesque body by the arms and feet. The Americans stood with sagging weapons.

The Germans looked at them through the sizzled flare shadows that stretched, diluted, and swallowed themselves.

Sergeant Dexter gave his hoarse, hesitant order:

"Okay. Let's move out."

PARKER WAS SENT stumbling back through the dark with the other Snafus to support a periphery guard set out in front of a battery of 105 howitzers. There was no mention of any relief. He was pushed and pointed to a prepared foxhole, hunkered down in it, and immediately nodded off, snapping awake at 0230 when the first German salvos opened up.

Swarms of screaming meemies came over: rockets with long tails of flame shooting out in a fast, regular series of terrifying screeches to explode in erratic patterns all over the front. Parker heard a phone ringing behind him.

Through the shadow play of momentary silhouettes, sky flashes, and drifting flares, he could see the head-high, lacy drapes of the camouflage net with loose white and gray ribbons that flapped in the wind. It covered a pit with sandbagged walls; and then a guarded flashlight over a field table—a section leader's loud, clipped orders.

He could hear what he couldn't see with the glasses, and imagined the rest of it: gunners scrambling out of sleeping bags, and running in from dugouts. They called out their crew numbers up to seven as they were already drawing back the camo net. He could hear the precise, practiced order of their loading and firing routine. They elevated the gun, set the traverse, popped open the breech, and loaded a charge.

He knew something about it from those manuals in the rec room and those brief, frozen bullshit sessions with the runaway gunners in Team Crazy, the pride they took in their military gymnastics.

"Set! Ready! *Fire!*"

UNG-OOMM!

The other three guns in the battery flashed and boomed from their neighboring positions. Parker stood in his hole, watched their moves, and heard the scuffles and clanks of their drill. He watched the howitzer bounce back. Its wheels were raised up, supported by the jack pad under the carriage, braced by the trail legs splayed apart like outriggers, their spades embedded in the ground.

One gunner yanked open the breech; another snatched out the hot casing; another shoved in a new shell. Others stuffed small powder bags inside and spun the wheels to adjust the traverse, and the deflection. The breech clanked shut.

UNG-OOMM!

Flame flashed out of the muzzle. Parker felt the concussions, the snow puffing around him, smelled the stifling smoke that wafted everywhere. Empty cases clanged on the pile tossed outside the pit. A wire-section detail ran in with another line. They cranked up field phones. Forward observers dictated corrections through the radio static as they plotted coordinates.

"A hundred right. Fifty over."

"Fire for effect. Keep it going. Lots of it."

"Sing it to me, ba-beee!"

The 105 erupted, banged, and hopped. The cannoneers danced in the middle of hot, glittering brass cases spilling around their feet. The handlers set the fuses, counted out the different-colored powder bags, and hustled the shells over from the stacks kept on the opposite side for safety reasons.

Parker could feel the monstrous coughs through the ground, could see the flashes, and the cushions of fog as the echoes filled the valleys with the resounding shock waves that trilled out of a mad giant's piano case. But he had no idea of what was being destroyed, or what was being killed. The gunners didn't know either.

He looked through his field glasses and watched the German barrage creep closer, the whole front lit up with flares. He saw tanks and men fading back, knew this thing was major, and knew the line could not hold. Men climbed out of the foxholes around him. The gun's firing rate went from three or four rounds a minute to three times that. Then a whistle, a command voice yelling out with a shrill pitch:

"Battery A. Displace to the rear! Load up and move out!"

They rolled up the net, collapsed the poles, and folded furniture. They handed up radio gear, powder canisters, and leftover shells into the trucks, tossing personal gear on top. They jacked the gun down on its wheels. They shoveled out the trail spades, folded the legs together into a single wagon tongue, and grunted the gun over to the hitch on the back of a truck. They clambered on top and the truck moved away.

The other three battery guns followed them out. Parker sank down in his hole with nothing left to guard.

Shells dropped closer. Bullets came in. Mortars coughed in the distance, then landed with hard slams. He tried the binoculars again and saw a chaos of things burning, shadows running through the flare light, the spark of muzzle flashes.

A broken line of GIs dodged back around him with boots that kicked and thumped with hollow sounds. They cursed to each other and wheezed out desperate questions. Some dropped into empty foxholes and the abandoned gun pit and turned to fire their rifles. Others kept running.

And then a rough and desperate but superior voice:

"Fall back! Fall back to those trees!"

The cry rippled through the darkness. Parker crawled out and ran for the woodlot. Another racketing uproar came from a sector a mile to their left rear. He guessed it to be Team Browne's position, and wondered about Lieutenant Stoklosa, and Sergeant Blavatsky. The circle around Bastogne was shrinking tighter as the Germans struggled to break in.

When a white tank charged the trees with both MGs firing, they all ran. Parker thought he saw a farmhouse and headed for it, but just before he got there the door was blown in. He heard the survivors' feet rustling around manure piles, and haystacks, heard the swearing and the groans. Parker went after them with his hobbled sprint. He heard a frustrated uproar of boos, and almost caught up to the crowd chasing after the crews of the two anti-tank pieces getting towed away by jeeps.

Too exhausted to keep up, he dodged along a straggly hedge to a wagon road, then made it alone to a little town where the moon gave him a quick look at three dead civilian women tumbled in the street. The sign said HEMROULLE. Bastogne was another three kilometers.

He raced to a house that flashed up in the dark, the second floor destroyed. He yelled out his identity as he ducked through a hole punched through a wall, and made out the shades of dueling GIs who peeked around the edges of windows to shoot fast, and cower away from the hot, spontaneous returns.

Something heavy shook the house. Pieces of the roof and the top of the walls broke off, and fell on the heaps of rubbish, and wrecked furniture. A fire started. Some beat at it with blankets, but others looked for a way to get out.

Parker followed three troopers feeling their way through a dark kitchen with muffled flashlights. Just as they found the back door, bullets came through it, the first man knocked back with a grunt, and a wail. The legs of the table scraped and shuddered before it went over. Dishes crashed. There were shots in the other rooms and a grenade went off. The three swayed and slipped, dragged the body away from the door, got it open, crawled outside, down two steps, and across the yard to the trees.

THE AIRPLANES CAME over with the daylight as they faltered along a farm road, the snow packed, and cleated hard by tanks, and half-tracks. The tall one squeezed a gushing arm and hissed one long, continuous stream of *damns,* and *shits,* and *fucks* through clenched teeth. The short one grabbed at his belly. They could see Bastogne up on its rise as they swayed around a bend, came to another house, and stood there, stooped over, and wondering, until they saw dogfaces signal them in.

Heavy American guns started in from somewhere up ahead. Parker could pick out that special metallic sound of a direct hit among the tree and ground explosions behind them. Then came the deep blats of diesel motors, first one, and then more, as the exposed Mark IVs, and Panthers, went into reverse to turn, and clatter away.

The three of them collapsed inside the house, falling into an empty pause, a bewildering suddenness of calm. The fireplace smoked. Somebody fiddled with the damper but couldn't get it right. A kind of soup simmered in a kettle on a hinged hook as five men squeezed in on a ripped sofa to watch the fire. Still more ganged up around the hearth.

Some dipped into the kettle with their canteen cups. Others spooned in K rations or worked on their wounds. One gulped from his canteen and checked around the edge of a window. One just sat and bled until the men next to him eased him over, stretched him out, and fumbled with a dressing.

One choked on his sobs as his buddy patted his back:

"How much more, Randy? We can't never make this shit."

The short one from the other kitchen slumped in a corner cross-legged and held his belly. The tall one sprawled, leaning on his good arm. Others lay on their backs, and stared at nothing.

Parker was still up, looking at the blurred, dim family photographs that hung in oval frames on walls that were papered in narrow stripes. He saw a Victrola on a corner table, took off the record, and blew away the dust. The label said *Mozart—Konzert*

21 *für Klavier und Orchester*. He wound up the crank, pushed the start lever, and set the needle.

They curled up and grabbed at their knees. They gaped at the fire and whatever was beyond. Zippos clinked open and shut—then a cough, a snuffle. Cigarettes burned. Muted guns rumbled somewhere, way off.

A voice came over a walkie-talkie:

"What's going on up there?"

The piano lingered and loved. Oboes and bassoons droned.

"Hollingsworth? God damn it, you there? Get moving!"

Static. The sergeant turned it off. The music came to a scratchy end and the needle grooved on an empty whisper.

The sergeant dragged himself up, slow about it, mumbling:

"Okay. Let's go."

Nobody moved.

"Hey."

A few cigarettes flared up. Somebody sniffed.

"We gotta go, fellas. Come on."

The sergeant dragged over to the door and turned. Parker watched him pull his pistol. He fired it into the ceiling.

"*Hey!*"

Dust filtered down. Canteen caps were unscrewed and clanked. Parker looked at the Victrola.

An interrupted, organized, grumbled din grew louder outside as an armored column came up, and jangled past the house. A lieutenant ran in, stared down the rifle shoved in his face, and went from room to room.

"How many in here? Who's in command?"

The sergeant hung his head and shifted his hand. No one else looked up.

"Everybody, let's go. We're starting a counterattack."

No movement. Nothing.

"That's an order. Let's move! *Now!*"

Hung heads, no groans. The fever had run its course, leaving a stunned, black sickness.

"You. Repeat after me. 'We are starting a counterattack.' Say it. Out loud."

The lieutenant got mumbled whimpers.

"No. *Loud*er! 'We are . . . starting—a counterattack.' "

One of them raised his knee and slid his boot on the floor. He hesitated, moved the other boot, and got up.

"Say it. I want everybody to say it."

A grumbled, broken chorus; no beginnings, no ends. The lieutenant went over and shook the short one.

"Hey, you. For crying out loud, wake up at least."

The short one looked up with fluttered eyes.

THE HEAVES AND flumps and the rattled equipment had no meaning as Parker reeled outside, unfocused. He scuffled along with the shaky, unwilling skirmish line, back past the same houses of last night, the fractured walls, and roofs in flames now, Hemroulle destroyed.

A mine exploder squeaked up from behind, a tracked vehicle with a bulldog undercarriage and double sets of five narrow eight-foot solid-steel wheels. Parker startled away from it, terrified of those explosion-proof, rolling things, those relentless wheels . . .

Up ahead, the fighters did their Doppler swoop, eeyowing low to poop out bombs, their wings sparking fire. Somebody ordered, or commanded, or screeched something about another mile, another town, this one called Champs.

Parker's mouth kept twitching. He was weeping and tried to snuffle up the snot freezing in his nose . . .

HE FELT A heavy thump across his chest, stepped back to shift his center of balance, and fell. As he went down, he could still hear it: the bullet that twanged off the skirt plate of a tank, then twittered, and whirred off to wherever.

He was down and hurting. He kept hearing that bullet, still twanging, again, and again.

"MEDIC! MEDIC!" The words bounced and faded. Somebody rolled him and unhooked his gear, eased away the sniper rifle, and the Schmeisser slings from his shoulder, cut away his bloody uniform, and pushed down on his chest with two compresses. He felt nothing at first, but the numbness gave way to sharp, zippered tears. He could only take shallow breaths.

"One thing about the cold, mac. It stops the bleeding real good. I was talking to this civilian farmer guy? He says this is the worst winter they've ever had. Just our luck, right?"

FEET CAME RUNNING, a medic with a folded litter over his shoulder. His gear flapped. Two harnessed kit bags rattled with tablets and pills. Medical scissors dangled from his wrist by a shoestring. His left arm and his helmet advertised his mercy: red crosses front, back, and on both sides.

The medic opened his musette bag and took out square patches cut out of a raincoat. He peeled off the two bloody compresses, dabbed at the wound, and turned his ear down to listen to Parker's breathing.

"Deep as you can. Again. Okay, you won't need these. They're for lung cases."

He took an envelope of white powder from a metal box, tore off a corner, and sprinkled it like salt on the wound. He put on a new compress, covered it with a long bandage pad, and taped it down. He opened a packet of twelve tablets and made Parker swallow one with water.

"It's a nasty cut. Deep, and jagged, but it didn't hit the chest cavity, so I can give you some morphine. It's just muscle. Some bone, maybe, but no organs. It's only a hundred-dollar wound. Maybe one-ninety-eight. You'll be okay. You're Class Two, so you'll go to a local hospital. What outfit you with?"

"I don't know. I'm Team Snafu."

"Shit. Ain't we all."

The medic used his scissors to cut a bare spot on Parker's shoulder, rubbed alcohol on the skin, and jabbed him with a syrette. He stuck another piece of tape across Parker's forehead and wrote on it with a grease pencil. Parker looked up at the medic's smile.

"It's okay. It's the time and the dosage I gave you."

The medic started to unbuckle the pistol belt. Parker pushed him away.

"Not my sidearm. I gotta keep my pistol. It's special."

"You can't have it. You're wounded now. You're a noncombatant by the Geneva rules. You have to be completely unarmed. No weapons are allowed in ambulances."

PARKER WAS DOWN on a stretcher, woozy. The medic said he'd be transported to the rear. But there was no rear.

A Catholic chaplain was wearing a purple stole. He and his assistant held a Mass, a paten of wafers and a chalice of wine laid out on the altar cloth draped over the hood of his jeep. Men knelt in the snow with clasped hands and took their Holy Communion. Behind them, four medics carried a litter, the terrified soldier leaning on his elbow, twisted around to see where they were taking him.

A guy mumbled on the litter next to Parker, taking deep but

careful drags on a cigarette as he told the whole story about the Santa Claus raid, and how the German commandos stole all their Christmas turkeys.

A GI wandered through the trees among the vehicles and foxholes, unshaved, in a filthy uniform, eyes hollow, a loaded duffel bag slung over his shoulder.

"Uh. Hi, ya. We got called out on a detail. Hadda help the chaplain open up Christmas packages that were air-dropped? But some of the guys got dead. Or lost somewhere. We took out the valuable things and sent them home. But, you know. The food and stuff would spoil, so we divvied it up to pass around. Here's a little something. You can eat, right?"

A pouch of twisted Christmas wrapping held a small handful of salted peanuts. Parker ate them one at a time.

A tracked utility cargo vehicle rattled up through the wind. It rolled and pitched over the snowdrifts like a boat, and fluffed up twin rooster tails. They called it a weasel.

Parker was wrapped with blankets, his stretcher hoisted into the open hull, and strapped to a rack of welded angle irons. The crew picked up another stretcher case, then met two gaunt GIs who dragged a shelter half by corner ropes. Their bleeding, unconscious buddy skidded along in the pouch.

THE WEASEL ROCKED and banged its way back to the battalion aid station, a house still in one piece. They had heat, and morphine, and emergency surgery. All but the gut-shot case were given a quarter inch of whiskey in a canteen cup with a little water. Parker shivered when he drank it down.

An aidman wrote out color-coded casualty tags and tied them to their jackets. The ambulance came up and the horn blew. Four were carried out and loaded on the racks, doped, in shock, saying nothing—the heater fans whining. Urine trickled down from the man above Parker and dripped on his blanket. Another gasped with deep, heavy, snoring sounds. The driver argued with the assistant between puffs on his cigarette.

"No, dummy. Sulfanilamide. How many times? Not suffalide. Not sulphermilanoid. It's sulfa-fucking-*nil*-amide."

Parker trembled and floated—the Crown Prince of Atlantis setting his sails.

He heard the talk about the regimental clearing station and the division collecting center. Doctors and orderlies hurried around with shower caps and dangled masks. Litters were carried this way and the other with limp, bloody loads that moaned, and whined.

They leaned over him, scribbled something on his tag, and left. He was not an emergency.

A work detail sawed and hammered on the blown-away part of the schoolhouse roof. He could still hear the banging as they carried him in under the lights. A doctor buzzed out his bored efficiency:

"Take those stitches and drains out of his face. His thigh is okay. His shoulder, eh. So-so. Somebody should have stitched his head. His chest needs to be debrided. Rule out any breaks in his sternum."

PARKER WOKE UP in a pyramid personnel tent. He felt the pressure of heavy, sharp teeth clamped on his chest whenever he took small sucks of air. Seven men lay on the other cots, duckboards on the ground. There was a hot stove, but he felt cold. When somebody zipped open the tent fly with an armload of firewood, Parker could see they were camped in a cemetery.

Artillery came in again, even closer. He woke from a doze, jerked up, and yelped stiffly around for his weapons. They bellowed at him. He barked back, desperate and enraged. An orderly zippered inside and got Parker under the blankets.

THE WORD THRILLED from tent to tent. That puny morning thing was the last fumble. The Krauts were pulling back, out of gas and ammo, and out of luck. The planes were still coming over to drop in food, mail, medical stuff. More of everything just fell right out of the blue sky.

After sunset, Patton charged up from the south and broke through the ring. Bastogne was relieved.

"Hey, man. We're rescued."

"Yeah? No shit? Does that mean it's over? Hell, no."

"All the papers Stateside are saying we're a bunch of heroes. Get this: We're the 'Battling Bastards of the Bastion of Bastogne.' How's that one? Ha? We circled the wagons all around and the cavalry comes galloping up. Ya-hoo! Man, pass the fucking popcorn!"

"They're taking out the serious right now. We're next."

SEVERAL HUNDRED were loaded into ambulances and trucks in a line that stretched back over a mile. Supply convoys zoomed in the other way, sizzling past the local citizens who pushed wheelbarrows, and baby carriages, and dragged overloaded carts, and kids' wagons, desperate to get through the new corridor before the Germans squeezed it shut.

They were driven eighteen miles to the evacuation hospital at Neufchâteau, put in open wards with warm air where orderlies helped them shave, and steered them into shower rooms. They sponged off Parker's face and arms, scrubbed everything from his chest down with hot water, and disinfectant soap. Then he got flannel pajamas and clean, white sheets: dry and smooth to go with his smooth, clean skin.

They ate hamburger steak, carrots, mashed potatoes, and applesauce served on bright metal trays stamped into separate compartments. They had coffee and pumpkin pie, got shots of penicillin, and shots for pain.

They wore socks and slippers, and red corduroy bathrobes that had "MD USA" over the front pocket. According to the ward boy, that meant: "Many Die, You Shall Also." Some of them played cards, wrote letters, or listened to the radio. Some read the *Stars and Stripes*. But bad shadows flickered among the muted night lights. Moans, babbles, and hot arguments struggled with relentless demons. When a pitcher was knocked to the floor, a man scrambled out of bed, croaking:

"Somebody cover the left! The left! They're coming in!"

Then he jerked out in spasms until soft feet on crepe soles rubbed up to save him.

THE RADIO SYSTEM played AFN programs. "Amapola." "Frenesi." "Don't sit under the apple tree with anybody else but me — anybody else but me. . . ." Dennis in the next bed had frozen feet. He pretended to be asleep when a nurse came by but then sprang his ambush and popped her one in the ear with a rubber band and a spitball, covered his head, and giggled.

Dennis's buddy on Parker's other side had snow-white legs and feet that were purple, spongy, and swollen double, his toes like short, rotten bananas, the nails gone, each one separated with a wad of cotton. There was a bad stink. Colby worried about getting gangrene. But maybe that penicillin stuff would work.

"I'm probably . . . lose some toes. But damn, not my feet. I mean, *shee-it!* And they're thinking it's deliberate so I don't even get no Purple Heart. Dennis got frozen feet, and that's okay. But trench foot is personal carelessness. We're out there together in the same fucking holes? Freezing and getting shot at? But me, I'm *preventable?*"

Across the aisle a man curled up with his arms around his knees, the covers up to his nose. His neighbor sat on the edge of his bed, his arms and fingers jiggling out a private semaphore. It took several tries to get the cigarette in his mouth. Then he wrestled his wrist to hold the light. Ward boys passed bedpans and urinal ducks. When a cleaning bucket clanked on the floor, three heads flinched from their pillows.

One ward was for amputees, one for burns. Theirs was a general exhaustion unit. Larry worked days in their ward. He knew everything: who was what, and why, and when, and was delighted to tell it all. A first-year medical student dropout, he was put on LTD in the Medical Corps, light duty because he had one bad eye.

Larry finished with that smelly stuff on the floor, pulled the mop through the bucket wringer, and came over one last time. He sucked his teeth and checked around, tasting that tart sweetness of conspiracy.

"Parker? Hey. Listen. I don't much believe in latrine rumors. But I heard something about you that's really hot. They're gonna give you a Bronze Star for something. Next time they go around and hand out the Purple Hearts."

"Bullshit. What did I do for a Bronze Star?"

"Hey. I don't know nothing. But I'm telling you. They got you down. But don't let it go to your head. It's like the entry grade of hero thing. We got a doctor here, got one for meritorious service. The story I heard, this forward artillery observer, and his radio guy? They stay overnight in a foxhole with some frontline dogfaces. Usually they go home at night. So for this they both got Silver Stars. Figure that one. But go ahead, enjoy it. Thing might come in handy."

Not a Bronze Star. Probably just a Purple Heart and he'd get a one-for-five. Unless Sergeant Blavatsky did it. Headley didn't live to get his Silver Star; Bucket; all those Task Force Crazies. Klaskin's Iron Cross would end up in a hockshop window in Peoria. Fuck it. He'd tell them to shove it.

THE EXIT DOORS were guarded, but they liked him to move, to swing up and down the corridor. He could look out the window at one end and watch the detail of German PWs digging graves, guarded, and directed by a crew from the Grave Registration Unit, the buzzard detail, all colored guys but the sergeant.

A truck backed in. The bodies were unloaded. The sergeant stripped them, helped by a colored corporal, experts with their enormous tailor's scissors that cut along the outside of the legs, the torso, inside the arms, and across to the neck. The uniforms were ripped off with one snatch, an actor's quick-change trick that left them naked.

The sergeant and the corporal went through the pockets for money or wallets, for photographs, letters, combs, wads of toilet paper. They took off the occasional watch, ring, a crucifix, or Mogen David and put them in small canvas bags that were tagged and tied. Ammunition and grenades went clanking into a GI can. Other things went into another can. The uniform rags were thrown on a pile. Forms were filled out on clipboards, notations made.

Some bodies had dog tags stuck into the gaping mouth, the notch end between the incisors, the other end jammed between the lower teeth. One of the GRUs copied down the name, rank, number, and religion. If the other tag was still there, hung on his neck, the sergeant clipped it off, and dropped it into a bucket. If the body had two tags, the sergeant clipped off one and put the other into the teeth with a tap of a small mallet. If there were no teeth, he stuck it into the mouth.

Parker watched them zip the body into a mattress cover. The

PWs carried it to the next grave and started filling it in. A GRU took a numbered white cross from a pile and banged it into the ground with a maul. Larry came up to the window and they stood there, quiet. Parker asked him:

"What's that they're throwing in that other can?"

"The embarrassments. Condoms, French ticklers, dirty pictures. But if he got letters from two girlfriends, ah-ha."

One had no head, only one leg and an arm. The sergeant and the corporal leaned over it with things from a metal box.

"What's this?"

"They inject something in the fingertips that swells them up and they can ink them with a pad and roll out a set. They send the prints in for a match. If it's just a head they do a dental chart. Until then he's a number."

"Do they ever get nothing? No heads, no hands?"

"Sure. Those are automatic 'unknowns.'"

"Does just an arm or a head get a grave all by itself?"

"Now you got me. When they're in for chow, I'll ask."

"Never mind. I don't need to know."

"They do try. I know those guys. But I wouldn't want to bet on who is exactly where."

Larry lit up a smoke. They were quiet until catcalls came from the window at the other end of the corridor, four patients jostling for a look. Parker and Larry went over and stretched around to see out at an empty, snow-covered parking lot. One of the four pulled Parker over and shared his space.

A man with a war correspondent shoulder patch held a hand-wound, spring-operated combat camera to his eye, squatting as a skirmish line advanced past him on both sides, rifles ready. Their pants had creases. Their clean snowsuits were the latest GI issue, rushed in by air; and they all wore those brand-new shoepacks. Another correspondent yelled out directions:

"Straight ahead, not at the camera. Look at me—serious."

The four patients tapped on the window and mugged with crossed-eyes and wagged tongues. They sucked and steamed on the icy glass with slobbered lips, and yelled "woo-woo." One GI turned and gave them a finger. The cameraman waved.

"Cut! Cut! For Christ's sake, you just ruined the shot."

"It's already ruined. Those bozos yellin' and screamin'."

"No, *NO!* We dub the battle sounds in *later*. All right? Okay, everybody. One more. Places. Back to the start line."

Two assistants broomed away the footprints. Their feet re-stirred the snow. They fired at a stone wall from the prone and the kneeling positions. The cameraman took his close-ups.

P arker woke up when a nurse came to take his temp and his pulse. The touch of her hand sent a prickling up the back of his head and he had to raise his knees to tent the covers over his erection.

His bed was near the door. He looked out and saw Major Beynon, the head doctor, standing in the corridor with a bird colonel and an MP sergeant. The colonel wore a white silk ascot with his tailored uniform, four rows of campaign ribbons, and a World War One French *fourragère* over his left shoulder. He carried an ebony baton with an engraved silver knob that he tapped into his hand.

"How come these SIWs aren't segregated? Those scumbag yellow-bellies haven't got the guts to stand up and fight like men? This them over here?"

"We have treatments for exhaustion cases now, Colonel. We keep men for three days for consultation and sodium pentothal sessions. Generally, we can return them to their units. But this ward is also for physical wounds. They are cross-category with compound diagnoses. But they do also have combat fatigue. The SIW question, that's a matter of law."

"There's no such a goddamn thing as combat fatigue. Bullshit. That's just a made-up, sissy word for cowardice. They don't even have the guts to maim themselves like these other bums. Hanging's too good for these creeps. They should be drawn and quartered, their fingernails ripped out. Anybody won't fight for his own country isn't a man; he's a thing."

"Colonel, we get about ninety percent RTUs. Most just need to unwind, to warm up, to catch up on their sleep."

"Not these assholes."

"Well, no. Maybe not all of them, no."

The colonel took the clipboard from the MP.

"Where's this Dehlin? And Monahan and Tardif?"

The major pointed to a bed on the other side of the room. The colonel charged over with the MP, the embarrassed, awkward major tossing in their wake.

"What happened, Dehlin? You blew your finger off just so you could get out of combat? You figured we'd send you home?"

"Sir? The grenade had a short fuse and went off soon's I threw it. Nothing self-inflicted about it. Not one finger, two. They was just hanging there by pieces of skin. I had to cut the rest off with a knife. Lucky I didn't lose my arm."

"Don't try to shit me, soldier."

The man sniveled.

"If I shot myself there'd be powder burns, right? Sir?"

"Not if you were wearing gloves. Not if you fired through a loaf of bread. You think we're not wise? The wounds are always on the left. Why? Because everybody's right-handed."

The MP got into it:

"His Form Twenty says here, there *were* powder burns."

"Maybe. From the grenade, I guess. But I'm left-handed."

The colonel pouted his pencil mustache from bed to bed, checking the name cards. He aimed the swagger stick at the fidgety one's throat. The cigarette fell out of his mouth.

"Monahan, Jeffrey T. Shot through the left hand. Stray bullet, you said. But you weren't even in a fire zone."

Major Beynon made a move, but stopped himself.

"Colonel Dorcas. Please, sir! These men have problems.

They are neuro-psychiatric. Above all else they must have quiet. They can't tolerate any form of stress."

The patient snatched the butt off his bed, brushed off the ashes, and tried to put it back in his mouth. Colonel Dorcas pulled the covers off the curled-up man. Curly tightened up his shell even harder, his left foot in a cast, his arms around his head.

"Tardif, Emanuel J. Shot in the foot, right?"

"I did not shoot myself, sir. I stepped on a Schu mine."

"That's a lot of horse manure."

"No, Colonel, honest. It's a little wooden box like a box of kitchen matches."

"I know what they are. I know all about them."

"But, listen, sir. They got TNT inside, a quarter pound of the stuff. It feels just like Fels Naptha soap."

"Yes. I know. Box mines, Schu mines. Anti-personnel."

"Not Bouncing Betties. They're different. A Schu mine."

"Soldier, for Christ's sake, you don't get to be a colonel in the infantry without knowing something about weapons."

"You step on it. The pressure on the lid forces this nail down into this detonator. It blew me right over on my back."

"Will somebody please chloroform this guy?"

"Sir? Sir? I was just lucky it didn't take off my foot. Break my leg, easy. Luck, that's all. Just one little hole."

Major Beynon kept trying:

"Peak efficiency is reached in ninety days. Two hundred is maximum in combat. But Type One shows up the first five days. Type Two, we get irritability, apathy. Men get careless, no initiative. Finally the hysterical sobbing. One out of every four battle casualties has a psychiatric base."

"You and this other yo-yo singing me a duet, or what?"

"Their eyes have that hollow look, their jaws open. Lifeless, hopeless, unable to see anything right in front of them. For them, dying is easier than living. We've had some here three times, rested, pumped up, and dreamed out. And then returned to unit. We call them the Ragmen. We send them back—but they're limp, like scarecrows, stuffed with rags."

"What kind of a fucking army do I have here? *Ragmen* now?"

"Sodium amytal or pentothal is a dirty business, but it's quick. It gives them twenty-four to forty-eight hours of solid, profound, restorative sleep. When they come out of it they're numb. They slip and fall all over themselves. But after they get fed and showered up we can return them. Or try. Doesn't always work. But if they can still walk and they can still see, we have strict orders to ship them back, regardless."

"You're damn right, you do. You got that part, at least. Jesus. And other men are out there *dying* for their country!"

A short captain hurried up from outside and broke in without apology. The colonel bent to listen, eyes up, bewildered.

". . . journalists? When?"

A moment. He clubbed the ebony stick into his hand.

"Holy Mary and Joseph! It must be fucking contagious. Let's get out of this nut factory."

He gripped the stick like a giant's pen and wrote with it.

"And you, Beynon? You'd better watch your mouth."

THOSE WHO COULD walk were sometimes bundled in blankets, overcoats, and boots and were allowed to sit in a little park behind the hospital buildings, the hedges capped with snow, the benches swept off. Four strands of barbwire angled through the trees around them. If the wind was right, Parker could hear the grumbling snore of the big guns above Bastogne.

They could smoke. A few could talk, even some with paralyzed faces, the tweaks, and tics. But they talked around each other, their jaws sagged, appalled.

One of them even laughed:

"Was I low? *Low?* Shit, my buttons got in my way. Never saw a barrage like that one. Like sticking your head in a bucket and somebody's beating on it with a hammer. All *day.*"

One sneered:

"I know that Dorcas prick. Wears the Combat Infantry Badge? Shit. He's strictly headquarters. What they do, drive up in a jeep, watch the action five minutes through binoculars, and drive back. Then they put in for a CIB."

One was still excited and still had trouble breathing.

"They fucking *screamed* right up to our *holes.* They were on dope or *something.* Had to be. We kept knocking them down. We had to jump out and grab their weapons and ammo 'cause we were *totally* out. And then *more* came up. And we knocked *them* down. Pretty soon we couldn't even *see* over them."

The one with hands and wrists drawn up into tight claws always twittered about baseball teams. The redhead kept explaining about dead men. He couldn't stand to look at dead men, count dead men, smell dead men, or see men get dead.

Then they shuffled back to their pajamas and bathrobes, booties, and slippers, the radios low, the voices soft.

A MEDAL MIGHT be nice to show off but only a quick flash, not like having a new car. Everybody would be coming home with ribbons, but after that big celebration it would all go to the back of a drawer. Mention it, means you're bragging.

But this could lead to a promotion. His mother would like it. He made out his $10,000 National Service Life Insurance to his mother, but she didn't even know where he was. A medal might make up some for his nose. Might even impress Daddy.

He borrowed a compact from one of the Doughnut Girls and looked at those wino eyes staring out of a dead-end alley, at the bruises on his jaw, the streak across his scalp, the one across his cheek, his nose shrunk, and warped into fine, knitted red scars.

He held the wrapper from a Baby Ruth candy bar up to his left chest, stretched his right arm out with the mirror, and twisted around to see how it might look.

ORDERLIES CUT OFF the cast and made him stretch and bend. When the stitches came out, he had his first real bath in a month. They let him linger in the shower.

They had movies, toothbrushes, coffee in real cups, haircuts, all they wanted to eat. But when a fighter plane flew low over the chow hall, one GI dumped a tray in his lap. Another crawled on the floor. Men howled, banged their fists, and punched at their own faces.

PARKER WAS NODDING off when he heard the excited heels and busy rustles, the council of pleasant voices. Major General Markham came in with his executive officer. Colonel Reno Dorcas walked one pace behind and to the left of the general, hands behind his back, his baton tucked under his arm. Major Beynon stayed in the rear. All of them wore full dress.

A sergeant offered up a velvet-lined tray of Purple Hearts, Bronze Stars, and Silver Stars. A lieutenant held a folder with a thin stack of citations and a typed list. A somber cluster of army nurses, and Red Cross Volunteers, spaced themselves and stood with their hands clasped in front. The men kept their hands behind them. All was quiet and grave as the general read out the citation in a steady purr.

" ' . . . as a direct result of hostile enemy fire . . . ' "

The witnesses applauded when the general pinned the Purple Heart to the man's Johnny coat, next to the stump of his left arm. He shook his hand and smiled. The flashbulb attached to the four-by-five Speed Graphic went off. A war correspondent made notes, his fingers slow.

The group re-formed around Colby's bed. The lieutenant leaned over to murmur to the general, who frowned and nodded. They shuffled over to Dennis' bed and began the next ceremony. Dennis sat straight up.

"How come Colby don't git no Purple Heart?"

"He has a different wound category," the lieutenant said.

"We both got bad feet. We're in the same hole together."

The general smiled a pleasant, soothing smile.

"He's NBC. Non-battle casualty, considered preventable. Some of these rules are—there's a thin line here, it's true."

"He don't git one. I don't neither. We landed on Omaha together. We buddies."

The general looked at the colonel. Who screwed up here? The colonel tapped the baton against the side of his leg. Parker watched and listened from his bed. He chewed his lips. Hard to believe that Dennis was crazy enough to actually do this. Turn down a medal and talk back to a general?

Major General Markham was tolerant, even serene.

"You truly earned this, soldier. It's a gift from your country, which is grateful for your heroism and your pain."

"Hell, I didn't even git shot up like these here other guys. I didn't bleed none. My feet froze is all. But if you'll give one to Colby then I'll take one too."

"Nobody *refuses*. It's an *honor!* You will join a glorious legion of fighting men, part of an exalted brotherhood."

"Ain't no rule says I gotta take it. Give it to some poor shavetail lieutenant needs a promotion point."

Slow about it, the general straight, almost at attention:

"Son, we're trying to bestow a decoration for your wound."

"I fell asleep is what happened. Passed out, woke up, and my feet were froze. My boots was split open, my skin. I even had ice between my toes."

Dennis wiped away the tears with the heel of his hand and broke into sobs. The group watched him shudder and gasp.

"I don't give a sweet fuck-all about any of this fancy shit. It's crazy! The ground out there is covered with dead men. I got crippled feet. Now I get a Cracker Jack prize?"

Dennis snuggled down and pulled the covers over his head. The general stared at his bare, swollen black feet sticking out. Major Beynon was quiet.

"It's very painful. We have him on round-the-clock meds."

Tight lips and squints. Nobody moved. Nobody actually heard any of this. Parker shivered. The general bent down to look closer at Dennis' feet, took a little sniff, and went over to look at Colby's. The colonel's mouth was working. He stepped up and prodded Dennis on the chest with his baton.

"What did you just say, Private? What was all that?"

"Forget it, Reno."

"Hank. I can't overlook this. You're a general officer."

"Reno?"

"Okay then. All right. A court-martial would be messy anyway and he'd just get to sit out the rest of the war. But no Heart either. I'll put it down—refused."

"No. Just get him down properly awarded so it'll go in his service record. Some day he'll change his mind."

"This little bastard's got no right to talk to you like this. This is a court-martial offense."

"Let it go, Reno. Just let it go. Under*stood?*"

"Yes, *sir.* Sir? I'll supervise his two-o-one file personally."

As the general stooped to look at Colby's feet again, the entourage darted and wavered away to another bed. The general read his commendation to a burn case whose arms hung from pulleys. He pinned a Purple Heart to the man's pillow. He grinned from a red, raw face. A flashbulb went off. There was applause.

The colonel held back. He pulled at Major Beynon's elbow, and led him over to Dennis with a soft growl. Parker lay behind them.

"You're head surgical officer here. As soon as you can get this bastard on his feet, even if it's just one foot, I want him shipped out. You got that? I'm going to check, Major. Make sure you don't fuck up. This is—a direct order."

"Yes, sir. I understand. But this is a psych thing here. All of them suffer from some hysterical conversion syndrome."

"Major? Did I ask you for a medical opinion?"

"Sir, at Normandy, as many as twenty percent had psychological problems in less than ten *days*. They either ran away or were sent back. Prolonged sleep deprivation alone can drive a man mad. In some parts of the world this is a basic form of routine police torture."

"Doctor, you don't get the big picture. We have a severe shortage of rifle replacements. I mean, it is critical."

"They have all the classics. Besides the twitches, there's the terror, the anger . . . They—just can't move."

The colonel squinted one eye. He took aim and stirred with his stick.

"That's goldbrick *bull*shit. And let me remind you, *Doctor*. You are an officer in the Army of the United States and you do follow the orders of your superiors. You don't have to eat shit with chopsticks to be crazy. I know that. But this one's a fake."

Dennis whipped down the covers, his face dripping.

"All right, Colonel. All right. If it's that important I'll take the goddamn thing."

A shrewd, vicious smile. Chin up high, his lips puckered, the mustache in a tight knot.

"Too late now, sweetheart. You done fucked up, for real."

The general called over, testy, impatient.

"Reno? Are you with us here?"

"A second more, please, General."

Colonel Dorcas hissed down at Dennis.

"You, are—number *one* on my shit parade. Forget about any discharge. You will be pulling shit details for the rest of your unnatural life. And someday, when the imps and the demons ask you, Why? you will whimper, and weep, and you will tell them: 'I sassed a two-star general.'"

Dennis' hand went up to his eyebrow, then out, casual, more of a good-bye wave than a salute. The colonel's face turned into a red spasm as he left to catch up with the presentation committee still going around the room, the applause milder, the enthusiasm restrained.

THE GENERAL STALKED to the door and waited for the rest to catch up. He crossed his arms, pinched his nose, and spoke to the lieutenant who nodded at Parker.

The committee took up positions around his bed and waited with dignified military courtesy. The general came over, took the certificate, and read the standard citation for the Order of the Purple Heart.

"'... direct result of hostile enemy fire ...'"

Which one was this for? Parker had five.

"'... twenty-first December ...'"

Damn. The day he finally made it in. The day they shot him down and killed that German kid.

The general smiled at the waiting formation. He laid the citation on Parker's bed and started another.

"'Private Tobias Parker, number four-four-zero-zero-seven-four-nine-nine. Infantry. Army of the United States. For meritorious conduct in connection with combat operations during the defense of Bastogne, Belgium. While serving in a provisional unit . . . heavy enemy fire . . .'"

Parker had to decide. Take the ride or walk alone?

"' . . . well in advance of his own lines and with utter disregard for his personal safety . . . previous wounds . . .'"

That crazy Dennis over there. That crazy shit.

"' . . . while under continuous small arms, tank, and artillery fire, did . . . on his own initiative . . . moved forward alone . . . hampered by sleet and snow . . .'"

The war wasn't over yet. He could go back out and do better next time. He wouldn't be new. He could . . . and Leora would know.

"' . . . magnificently and fearlessly . . . actions reflected the highest tradition of the military service . . .'"

General Markham pinned the Purple Heart on Parker's bathrobe and then the Bronze Star. He gave his hand a soft shake. Parker grinned at the applause that seemed forever, but his eyes were wet, and he had to turn his head. He heard a rattle of bedpans on a cart in the hallway, the clank of Larry's wringer bucket, a click of heels, and from somewhere, a moan.